Book One

Klaus

& the First of the Favored

WRITTEN BY

Juliet Pierce

This is a work of fiction. Names, characters, businesses, places, events and incidents are either the products of the author's imagination or used in a fictitious manner. Any resemblance to actual persons, living or dead, or actual events is purely coincidental.

KLAUS: First of the Favored
by Juliet Pierce

Cover design and photography by Catch Cloud Multimedia

For my Dave…
whose thoughts run deep,
whose spirit shines in the darkness.
The most interesting human being
I have ever encountered.

Contents

ACKNOWLEDGEMENTS

THE FIVE LAWS THAT GOVERN THE LAND OF

Klaus are prominently posted on the old stone sanctuary located on the outskirts of the elfin village, Kringle:

I Law:

Defiance to the King's supreme authority will receive execution

II Law:

Haughtiness in the eyes is punishable by imprisonment for seven days

III Law:

Anyone caught stealing food will lose a finger for each occurrence

IV Law:

Mischievous children will receive twenty lashes

V Law:

Don't eat the red berries from the shakel tree

I defied the fifth law when I was eleven years old because it was the only law that didn't carry a penalty. The second I secretly plucked a handful of berries and crammed them into my mouth, I understood why the King had made the law. He wanted the berries all to himself. The berries were about the same shade of color as my red locks of hair and the sweet crimson juice that flowed out of my mouth and dripped onto my hands that day betrayed me. At least to my grandmother, Grandmullie, as I call her, who had half a mind to lash me with a switch herself when she found me under one of the shakel trees outside the forbidden premises known as Oldenwald.

For as long as I can remember, Grandmullie has protected me from the eyes of the Cavaliers—knights that serve the King and ensure the laws are maintained. She has gone to great lengths to ensure that I would never behold a loss of fingers, legs lashed with switches, nor time in the dark dungeon under the grand stadium that housed the Kingdom festivities. She inherited me when I was a mere four years of age, when my parents were killed in the uprising of the masses who were starving for food. Their dead bodies, along with hundreds of others slaughtered on the footsteps of the sanctuary, were hung along the entrance of the forbidden premises as a warning to the masses not to break the laws.

I never understood why Grandmullie and I lived such a concealed life. Our small home is tucked into the rolling hills of Klaus, along with a smattering of other poor families eking out their existence in our settlement. A thick forest forms a barrier between us and the forbidden premises—where the palace and the headquarters of the reigning monarch reside. The only time we see outsiders in our region is during hunting season when the Cavaliers compete with the masses for the large deer that call the forest home.

When I was twelve years old, I ventured into the forest with Sir Throck, an older elf who let me accompany him and the other elves from his village on a morning hunt. These small elves are called Kringles, bearing the same name as their village, Kringle. They reach the scant height of three feet and have milky white skin, silver hair, and the most piercing blue eyes I have ever seen.

An early morning fog had settled upon the forest this particular day, clinging to the low hanging branches of the thick shrubs and trees. I could see only a few feet in any direction. My breath joined the mist swirling around me. I hugged my brown robe closer to my body which was starting to feel the penetration of the chilled air.

That's when we heard quiet footsteps behind us, followed by whispers. Sir Throck held up a cautious finger to his lips. I pressed my back closer to a nearby tree as they took cover under some shrubbery. The Cavaliers didn't take kindly to the masses hunting when they were in the forest. Many innocent people had lost their lives due to an unfortunate meeting with a Cavalier during hunting season. They considered us as much of a target as the large deer.

I was starting to second guess my decision to go into the forest. Grandmullie wasn't even aware that I had gone. The reality of the danger struck me as I pressed into the tree. Its bare branches didn't offer much cover. I could only hope the brown robe helped me blend in so I would go unnoticed by those headed in my direction. I pulled the hood over my head, waiting with bated breath.

It was then that a large deer reared up about twenty feet in front of us. It was a massive beast with large horns adorning its head. For a split second, I felt paralyzed at the sight of one so close. Commotion broke out behind me as a handful of elves rushed out into the open, a mere ten feet from the deer and me, trying to aim their spears at the beast. They weren't part of the elfin villagers, the Kringles. These were the Juuls, menacing elves who reside within the forbidden premises. Their appearance was as dark as Kringles' fair looks. Black curls framed their olive skin and equally dark eyes sunk into their faces like pieces of coal. They flicked their black forked tongues in the air to sense the vibrations of the deer's locations. I had never been in such close proximity with a Juul and a tremor ran through my body at their dark and threatening appearance.

"Stop!" I shouted.

My words surprised me more than them. Everyone froze, including the beast. I refused to be a witness to the creature's death. They would have to hunt it another day.

"What are you doing?" came Sir Throck's voice from the shrubbery. "Get down."

A ray of sun broke through the thick mist at that instant to envelop the forest. It produced an almost rainbow effect with translucent colors dancing all around us.

The beast remained very still, its eyes never leaving me. Very slowly, it lowered its head. I thought it was getting ready to charge. But it was bowing. Submitting.

Confused, I looked at the Juuls who seemed paralyzed in time, staring at me in wonder. "What?" I asked them.

"You are the Favored One," Sir Throck whispered, creeping closer to me in the small clearing.

He and the other Kringles joined the beast in bowing before me. I stifled a sudden desire to laugh and make them rise to their feet. I was not the Favored One—I couldn't be. The ancients had foretold of a Favored One who would arise to bring order to Klaus. The masses had been looking for a boy who would have the sign bestowed upon him. No one expected a girl.

From the forest, animals started arriving into the clearing. They silently stared at the sight before them, as if offering obeisance as well. And for a strange few minutes, all seemed at peace in the forest.

Until a gunshot rang out. The animals immediately dispersed. The large beast disappeared, crashing into the forest and the menacing elves suddenly sprang into action. They took their spears and aimed them at me.

"Run!" Sir Throck yelled.

I whirled and started running through the forest, not caring that the branches scratched my face and ripped at my clothing as spears whizzed by precariously close to my head.

I knew the forest well as I played in it often when it wasn't hunting season. When I felt I had enough distance, I scurried up a tall tree to hide among the thick branches above. I was too high for the menacing elves to find me. Besides, they would never be able to climb the trees to search for me.

I stayed in the tree for what seemed like hours, my heart still beating from my close encounter with death, my mind whirling over the implications of being the Favored One. It was only when I heard the low whistle from Sir Throck that I climbed back down the tree.

"We must hide you," Sir Throck said gruffly. "They will alert the King. He'll send out a search party for the Favored One."

"Stay low and follow us," an older elf with a long wispy beard ordered.

I crouched and followed him. The other elves surrounded me, spears poised and eyes darting about fearfully. We heard a crashing of feet to the right. The older elf stopped, his hand raised as a warning. We didn't move again until the footsteps disappeared in the opposite direction.

"Who is that?" I whispered.

"The Cavaliers. They are either hunting for food or hunting for you," the older elf said quietly. "Let's keep moving."

We didn't say another word as the elves led me through the forest to get me back to the safety of Grandmullie.

That was five years ago. Grandmullie has never spoken of the occurrence again, but she banished me from the forest. I understood the severity of her punishment. My life was in grave danger. The only clue the Juuls' had was that I was a young girl. They would never be able to identify me because the brown robe had concealed me from their view. But that brown robe betrayed the fact that I lived with the masses in the rolling hills. We all wore brown robes.

The King assembled a massive search party for the sole purpose of finding me. Sir Throck and the others that accompanied me that day went into hiding. Several innocent Kringles lost their lives during the King's interrogations. But I was kept a secret. I don't know how I would ever repay them.

***

"We need to find you a husband, Vixen," Grandmullie surprises me with her words on a cool morning as I stir porridge in a small black pot over the fire.

I look up at her and grin. "There's not a boy in these parts that I fancy, Grandmullie."

Indeed, there are only four boys near my age in the rolling hills. Two are a year younger than me, twins—Wilfre and Weldon; one boy is my exact age, George, who fancies Lila, my best friend in our small settlement; the last boy, Hugh, recently celebrated becoming a man on his twentieth birthday. He is preparing to enter the King's army, much to the disgrace of those in our settlement.

All of the boys are quite frightened of me as I have beaten their backsides on more than one occasion and I'm probably too outspoken for my own good. When I developed breasts, that seemed to petrify them even more, and they go out of their way to avoid me.

No one in the rolling hills is aware of the occurrence in the forest five years earlier. The Kringles never came near us again lest they endanger my life and the lives of the masses. But Grandmullie and I still receive secret gifts from them—loaves of freshly baked bread outside our doorsteps in the early mornings, fresh vegetables during the summer and potatoes in the winter provide sustenance for Grandmullie and me.

"Perhaps we look at leaving Klaus," Grandmullie suggests quietly.

I search Grandmullie's face. Her faded blue eyes meet mine, unwavering, and I know she is serious. I drop my eyes to the porridge, scraping the sides of the pot so it doesn't stick.

"I have time, Grandmullie."

"But I may not," she retorts.

My grandmother is getting older. I have silently ignored her graying hair and declining health the past two years, as if by ignoring it, she won't get worse. Her words force me to acknowledge that she may not have as much time as I tried to pretend.

"I will have to leave without you, Grandmullie. You won't be able to make a long trip and start over."

I hear her sigh. She knows my words are correct. Silence creeps between us as we ponder our situation. Perhaps it is time I think seriously about finding a husband who can take care of both Grandmullie and myself. Not that I'm really too concerned for myself. I'm able to grow vegetables and hunt for wild berries. We don't eat meat so I've never learned the art of hunting. If protection is what Grandmullie is concerned about, I will just ask the twins to show me how to use a spear.

"I want a great-grandchild," Grandmullie says suddenly. Protection isn't what she's seeking from my husband.

"I'm only seventeen," I begin, but she waves her hand at me and I close my mouth.

"I had your father at the age of fifteen. I want to hold my great-grandchildren before my last breath is taken from me."

I'm very much like my father, so Grandmullie tells me. Not only did I inherit his chestnut-colored hair and green eyes, but also his feisty spirit. He raged against the dictatorship of the King. My mother shared his haughty spirit. She readily accompanied my father on that fateful day when the masses marched to the sanctuary, demanding more rations of grain. Their lives were cut off, as was the support of the Kingdom to the masses. We were now on our own for any food supplies. Poverty and death has been our reward for their bravery.

Grandmullie and I drop the subject of a husband. It isn't to be solved in one day. We set about our daily routine of gathering firewood at the edge of the forest to cook and care for the poorest and most feeble among our settlement.

I'm startled early one morning when Grandmullie asks me to take a pot of stew to Kringle. It's an unexpected request as it has been far too long since she's allowed me to set foot in the elfin village. I don't question why she is sending me. Normally, she would have sent one of the twins on her behalf.

"Take the stew to Lady Sysselye at the edge of the village," she instructs quietly.

"Why are we taking her stew, Grandmullie?" I ask as she ladles the stew into a clay pot. My hands tremble as I take the pot from her.

"No questions, Vixen. Just take the stew and be back before darkness falls."

The unspoken law of Klaus is that no one is to wander about at night. No formal curfew has ever been established, but the Cavaliers have orders to detain, and in some cases, kill any unfortunate soul caught in the evening hours without a sealed pardon from the King.

I hurriedly braid my long hair and slip my brown robe over my shirt and trousers. Though it is frowned upon for girls to wear them, all girls in our settlement don trousers. Of course, we would be banned from Oldenwald, the forbidden premises, for wearing such an atrocity. The girls there wear long sweeping gowns made from colors that would rival the wildflowers gracing our rolling hills in the summer. But only nobility lives in the forbidden premises. The girls there have probably never lain eyes on the likes of me.

"Go through the forest. It will be much faster," Grandmullie whispers, even though no one else is around.

I look at her in surprise, but she gives only a slight shake of her head. No questions.

So I set off for the elfin village with the stew securely wrapped in a thick reed basket. It's been so long since I've made my appearance in the woods that it takes several minutes to get my bearings, find my markers on the large trees again.

"Vixen!" My only friend, Lila, shouts my name from within the forest.

Understandably, she's surprised to see me in the forest. She believes that my grandmother bans me from the woods because of superstition.

"Where are you off to?" I ask.

Lila is exactly fifteen days younger than me and strikingly beautiful. Her long blonde curls fall to her waist, and her green eyes seem to sparkle like the sun glinting off the surface of the precious emerald jewels secretly jutting from the hillside of our settlement that I discovered several years ago with the twins. Today, Lila's trousers are rolled up to her knees and the cuffs are wet. She's been fishing in the creek running through the forest.

"Does your grandmother know you're in the forest?" she laughs.

I hold up the reed basket and look behind her expectantly. "She sent me on an errand. And why are you in the forest without an escort?"

Lila looks guiltily behind her and giggles nervously. "Don't tell anyone, but George is with me."

Lila's parents require her to have an escort when entering the forest even though it isn't hunting season. George is not an acceptable escort. Girls are not allowed to be alone with boys. Lila would be forbidden to enter the forest again if her parents knew.

"You won't tell, right, Vixen?" George asks anxiously as he steps from behind a tree and glances at Lila.

I am so surprised at the sight of them together that I can't formulate words. Instead, I shake my head no. A foreign feeling wells up inside me—jealousy. And I can't tell if I'm jealous because Lila has replaced me with George and never shared their relationship with me or if it's because I want a boy to look at me the way George looks at Lila.

"Do you want us to accompany you?" Lila asks, her uncertain eyes probing mine as she searches for reassurance that I won't reveal her secret.

"I'm fine," I manage to say.

Without another word, I duck my head and start making my way further into the forest before they can see the sudden swelling of tears in my eyes. Lila softly calls my name, but I pretend not to hear. My excitement about being in the forest for the first time in five years is diminished. My feet feel heavy trudging through the thick pine needles.

I'm almost through the forest before I realize I'm being followed. Suddenly, my ears pick up the sound of footsteps to my right. Cautiously, I look in the direction of the sound, but I can see nothing. I know it's not a figment of my imagination.

Then the sun glints off something shiny. A Cavalier is following me.

I slip the hood of my robe over my head and increase my pace. The footsteps quicken until, suddenly, the knight makes his appearance about five yards in front of me. I freeze.

The Cavalier is young, at most four years older than me. His sandy brown hair is cut short like the rest of the Cavaliers. He isn't lanky like Hugh. The armor doesn't conceal his broader shoulders and muscular frame.

I give a polite bow and tighten my grip on the basket. He doesn't say anything as he takes in my appearance, or what he can see of it hidden under the brown robe.

"Remove the hood," he orders in a low voice.

I slowly push back my hood, feeling self-conscious about the wisps of hair that have escaped my long braid. Again, I give a bow, this time sinking lower to the ground.

"You know that hunting is forbidden?" he asks, his eyes never leaving my face.

"I'm obviously not hunting, sire," I respond.

"What is in your basket?"

I hold out the reed basket as though he can see the contents from where he stands. "I'm taking stew to a sick friend."

"Stew? That proves you've been hunting in the forest."

"No, sire," I protest. "This is vegetable stew. My family doesn't eat the flesh of animals."

I see an unexpected smile curl the corners of his lips. "What am I to do with you then? You're trespassing."

"Not so," I say more forcefully. "The forest is only forbidden during hunting season."

"Are you arguing with me?"

His voice is lower, almost threatening. I sink into another bow and shake my head no. Grandmullie says I must always bow before anyone that serves the King. And when I feel disdain rise up inside me, I must bow even lower. The Cavalier clears his throat, and I look up to see him gesturing for me to rise.

"I mean you no harm," I try to say in the most sincere voice I can muster.

My words produce a short laugh from the young knight. "You? Harm me? Come here."

I look around the forest, considering my options. If I try to run, he will be able to catch me in no time. I don't know what the Cavalier's intentions are, but I must be prepared to fight him if necessary.

I sink into the lowest bow I can manage. "I have been detained for too long, sire. I'm asking for the right to pass."

His eyes narrow and the smile that curled the corners of his mouth stretches across his lips as he considers me. "Request is denied. Come here."

I lower the basket to the ground. Slowly, I untie the thick robe tied at my waist and slide the robe off my shoulders. It will only slow me down. The autumn breeze feels cool on my white cotton peasant top.

"I gave you a chance," I tell him before rushing full force in his direction and ramming my head into his chest.

The armor is hard and my head takes the brunt of my rash action. The Cavalier falls backward. Instinctively, he grabs me as he falls to the ground. I land with a hard thud on top of him. Before I can move, he clasps my wrists in a tight grip and wraps his legs securely over mine.

One might think this a precarious situation for a young lady. But I have an uncanny strength and ability to maneuver myself in various fighting stances. The only strategy I can employ now is to relax against the knight's body.

We are both breathing heavy, weighing our options. My head is throbbing and I can feel a sting above my eyebrow. His armor must have cut me.

"Is that haughtiness in your eyes?" he questions. "You know the punishment for breaking the second law."

I lower my eyes to his chest to conceal the amount of haughtiness I was actually feeling at the moment. "Unhand me, sire."

He gives a hearty laugh and I fight an instant attraction to him. He is a handsome young man. Now that I'm up close, I see his eye color is hazel—warm brown with flecks of green around the pupil. "I don't believe you're in a position to give orders."

The second I feel his grasp loosen around my wrists, I twist my arms to free them. His legs instinctively tighten over mine. I'm able to grab a large rock near us and poise it over his head to strike, but he's too fast for me and rises to a sitting position, knocking me to the ground.

At least that frees my legs. Without thinking, I swiftly roll off him and jump to my feet. I'm about to take off running when his hand grabs my braid.

"Not so fast," he murmurs, pulling me closer to him.

Just then we hear a loud snort. We both turn to see a large doe with her young calf in tow. The deer charges straight at us and rises to pummel the Cavalier with her hooves.

"Run," the young knight yells to me.

I break away and dash to my basket. I'm prepared to run, I should run, but I look back to see the deer pummeling the young man.

"That's enough," I yell loudly, hoping to distract the doe.

She stops at my voice and turns to me, snorting loudly. I know what's going to happen before her next move. It happened five years ago and many times in my dreams since then. The doe bows her head and steps back. The young calf steps closer to her for protection, its eyes staring innocently at me.

The Cavalier, breathing heavily under his now dented armor, casts a quick look in my direction. "Are my eyes deceiving me?"

Hurriedly, I slip on the brown robe, tying the rope at my waist. The doe is helping me escape, although, strangely, I don't feel I was in real danger with the young knight.

"Wait," he yells after me. "I never caught your name."

I don't respond and I don't look back as my legs start running through the forest. It is my first encounter with the Cavaliers. I should be frightened, but the young man only incites a longing to see him again.

Two

LADY SYSSELYE IS A FEEBLE WOMAN IN THE
elfin village. When I was younger, I would sit at her small feet
as she knitted and relayed fantastic stories of her ancestors and
their feats. Age has shrunk her even smaller than I remember.
She barely reaches my waist now and is hunched over a cane
to help her stand upright.

"My sweet Vixen," Lady Sysselye says in a soft voice, so soft
I have to lean in closer to hear her. "I have seen your precious
face one last time and now I can die in peace."

"Hush," I scold. "No talk of dying, Lady Sysselye. You will
live another hundred years."

"I hope not," she responds in a raspy voice, her eyes crinkling with laughter. "You have grown into a fine young woman. Is there a lucky young man in your future?"

I can feel the heat flood my cheeks, but it's because of the memory of the Cavalier rather than her directness. "No one special, Lady Sysselye."

"What has your grandmother brought me?"

I hand her the basket and take a moment to look at the small, earthen home she has lived in all of her life. Her parents had passed it on to her and her husband upon their marriage. The dirt floor carries many memories of me sitting and playing on it for hours at a time while Grandmullie and Lady Sysselye visited. But that was before I was twelve years old.

The elderly elfin woman isn't interested in the stew that Grandmullie has sent. Instead, she places the clay pot on her small table and removes the lid to pry at it.

"Is something wrong?" I ask.

Her delicate fingernails forcefully dig at a tiny opening in the lid, and she reaches inside to remove a small piece of paper. Grandmullie has sent her a note. I watch the small woman read with shaking hands. She finally looks up at me and smiles.

"What is it, Lady Sysselye?"

Carefully, she folds the piece of paper and tucks it into the pocket of her apron. "If your grandmother had wanted you to know, she would have told you herself."

"That's not fair," I protest. "I didn't know I was delivering a secret letter."

Lady Sysselye gives me a smile. Her teeth have become rotten in the last five years, and the sight is only another painful reminder of how little time I have remaining with her and my grandmother.

"You were delivering supper, as well, Vixen. And I will make you some blackberry cobbler, too."

I smile at her and remove the brown robe, draping it over a small chair. "How are things in Kringle?"

The smile fades from her face and she busies herself in the small kitchen, leaning on her cane as she kneads dough. "We are hopeful that the change in the monarchy will bring an end to the oppression."

It was with joy that Grandmullie and I received news that the old King had finally passed. He had ruled Klaus with a fist of iron. His son, Lawrence Oxneed Sinter the fifth assumed the throne with his death. The Sinters have held dominion over the lands for so many generations that no one even questions their right to rule. We're hopeful the new King will ease the tight restrictions on food to the masses.

I spend the day with Lady Sysselye, filling my stomach with stew and cobbler. It takes the long shadows streaming through the windows of her small home to alert me that I must make my exit. I cannot be caught in the forest at night.

When she falls asleep in her rocking chair, I quietly slip on my robe. She has filled my basket with some jams and the remaining blackberry cobbler to take to Grandmullie.

"Leaving already?" Lady Sysselye asks.

I turn to her with a smile. "I thought you were asleep. I will be back for a visit."

"Promise me that you will."

I crouch down beside the chair and plant a kiss on her forehead. "I promise. Perhaps next time I can see Sir Throck?"

Lady Sysselye softly pats my cheek, sadness creeping into her eyes, creasing her brows. "Throck and some others have been thrown into prison."

My chest tightens at her words. "When did that happen?"

"Last month. We have been petitioning the King, but he isn't responding."

"What for? What are the charges against them, Lady Sysselye?"

"Hunting in the forest. But I don't want to worry your young mind. Best you be on your way before the sun sets any further."

With one last hug, I leave the dear old lady, but my thoughts are filled with images of the small elves chained to a wall, hungry, perhaps beaten by the guards. Sir Throck protected me at a time when I was vulnerable. I will do whatever is in my power to help free him and his companions. The only problem, if one must label it that, is my lack of influence—and quite possibly, my age.

The elfin village is quieter than I remember. No longer do the small children play in the dusty streets. So much has changed since I last visited. At least the small twinkle lights still greet me. As a child, I tried to figure out how the very dust particles in Kringle seemed to sparkle and glimmer. No other place in the lands experienced such a phenomenon. Grandmullie told me I would spend my life trying to figure it out as thousands had before me—and the conclusion I would ultimately reach is that the mystery is not for anyone but the Kringles to understand.

There is a shortcut from the elfin village to the forest that will take me beside the old stone sanctuary where the laws of the land are posted. I had avoided it on my way to Lady Sysselye's home but will have to pass that way to ensure I'm home before dark.

I wrap my arms around my waist with the basket swinging from my hand as I scurry by the stone structure. Yet, something draws me near its entrance.

I look about me and see not one person, so I cautiously make my way up the stone stairs. The wooden plaque that holds the five laws has weathered considerably since I last laid eyes upon it. But the laws haven't faded. It's almost as if they have a voice of their own—spanning across time. If all else withers away, those five laws will survive the passage of rot and mire that the masses encounter in the lands.

"How very nice of you to visit us."

The hairs on my neck raise from the soft, raspy voice behind me. Nicklaus. He is the bishop appointed over the sanctuary. He calls himself a saint and is supposed to offer aid to the masses, but he actually terrorizes the unsuspecting that cross his path.

Very slowly, I turn to face the character that I have only heard stories about since my youth. Nicklaus is an old man. His thinning gray hair hangs down to his shoulders in greasy strands and his wiry white beard falls into an unruly mass upon his chest. Wrinkles etch his weathered face with purple spider veins protruding through his paper-thin skin. He is wrapped in a cape, dyed scarlet from the innocent blood of the masses I've been told. The softest and purest white fur lines the cape, taken from a now extinct animal—the snow-angel jack rabbit.

"You seek sanctuary perhaps?" he asks quietly, his eyes poring into mine.

I take a step back from him. His foul breath smells like regurgitated rotten fish. Something about the gleam in his eyes and the way his tongue sneaks out to lick his dry lips makes me want to run.

"No," I manage to say. "I must get home."

He just smiles in response. Not a warm smile, but one that makes me feel like he's in control.

"So soon?" he murmurs, eyes narrowing.

I move to pass him, but his hand snakes out, and he clutches me in a surprisingly tight grip, wrapping his bony fingers with their thick, long nails around my wrist. A slight gasp escapes my lips. I don't want him to see any weakness lest he thinks I'm a victim.

"Pardon me, sire," I say in a loud voice.

The look he gives me makes my skin crawl. His tongue flicks back over his lips and he murmurs, "I can pray for your soul."

With a twist of my arm, I free myself from his grasp and take off running down the stairs. His low laugh follows me, driving me forward to the forest. My lungs are burning and my chest heaving by the time I enter the thick, wooded shelter.

Shadows are already looming in the forest as I pause to catch my breath. I should have left Lady Sysselye's home earlier. I shouldn't have stopped at the sanctuary.

"I've been waiting for you."

I whirl to face the young knight I had encountered earlier. He's lounging against an old tree, watching me.

"Don't you have to report to the King?"

A laugh escapes his lips. "What do you know about reporting to the King?"

"It's getting dark, sire—."

"Stratton," he breaks in and gives me a bow. "My name is Stratton Foustworth."

I pause as he looks expectantly at me. "Thank you, sire, but I shall not be calling you by your name."

He pushes himself from the tree and draws closer to me. "Why not? There's no law that you can't say my name."

"There's no law about hunting in the forest, but it doesn't stop the King from imprisoning innocent people."

Stratton stops a couple of feet away and shrugs. "The King can do as he wishes."

"But it ought not to be that way."

I shouldn't have said those words—especially to a Cavalier. I'm merely one of the masses. We have no voice in decisions the King makes. My words can be considered treachery.

"What is your name?"

Stratton's question is more like an order. I give a quick curtsy. "Vixen St. Ridlington."

He smiles broadly and holds out a hand. I slowly place my hand in his and, without his eyes leaving mine, he turns my hand over to press his lips into my palm. "Very nice to make your acquaintance, Vixen St. Ridlington."

My breath catches in my throat as I stare into his eyes. I haven't really thought about what type of man I will marry one day, but at that moment, I desperately want my future husband to make my heart race like it is now.

I force myself to break Stratton's gaze. The impending dark shadows are reminding me of my need to keep moving through the forest.

"Allow me to escort you home," Stratton tells me.

I nod my head and start pushing through the trees. There are half trails that seem to dead end at thick brush, so maneuvering through the forest is an art.

"Don't you have a horse?" I ask after we have walked for several minutes in silence.

"I lost my steed when I first met you. I thought he was tethered to a tree, but the sight of you distracted me, so it's quite possible I neglected that detail."

I laugh at his remark. "Are you always so distracted by young maidens in the forest?"

"Only one as fair as you."

I clench my fist and stop in my tracks to confront him. "You cannot say things like that."

He draws nearer me until he's close enough that I feel his breath on my cheek. "Why not? There's something quite mysterious about you, Vixen St. Ridlington."

"It's the brown robe," I quip, but he shakes his head no and reaches out to touch a tendril of hair that has escaped my braid.

"You are the fairest in the lands."

His words sound sincere, but I laugh them away. "My friend, Lila, is the fairest in the lands. She has honey blonde hair and the most beautiful—."

My words are cut off suddenly as he reaches in to plant a kiss on my lips. I turn my head just in time to feel his lips graze the side of my cheek. My legs start to quiver and I reach out to grab him for support. His strong arms encircle my waist as I lean in to him.

"Why did you do that?" I whisper.

"I've wanted to do that since I first laid eyes on you and I'm afraid I'll never see you again." His voice is low and husky, and I get the sensation that it is caressing me.

"My first kiss is mine to give, not for you to just take."

His eyes soften with a smile. "I would have enjoyed sharing your first kiss."

I push back from him and almost regret that he releases me from his embrace. "You may be accustomed to that sort of behavior in the palace, but out here, we don't engage in—in kissing strangers."

His eyes narrow. "If you must know, I don't engage in that sort of behavior, as you call it. Who are you? Something about you is a mystery. I've ridden in this forest for years and I've never encountered you. And the animals—as far-fetched as it is, they seem to listen to you."

I frown at him, a sudden thought striking me. What if he tells the King about me? The King may suspect I'm the Favored One and come for me.

"The animals don't listen to me. They were just startled by my voice. They're instinctive creatures, you know."

Stratton cocks his head to consider me. "I do know creatures' behavior as I've hunted all my life, but I've never seen anything like that."

"Yes, well, I didn't notice anything too strange," I say dismissively and start back through the forest.

He doesn't say anything else about it as we push our way through the woods. By the time we've reached the middle of the forest, perspiration is dripping between my breasts. I stop to catch my breath and loosen my robe.

"Darkness falls fast in the forest," Stratton remarks. "We need to keep pushing forward."

No sooner have the words left his mouth then we see a light approaching fast from the east of us. It's a Cavalier riding his horse swiftly toward us, bearing a torch to light his path.

"Get behind me," Stratton orders softly.

I do as he says and place the reed basket on the ground beside me. I may need to run and it will only weigh me down.

A large man wearing the same armor as Stratton pulls his steed up by us, swinging the fire-lit torch in our direction. His dark hair is pulled into a ponytail and his face is covered with a full beard. He looks from Stratton to me, and a slow grin breaks out over his face.

"What do we have here?"

"I'm escorting the lady home," Stratton says.

A deep laugh emanates from the man. "You don't say. And you call her a lady?"

He's a dangerous fellow. I can tell by the wicked gleam in his eyes. He drops from his horse and crosses to us. "Where's your steed, young knight?"

"I've lost him in the forest, sir."

"The wench stole your attention, distracted you from your duties as a royal Cavalier."

"Not so," Stratton protests, but the older man raises his hand warningly.

"Go find your horse, son. I'll take care of the likes of this one."

His eyes leer in my direction and my stomach tightens. With his large size, I'm not sure I can fight him.

Stratton doesn't move, even when the older man thrusts his torch mere inches from his face. The air is full of tension as the two square off. From my perspective, Stratton looks no match for the man's large frame.

"Are you sure you want to defy me?" the man asks in a low, threatening voice.

"I don't wish to defy you, sir, but I've given my word to the young lady to escort her home safely."

A harsh laugh pulsates from the man's tight lips as they twist into a cruel smile. Slowly, he pushes the torch into an opening on the saddle. "It's your honor at stake then? By my word, you are relieved of your duties. I've been riding the length of this forest for the past four days and I need some relief. This wench will do quite nicely. Off you go."

He pushes past Stratton and reaches for me, grabbing my robe tightly in his hand to pull me toward him. Stratton unsheathes his sword, causing the man to look at him in surprise. He drops my robe and turns to face the young knight, swiftly drawing his sword.

"You would dare to come against me in defense of this filthy settler?"

Stratton doesn't respond. He circles him to place himself between me and the imposing figure of the older man.

Despite his size, the large man lunges forth with surprising speed and unexpectedly thrusts his sword through Stratton's armor, driving it deeply into his shoulder before extracting it. Stratton stumbles back against me and drops his sword onto the ground. In horror, I see blood gushing out over his armor.

The older man snarls and raises his blood-soaked sword to his mouth, sliding his tongue over the blade to taste Stratton's blood in a show of victory. "You could never win against me, young knight. Now I'll take what I stopped for."

He easily pushes Stratton to the ground and grabs hold of me again. I try to fight him, but he's far too large. I hear my robe rip as he tries to gain control of me. My fingers curl to claw desperately at his eyes. I'm able to hook one eye, and I press my finger into it as hard as I can. It forces him to let go for a split second, but before I can turn to run, the man delivers a blow to my face with his mighty fist.

I can feel my eyes rolling back into my head and blackness overtaking me as I fall to the ground. Not even the scraping of the scraggly branches against my skin can compare to the pain I feel in my head.

On the ground, I hear a guttural snort. At first, I think it's the large man trying to catch his breath as he looms above me. But the noise comes again, closer and louder this time. Into the opening a large bear appears, his nostrils flaring as he reels on his back legs, his thick, cinnamon-colored fur standing on end.

The older man is stunned. He grabs his sword and defensively holds it out toward the bear. The huge animal extends his long, sharp claws to swipe the sword out of his hands, leaving a trail of blood across the man's face.

I know the Cavalier has only death to look forward to. I close my eyes when the great beast opens his mouth and roars a deep-throated, threatening sound. It lasts only a few seconds, the life being taken from the man. I hear his body crash to the ground. And then silence. And pain.

I lay for what seems like hours before I'm able to rise carefully. My cheek has swollen so much that I can hardly see out of one eye.

Stratton lays motionless on the ground. I have to walk around the mangled body of the older Cavalier to get to him. I try not to look at the remains of his body, ripped to shreds by the great bear who is no longer around.

Stratton's skin is cold, but he's still breathing. Somehow, I have to get us out of the forest, and there's only one way I can think of to get us home swiftly. The older Cavalier's horse. I'm surprised the steed is still where he left it. *Why did the horse not flee when the bear attacked?*

I've never been close to a horse much less ridden one before. The large animal frightens me, but he's my only hope of helping Stratton. His soft eyes watch me as I carefully take the reins in my hand to lead him to the young knight.

"Please help me," I whisper to him.

As if comprehending what I say, he lowers his body to the ground so I can drag Stratton across his back. I climb on behind Stratton, and the great steed raises up and takes off in the direction of my home.

The horse is familiar with the woods, masterfully jumping over logs and maneuvering through the brush. I cling to the reins with all my strength, my body half laying over Stratton.

By the time we reach the small house Grandmullie and I share, the lands are completely enveloped in darkness. I'm grateful for the shroud of protection from curious eyes as Stratton may not be welcomed here.

I tug at the reins to alert the horse to stop. He snorts softly and obeys. Grandmullie flings the door open, her face registering fear at the sight of the horse and the motionless Cavalier.

"What have you done, Vixen?"

Wearily, I slide off the horse. "Help me get him into the house."

Without another word, she crosses to help. Between the two of us, we are able to slide Stratton's body off the horse and drag him to the front door, leaving a trail of blood.

I cross back to the horse. Stratton's blood is all over the saddle and blanket covering the horse's back. Hopefully, when the steed is found, they will assume it's the older Cavalier's blood.

"Go back to the palace," I whisper in the horse's ear.

He whinnies softly and turns back toward the forest to make his journey to Oldenwald. The torch is still lit on his saddle and I watch him gallop into the darkness until he's out of sight.

Grandmullie is waiting beside the door, arms crossed and uncertainty marring her soft features. "What are we to do with this young man?" she whispers.

"We need to help him, Grandmullie."

We manage to drag him inside but are forced to leave him on the floor. I have no more strength to try to get him onto my small cot. Grandmullie leaves me to clean his blood off the stones outside. We can't afford any questions.

Alone with Stratton, I carefully remove his sword and armor until I can cut off his shirt with a kitchen knife. It's a slow process with my vision only good through one eye.

Stratton's wound is still oozing blood. I take my pillow and press against it. Grandmullie will know what to do to stop the bleeding.

"Oh, dear," she murmurs at the sight of Stratton's bare torso.

"He's been injured, Grandmullie."

"He's not the only one," she says and tips my head toward the candle light to examine my swollen face.

"I'm tired," I say softly and close my other eye. I can feel exhaustion sweeping over me.

"I'll take care of the young man after I get you in bed."

I let her help me to my cot. I don't care that I have no pillow. The throbbing in my face beats to the blood pumping into my veins. I only hope no bones are broken in my face.

Grandmullie places a wet cloth on my skin. A moan escapes my lips, but she keeps it on as she grinds some herbs into oils she's placed in a wooden bowl. The cloth is removed, and her delicate fingers lightly apply the mixture to my face. The scent of lavender and lemongrass fills my nostrils.

I'm conscious of her moving to Stratton to assist him. I can't seem to open my good eye. If anyone can help the young knight, it is Grandmullie. Because of her vast knowledge of healing herbs and oils, all of the members of our settlement come to my grandmother when they have ailments.

"The wound is very deep," her voice floats through the air. "He's lost a lot of blood. I don't know if he'll last through the night."

In these lands, the masses rely on prayer. Sometimes it's the only hope we have. So I say a prayer for the young man who has arrested my attention in my brief encounter with him. Of course, I know it's my imagination that makes me fancy the young man, but I can truly say that I have never experienced the emotions that I have today.

"Don't fall asleep just yet," Grandmullie warns. "I need to make sure damage wasn't done to your brain."

"I'll try not to, Grandmullie, but I feel so tired."

"Talk to me. Tell me what happened."

I relay the events of the evening, skipping over the part where Stratton tried to kiss me. That was a private moment that I wouldn't share with anyone, not even Lila.

When I'm finished, Grandmullie crosses to my cot to sit on the edge. She softly caresses my hair. Her soothing touch has a way of relaxing me and I feel myself drifting off, only to be shaken awake by her voice.

"The animals protected you again, Vixen. I thought you would be safe to go back into the forest. Perhaps it's time I share some news with you."

I force my good eye open to look at her. "Go on."

"News from the palace is not good. There's talk of a great sporting event in the stadium. The King is inviting royalty from the neighboring lands."

My chest tightens at her words. The stadium is a massive coliseum built to hold thousands of spectators. Annual festivals are held in the stadium, but no sporting events.

"What's the sporting event?"

Grandmullie gives a heavy sigh. "The King will call for the Kringles and single young lads within the masses to battle the Cavaliers."

Then I understand the note to Lady Sysselye. Grandmullie was warning her. Innocent elves and young lads would prove no match for the great knights and their weapons. But they would provide sport for the royal spectators invited to attend the event. And for the masses who will be present at the spectacle.

"Is that why Sir Throck and the others aren't being released from prison?"

Grandmullie stands to pace. She paces when she's consumed with worry. "I wasn't aware they were in prison."

"Lady Sysselye told me."

"If they're still in prison by the time of the event, you can be sure they will participate."

"When is it to occur, Grandmullie?"

Grandmullie stops pacing to look at me. "No one knows the timing yet. We await word from the palace."

I look at the young knight on the floor and wonder if he will participate in the slaughter of innocent elves and young boys. Grandmullie has covered him with a blanket, and he seems to be breathing better. Are we saving someone who will take the lives of others?

"We were placed on this earth to help bear the burdens of others," Grandmullie says as if reading my thoughts. "I know you understand that better than anyone. I've seen you go to great lengths to help those more in need than ourselves. If you are the Favored One, a weighty responsibility will be placed on your shoulders to bring order to the lands."

"How can I be the Favored One? I'm a commoner like the other masses. My life is in jeopardy if the King even suspects me. And exactly how is the Favored One to bring order to the lands? Am I supposed to battle the monarchy—perhaps bring the animals against the Kingdom?"

Grandmullie stares at me in silence. "I don't know, my child. But perhaps there are those who can help."

She doesn't have to tell me that she's referring to the Council of Elders, a select group of wise old men that make their living in the caves on the side of massive cliffs high above us. It's several days' journey to get there and a treacherous climb up the cliffs. They live there to discourage visitors. Only the most desperate attempt the climb for their counsel.

I'm not sure I'm feeling desperate enough. Besides, Stratton will need my aid to recover. And time with him is a more attractive prospect anyway.

"Don't let your eyes shirk your responsibilities," Grandmullie warns softly.

"We don't even know if I'm the Favored One."

"But the Council of Elders will know."

"I'll go to them when the Cavalier departs. I want to make sure he's healed before I take my leave."

Grandmullie nods her head in agreement. She's not sure she wants to be left alone with a Cavalier anyway and I need to be able to see out of both eyes before I can attempt the climb up the cliffs.

I close my eyes again. This time, Grandmullie doesn't say anything. I already feel some of the swelling dissipating from my face from the mixture of herbs and oils. The bruising will take time to fade, however.

"Sleep well, my child," Grandmullie says softly as I feel myself slipping into a dream state. It's filled with violent images of blood and fighting.

Will the lands ever experience peace?

Three

THE KNOCK ON THE DOOR IS LOUD AND INSISTENT.
For two weeks, we have sheltered Stratton. The encounter with
the large Cavalier changed him somehow. He has become
more withdrawn with each passing day. I stare at him from
across the table where we are eating breakfast. Grandmullie has
gone to help Mina, a young woman in our settlement, deliver
her first baby. It's the only time in two weeks that Stratton and
I are left alone and I hope to have a conversation with him.
The knock is most unwelcome.

Stratton places a warning finger to his lips. We wait in
silence as the knock comes again.

"Keep whoever it is distracted so I can leave," Stratton
whispers.

I feel my heart sink. "Where will you go?"

"Back to the palace. The longer I linger here, the greater the danger for you and your grandmother."

He crouches under the table when I move to the door. We can't afford for anyone to discover his presence. It will put all of us at risk—us for harboring a Cavalier, Stratton for consorting with the settlers. Once the young men enter the royal duties as a Cavalier, they are forbidden to interact with us. Though he hasn't voiced it out loud, we've all known that he would be leaving any day to resume his duties as a knight for the King.

Slowly, I creak open the wooden door and come face to face with a royal party. Two Cavaliers sit atop their fine white steeds. In between them is a gold carriage bearing the royal seal, pulled by a team of four white horses. Seated upon the pristine white velvet seat is none other than Nicklaus, his scarlet cloak wrapped around his body to shield against the cool morning mist hovering over the rolling hills.

Nicklaus is accompanied by three of the Juul elves wearing black and red cloaks. They still look as menacing as I remember from my encounter with them five years earlier. Their eyes have a yellow hue as they stare up at me. One of them flicks his black forked tongue over his lips—it reminds me of the sand lizards.

"Can I help you?" I ask hesitantly.

Nicklaus squints his eyes to stare at me. His mouth slowly twists into an odd smile. "I recognize you. You were the young maiden that visited me at the sanctuary."

Visited? I would never willingly visit the disturbing figure of the man called St. Nicklaus. "I saw you there recently," I correct him.

His low laugh sends a chill down my spine. "Fate brought you there that day," he insists.

One of the Juul elves raises a scroll that looks rather large in his short stubby fingers. He clears his throat and bellows, "Hear ye! Hear ye! The King does hereby proclaim that all Kringle males and single commoner males between the age of fourteen and twenty are to report to Oldenwald on the appointed day of Winter Solstice for a great sport of combat against the mighty Cavaliers. All who refuse faces death by hanging in the hollows."

"There are no young men or Kringles here," I tell them, hearing the trembling in my voice.

Nicklaus' eyes narrow and he rises to step down from the carriage, carrying a long, deceptively thin tree branch in his hand—the dreaded switch that has brandished the skin of numerous children. He runs his fingers up and down it with a wicked smile twisting his thin lips. "Perhaps you've heard what happens to children that lie? Twenty lashes from a switch is a most unpleasant punishment."

One of the Cavaliers swings down from his horse and crosses to loom over me, his very large appearance threateningly close. "Move aside."

I give a small curtsy and open the door wider to allow him entry. Stratton has left through a small window. I'd heard the curtains rustle when he took his leave at the Juul's announcement.

"There's no one here," his loud voice booms after several seconds of looking through my small home.

"Such a pity," Nicklaus murmurs as he gazes at me. "I might have enjoyed delivering twenty lashes to this maiden's soft flesh."

With a swish of the scarlet cape, he turns to climb back on the carriage. The Juuls scramble onto side railings and hang on for dear life as the carriage lurches forward with a light jingle of the bells that are strung along the horses' reins. And off they ride to deliver the proclamation to all of the masses. I can hear the faint sound of the Juuls' scratchy voices chanting, "Jingle all the way," as they disappear from my view.

I turn back to look at the small empty house and a sudden loneliness washes over me. I know what the King's proclamation means to the masses. Control. Killing off the young men will stop the masses' population growth. The monarchy is always concerned about another revolt.

The time has come for me to consult the Council of Elders. I prepare for my journey and wait for Grandmullie to arrive home before I depart. She holds me close for a few minutes before letting me take my leave.

"You will be fine going through the hills," she says softly, "but danger will await you when you move through the desolation lands and then up the cliffs. Predators abound in the cliffs, Vixen. Travel in the day and light a fire at night. Those who hide in the darkness won't like the light."

I nod my understanding. I have flint rocks to start fires and there will be ample wood in the section of forest I'll have to cross through before I meet the desolation lands that stretch out to welcome any trespassers with the threat of death. If the desolation lands don't turn unwelcomed intruders away, then the daunting cliffs are sure to cause hesitation. Very few people have dared venture where I plan to go.

My supplies are tied in a wool blanket which I toss over my shoulder. It will take me a couple of days to reach the jagged cliffs. How long to climb up the cliffs is a mystery to me.

The mood through our settlement is one of somberness. I can sense the tension and anxiety lingering in the air as I pass each dwelling that houses an eligible young man.

"Vixen," Lila yells when I come upon her house. She scurries out to greet me, wiping her hands on a towel. I know she's in the middle of baking.

I set my blanket down to embrace her warmly. "I'm so sorry for George."

Unexpectedly, she laughs at my words. "The proclamation is good news for us. Our parents have consented to our marriage so George doesn't have to participate."

I don't know why I'm surprised—I shouldn't be. It makes perfect sense for Lila and George to marry, but I can't imagine my friend settled into the role of a wife and mother. She and I have spent countless hours laying in the grass, dreaming about leaving Klaus to live a life full of freedom and adventure.

She laughs at my expression. "Aren't you going to say something—anything? Are you happy for me?"

"Of course," I stammer. "But I thought, I mean, we always talked about leaving Klaus when we grew up. You know, taking Grandmullie and your parents and your sister out of here—."

She searches my face earnestly. "But those were just girlish dreams, Vixen. And that was before George and I fell in love."

I swallow the lump in my throat and blink back sudden tears. "I know. It's just that you're my best friend and now you're getting married and will be taken from me."

She laughs again and squeezes my hand. "We'll always be best friends. Marrying George isn't going to change that. You'll see. Besides, it's time you married too. You can save a boy in our settlement—perhaps Wilfre or Weldon."

"The twins?"

"It might not be so bad, Vixen. They're growing into men. And just think, we can live beside each other and raise our children together. Doesn't that sound like great fun?"

I shrink back at her words. I thought Lila of all people would understand that I'm not ready for marriage, and definitely not with either of the twins. "Wilfre and Weldon will need to find a wife outside our settlement. I just can't fathom the thought of marrying either one of them."

The smile fades from Lila's face and she puckers her lips in a pout. "You're no fun, Vixen. You're always talking about embarking on some grand adventure. Can't you see that marriage is the grandest adventure any young lady can experience?"

I firmly shake my head no. I have a feeling that being the Favored One is where my destiny lies, despite Grandmullie's encouragement to marry for the sake of a great-grandchild. Besides, the thought of spending the rest of my life with one of the twins is more than my imagination can take.

Lila laughs at my expression. "Well, I must finish my pies. Mother is excited to begin sewing my wedding dress—she's making it out of lovely lace she purchased years ago. It's been sitting in her trunk just waiting to be used for such an occasion. Of course you will be standing at my side when I say my vows, right?"

"Of course, Lila."

I release a slow breath as soon as she enters her house. My best friend is getting married. I fully expect the twins' mother to approach Grandmullie about the prospect of me joining in matrimony with one of them to save them from death at the hand of a Cavalier. I don't know what my grandmother's response will be.

The sun is setting by the time I'm out of our settlement. I've only traveled north a couple of times in my life, and never by myself. The settlements closer to the cliffs don't seem as welcoming as home. Settlers eye me with curiosity when I pass by. My brown robe identifies me with the masses, however, so I don't have any problems passing through.

I pause at an old shanty to catch my breath. An older man and his wife are burning something over a large open fire. They stare at me in silence, their faces flushed from the heat of the flames.

I force a smile to my lips and cross to them. "May I bother you for a drink of water?"

The old man motions his head to a well. Gratefully, I move to pull up a bucket and bring the cold water to my dry mouth. When I've had my fill, I lower the bucket back into the well.

"Which settlement do you hail from?" the man asks right behind me.

I whirl around to face him. He's unexpectedly close. "Beyond the bridge."

None of our settlements have names. We use land markers to identify our location. The man nods his head as though he's familiar with the settlement.

"You received the King's proclamation too?"

I nod. "It's just my grandmother and myself though."

"You're not married then?"

His question makes me uneasy. I sense he has an objective behind it. "No. It's just my grandmother and me."

"We have a son," the woman says, joining him. "We don't want him killed at the hands of the Cavaliers."

Then I understand. They're imploring my help. "I'm sorry, but I can't help you. There must be a young woman from your own settlement who you can ask?"

The man shakes his head no with a grim expression. "Our settlement has excommunicated us."

I know my face registers my surprise. Settlements are crucial for the survival of the masses. One can't really expect to live in Klaus without the support of others.

"Our son is responsible for trying to rally support for an uprising. That made folks fearful. Nobody wants to repeat what happened to the masses years ago."

He's talking about the uprising where my parents lost their lives. I nod my understanding. "My parents died in that."

"We lost loved ones too," the woman says softly. "It was a sad time in our history. Hann was too young to remember. He's a passionate youth."

"And strong and courageous," adds his father. "He would make a fine husband."

"Trying to marry me off to the first young maiden outside the settlement?"

A young man brushes past me to dip the ladle in the bucket. He's around my age, perhaps a year or two older than me. I eye him with curiosity as he takes a drink of water. His chiseled features are strong but rather plain with his dark hair falling just to his shoulders. He isn't wearing the brown robe that I'm accustomed to the settlers donning. His muscles ripple under his thin cotton shirt. Years of working the lands does that for most young men when they reach maturity.

"Hann, please," his mother pleads. "We want you to have a future."

"Is this the kind of future you want for me?" he scoffs. "Working these lands for pittance while the monarchy sits in their warm houses, getting fatter off the labor of the masses? I would rather fight for honor than die like a coward."

He faces me, his dark eyes flashing as he takes in my appearance. "On your way. I will not marry to save myself from death. On the contrary, I plan to triumph against the Cavaliers. The cowards may have swords inside the battle, but a cunning mind is the most fierce weapon a man can take into the ring."

I can't help the smile that crosses my lips. The young man before me is a demonstration of the courage the masses need to break the tyranny of the King.

"Are you mocking me?" he accuses.

I quickly shake my head no. "Not at all. I find your zeal quite refreshing."

His mother groans. "Please don't encourage his behavior. It will only get him killed."

"Or help me prevail against the Cavaliers," he says in a quiet voice.

I back away from them, keeping my eyes fixed on Hann. "I am in no hurry to marry, though I must say, if you ever hope to wed one day, it might be best for you to bridle your tongue. No young maiden worth her salt would put up with you."

I hear his mother gasp, but just the hint of a smile curves Hann's hips. I clear my throat and raise my voice. "If you'll excuse me, I must be off. I still have a long journey ahead of me."

"Where do you go?" Hann asks as his eyes take in my wool blanket laden with supplies.

"I seek the Council of Elders."

The words slip out of my mouth. Not many people would dare the treacherous climb to seek counsel from the wise men.

Hann's parents look at me as though I must surely be daft, but my words draw sudden interest from him.

"And you plan to make the journey on your own?"

"I do."

"I shall accompany you," he declares. "A cord of two strands makes a tighter bond against the forces of darkness."

"I don't need your help. This is a personal journey."

"But you're a young, helpless girl," his mother says, her brows knitted together in a disbelieving frown.

"I can assure you I'm not helpless. Thank you for the kind gesture of water and I wish you happiness in your life."

I turn quickly and stride away. I'll have to find shelter for the night, which won't be easy in the darkness that's already cloaking the lands.

"Stay with us this evening and depart in the morning," the father shouts after me.

I ignore him and keep walking. It isn't long before I hear hard footsteps behind me. I stop and face Hann who is bearing a lighted torch. "I don't need your help nor do I want your company."

A grin lights up his face and he whistles softly. "I like your spirit."

"Please go."

He looks out at the land beyond me, trees now silhouetted in the darkness. "I know the lands well through here. I can at least accompany you through the evening and depart at the dawn of light."

I chew on my bottom lip as I consider his offer. There is an uneasiness in being alone in unfamiliar territory at night. My plan is to push through the darkness for as long as I can before catching a few hours of sleep.

"Fine. But just through the night."

We continue the journey in silence. I look to the moon as a compass to direct my path. Dark clouds shroud it, but a silver crescent is still visible to let me know I'm headed in the right direction.

"Why do you seek the Council of Elders?"

My silence is my response. I hear Hann sigh in the darkness. He probably thinks I'm seeking a way to save the lives of the innocent in the sporting event. In a sense, he would be right. If indeed I am the Favored One, then I should be able to help the masses. Somehow.

"Should you light a torch as well?" Hann suggests. "The bright light will keep away the animals looking for easy prey."

"I'm not concerned about the animals. I have heard tales of evil powers that rule the darkness in this part of Klaus. No amount of light from a mortal's fire will stop them."

Hann gives a short laugh, but he isn't amused or mocking my words. "It's no different in the settlement where you live."

"Possibly, but that's my home. I think when you're familiar with an area, you cease to have fear of the unknown there."

He grunts in reply. I'm not sure if he agrees with me or not, but it's of no importance. Hann will depart in the morning, and it will be highly unlikely that our paths will ever cross again.

"Maybe it's better for two to journey together into unknown parts of the land then," Hann says quietly.

"No."

"Perhaps I should seek out my own counsel as well," Hann mutters.

I stop walking, forcing him to pause mid-stride. I can see the frown on his face in the torch's light. My lips tighten as I thrust a pointed finger into his chest.

"You listen to me. I don't know you, but it sounds like you're intent on organizing an army against the monarchy. How many brave young men have you rallied to fight with you?" His dead silence lets me know that he hasn't been successful in finding recruits. "Perhaps your parents are right. Rebellion has caused many deaths in Klaus. And the way I see it, you have no one brave enough to follow you. Seek the Council of Elders if you must, but I don't believe they will support your death mission."

His laughter echoes in the night. "Death mission? You talk about the evil powers in the darkness when Oldenwald is filled with mortal enemies that have no qualms about killing the masses. It isn't a government for the people. And if the people don't start fighting against the King and his tyranny, then many more innocent people will die."

I wonder how many times he's used those words to try to gain supporters. I stare at the passionate young man before me. How did he have such courage? Why did others not share his quest for deliverance from the monarchy? Had all of the brave men and women died on the steps of the sanctuary with my parents? *Was I brave enough to take on the monarchy?*

"Go home, Hann. Spend your last waking hours with your family."

"Are you so sure I won't prevail against the Cavalier?"

"Don't you mean Cavalier*s*? You may somehow defeat your first opponent, but there will be more than one, you know."

"I'm prepared for that," Hann says with dead seriousness.

I let out a long breath. He has accepted his fate. "There's nothing more to say then."

"Well, there is one thing I would like to say—or rather, inquire of you. May I have your name?"

"Vixen," I say shortly and turn to keep moving.

His laughter follows me. "Vixen. That name suits you quite well. You're a spirited girl; I'll give you that."

Grandmullie told me that my parents gave me the name, Vixen, with the hope that I would live up to it, defying those who would empower me and have the boldness of speech and courage of action to do what is right.

But I think Hann is referring more to my feisty demeanor. I've never been good at bridling my tongue. It's a trait both he and I should work on if we are to survive what is coming upon the land of Klaus.

Four

I'M AWAKENED BY A HAND GENTLY SHAKING
my arm. When I open my eyes, I stare into Hann's dark brown
eyes, so dark that his pupils almost blend in with the color. He
holds a finger to his lips as a warning to be quiet.

It took us two days to trek through the settlements—two
long days of silence. Hann led me through the settlements, his
pace fast and assured. When darkness had descended and
Hann was no longer familiar with the area we had moved into,
we decided to rest until daybreak. Sleeping on the ground had
proved to be a wise move. In the light of the day, we can see
the tall grass spread out around us, concealing our presence.

The tall grass is a sign that we've reached the desolation lands. Not only is it covering us, but it's also obscuring a multitude of predators on the hunt for victims.

"What is it?" I whisper as Hann remains frozen.

He leans over to whisper in my ear. "I felt the vibration of a herd of animals coming in our direction. We are surrounded by whatever they are."

"What do you suggest we do?"

He gestures for me to stay down. Slowly, he takes his torch, now encrusted with dying embers, and rises to look out over the lands. There is complete silence—not even the sound of birds can be heard flocking near the desolation lands.

And then a bellow of grunting fills our ears. Grunting unlike anything I've ever heard before. Hann reaches down and yanks me to my feet just as several massive wild boars come into view. They are ugly creatures, large with coarse black bristles standing on end down the center of their backs. Long, ivory tusks protrude from the sides of their foaming snout.

Hann holds my arm securely in his grasp and wields the torch as a weapon, swinging wildly at the boars. This seems to agitate them further. I don't like the wild look in their eyes nor the popping of their jaws as though they're preparing to make us their morning feast. Collectively as one, an ear-splitting grunting fills the air and they charge at us.

"No!" I hear myself yell and pull my arm free from Hann. "Stop!"

The boars' short legs abruptly skid to a stop, mere inches from plunging their tusks into our flesh. They stare at us, snorting, confused. I'm aware of a change in the atmosphere about us, misty from the cool air, but also a sudden brilliance from the sun that causes the swirls of mist to dance in the early morning light.

"Go away," I command in a loud voice, praying that they will heed my words.

They snort at me as if challenging my words, defying me. Despite the shaking I feel in my legs, I turn in every direction and meet their wild eyes.

"On your way," I order again, my voice ringing out in the hushed silence.

They aren't acknowledging my authority by bowing as the forest animals had done, but they are submitting to me. One by one, the boars disperse and disappear back into the tall grass.

Very slowly, Hann turns his head to give me a disbelieving look. "Do my eyes deceive me or did that just happen?"

I avoid his eyes and bend down to gather my supplies back on the wool blanket. It had provided warmth for both Hann and I as we slept in the chilled air.

"You shall not speak of this to anyone," I say firmly.

"I'm not going to pretend this didn't happen, Vixen. Are you some sort of witch or sorcerer?"

I sling the wool blanket back over my shoulder and look him in the eye. "The Council of Elders will never hold an audience with one who does magic."

"So that wasn't magic? Then explain to me what just happened."

"It's an odd thing, but animals will sometimes listen to me," I toss over my shoulder as I walk away.

"Why would they listen to you? Do you speak their language?"

I had to laugh. "Obviously not or I would have grunted like the boars."

"Now I understand why you weren't concerned about wild animals in the unknown parts," he says, hurrying to catch up to me and fall in line with my quickened steps.

I don't say anything. Instead, I let the whistling of the wind blow his words past me as it whips loose tendrils of hair across my face.

I sense that we won't encounter any further attacks from animals through the desolation lands. We'll reach the cliffs by late afternoon if we keep our fast pace. It's a journey Hann and I will continue in silence, both of us eyeing the tall grass warily as we push through it.

The dark cliffs loom ominously above us the closer we reach them. They are even more menacing than the tales I've heard whispered from the masses who dared venture past the desolation lands to see them firsthand.

By the time we reach the base of the cliffs, fear is threatening to force me to turn back. The jagged rocks are actually sheer cliff banks that hold very little promise of footholds for a person to scale up. The slippery cliff surface can be likened to climbing ice.

Hann and I are breathing heavily by the time we're able to touch the cliff's wall. His eyes dart over the surface as he tries to find a safe path upward. Finally, he sighs and throws me a somewhat defeated look.

"How experienced are you at climbing?" he asks quietly.

I rub my tired eyes. "I'm not."

"That's what I was afraid you would say," he mutters and turns back to the wall of rock towering above us, running his hands over it as though searching for hidden crevices that may help.

"People have climbed this before," I say with false bravado. "I'll make it to the top somehow."

I join him for a closer inspection of the cliff. Its brutal surface is unforgiving. Neither of us can see a safe path to take us to the top.

"Perhaps we eat and rest," I suggest.

Hann turns to me with a frown. "If we stop to eat now, it will be too dark to start our climb."

"I'm not going to attempt to climb in the dark. There has to be another way up."

Hann throws up his hands. "You're looking at the same cliff that I am. And I'm not feeling too good about our options right now."

I find a log to plop down upon and relieve myself of the weight of my supplies. The forest is sparse in this area with a narrow tree line the only barrier between the cliffs we will climb and the desolation lands.

"I have some dried apples," I offer.

Hann crosses to me and takes a small handful from the cloth I hold out. His face is marred with a frown as he considers our options.

"Have you actually spoken to someone who climbed the cliffs?" he asks quietly, slowly chewing an apple piece.

"No."

"Me neither. Do you think it's quite possibly a hoax? That there really isn't a Council of Elders?"

I had never considered that possibility. Stories of the famed Council had been recited to the masses for years. I've always taken the stories as truth.

"I hope the Council of Elders isn't a hoax." My voice is barely above a whisper. "It's the only hope I have right now."

"Your hope may be misplaced."

I turn my eyes to look at him until he catches my glare. "Please keep your thoughts to yourself. I can't afford to question my decisions right now."

"Even though your decisions may bring about sure death?"

I stand to face him, trying to restrain an unexpected anger at his words. "I don't receive your words. Why must it be a sure death? Why can't you just believe that there is a passage up the cliffs that we haven't discovered yet?"

Hann scratches his head and sighs. "We'll look in the morning."

I draw in a deep breath and consider the young man before me. He doesn't want to engage in an argument. Something about him makes me feel unsettled. He's dangerous, not worthy of placing my life in his hands. I should look for my own passage up the cliffs.

"You won't make it on your own," he says, eyes narrowed as though he has read my thoughts.

"How do you know?"

"If you don't have support, you'll fall to your death—that is, if you are able to scale even the first ten meters."

"I never asked for your help in the first place," I say between clenched teeth. "Telling someone they will surely fall to their death is nonsense. Don't you know your tongue can pronounce curses or blessings?"

A gleam enters his eyes and he relaxes. "You're the first person to ever acknowledge that. Of course there's power in words. Why do you think I keep proclaiming the masses' victory over the Cavaliers?"

"Then why do you pronounce death over me?"

He holds up his hands in defeat. "I didn't mean to pronounce death over you. I was just trying to make you see the folly of attempting to climb the cliffs by yourself. Can we call a truce?"

I stare at his outstretched hand for a few silent seconds before reluctantly reaching out to accept his handshake. His hand is rough with callouses as it closes around mine—marks of the hard labor settlers are forced to endure to carve out a living in the rolling hills.

I hear him draw in his breath as his hand lingers over mine. Quickly, I withdraw my hand. I don't want to give him the impression that I have an interest in him.

We avoid each other's eyes and silently set about to make a fire. Hann grabs nearby branches as I pull the flint rocks from my supplies. Within a few silent minutes, a small fire is lighting up the shadows.

I settle onto the ground in a fetal position on my wool blanket, as close to the fire as I can safely get. I hear Hann sit down several feet away from me. I can almost feel his dark eyes poring into my back as he stares at me.

"Why don't you wear the brown robe?"

"Why?" So that I fit in with the rest of the masses?" Hann asks sarcastically.

"So that you will be warm in the night air."

"I'm fine," he says shortly.

I feign sleep, hoping Hann will turn his attention away from me. It's a couple of hours before I hear his slow, rhythmic breathing to let me know his heavy eyelids have succumbed to his weariness.

The fire is dying, so I quietly rise to place several branches on it. Sparks fly up as the branches catch on fire. Through the tall flames, I see the eyes of night creatures watching me. I should be frightened, but I sense they mean no harm.

I stare at a pair of eyes just out of sight beyond the fire. A soft snort emanates from the creature. Slowly, softly, it advances toward the fire. It's a reindeer, smaller than the large deer in the forest, slender, graceful, with small stubs as horns. Its wide eyes watch me closely as if trying to convey a message or thought. I have heard tales of the reindeer being able to jump remarkable high and long distances. I wonder if it's true.

As if sensing my question, the reindeer lowers its hindquarters to the ground, beckoning me to climb on its back. Without thinking, I creep closer to the reindeer and hold out my hand to its nose. It's velvety soft to my touch. Carefully, I move to climb on its back and immediately topple off as it rises swiftly to its feet.

Hann's eyes fly open and he jumps to his feet. "What's going on?"

"Shh," I caution softly.

He freezes as the reindeer lowers its hindquarters again. This time, I wrap my arms around the creature's neck before swinging my leg over its back. I cling to the reindeer as it rises to its feet.

"What are you doing?" Hann yells. "Are you out of your mind?"

"It's my only chance to get to the top of the cliffs," I shout out.

The reindeer leaps into the air, soaring over Hann. He yells at me, but I ignore him. The reindeer heads toward the towering cliffs and up we rise. I clench my eyes shut, praying that I won't fall off the back of the reindeer as its hooves kick the air in a rhythmic movement to push us higher and higher.

A cool breeze blows across my face, but sheer terror of heights won't allow me to enjoy it. It seems like an eternity, but it's probably just minutes, before the reindeer alights on a clearing tucked into the cliffs—far above the prying eyes of humans.

My legs are trembling as I crawl off the creature. They buckle when my feet touch the ground, sending me sprawling to the ground. I think I see a look of pity on the reindeer's face before it takes a running leap from the cliff, descending quickly out of my view.

Without any trees to conceal its brilliance, the full moon above me illuminates the clearing. It's a grassy expanse of land stretching out several hundred meters in front of me, leading to the large mouth of a cave. But it's late and there isn't a sign of any living being here.

I crawl away from the cliff's edge to place myself out of harm's way. After the experience of flight on a reindeer, it would be rather foolhardy to perish from falling off the edge of a cliff.

"Hello?" I call out hesitantly.

I listen for any sound of activity, but nothing is forthcoming. I call out again, louder this time. I hear someone or something stirring inside the cave. It's several minutes before the stooped figure of a man in a robe appears. He's carrying a lantern and squints out at me in the darkness.

"Is someone there?" his raspy voice calls out.

I rise on my still trembling legs and make my way to him. "How are you this evening, sire?"

He's startled by my presence and takes a step back. "Do you know what time it is?"

"I understand it's later than customary to receive visitors, but I've come to seek guidance from the Council of Elders."

"Come back in the morning," he growls and turns back to the cave.

"Please, sire," I beg. "May I take shelter in the cave?"

"Shelter from what? Animals? There are none. The weather? It's a fair night."

He turns again to depart, and I feel the sting of his rejection jolt down my spine. I don't have much tolerance for ill-tempered people.

"Your hospitality is lacking, sire. I hope you are not a member of the Council of Elders or I shall be most disappointed."

My words cause him to pause at the cave's opening. Slowly he turns around, holding the lantern higher in an attempt to get a closer look at me. A gruff laugh escapes his lips.

"What's your name?"

"Vixen St. Ridlington."

"We've been awaiting your presence for some time, Miss Vixen St. Ridlington."

"You know me?"

"We make it a point to know those who can change circumstances."

I don't have a clue what he means, but at least he sounds more accommodating. "Am I in the right place then?"

He nods and waves for me to follow him into the opening. "I'm Elder Elof."

Silently, the old man lights other lanterns inside the cave so that a warm light fills the room. He's a curious man, frail with thin strands of whiskers hanging from his chin to form an odd sort of beard—if he indeed he has enough whiskers to really call it a beard. He peers at me over his beak-like nose until I shift uncomfortably.

"How did you climb the cliffs to get here?"

"I didn't climb, sire. A reindeer provided my transportation."

He stares at me for a long minute before a smile breaks out across his face, revealing surprisingly white, healthy teeth. "That's fine. A sure way to escape the travails of climbing."

"How do people usually reach you? The cliffs seem almost impossible to climb."

"They are," he says simply. "It's late, young Vixen. Best you get rest before the morning greets your tired eyes too soon."

I watch him fold a blanket on a pile of hay tucked in the corner of the cave. I'll sleep there for the night. As exhausted as I am, any place to lay my head to rest is most welcome.

"Will I have the opportunity to meet with the Council of Elders tomorrow?"

"You will," he says and waves for me to lay down. "Sleep so that your thoughts are clear for what tomorrow brings."

"Can I ask you a question first?"

"Only if you're prepared for the answer."

I nod my head. "Fair enough. I wonder what you meant about making it a point to know those who can change circumstances."

Elder Elof pauses before responding, as though carefully choosing his words. "You must know that there's something unique about you?"

"Yes," I whisper.

"The stars alert us to things of utmost importance—like the birth of a special child, a shift in rulers, climate change."

"So the stars told you of my birth?"

He inclines his head with a small smile. "And where you were born."

"But how did you know my name?"

"The birds in the air keep us informed of such matters."

I suppress a smile at his words. "A bird told you my name is Vixen St. Ridlington?"

His brows raise at my question. "Why does someone who communicates with animals find that so hard to believe?"

"Well, it's not like I hold conversations with them," I object. "They just seem to understand what I'm saying."

"Have you tried?"

I swallow hard. The truth is, I'm rather frightened at the prospect of understanding animals. The memory of the wild boars is enough to keep me from wanting to engage any creature in a lively conversation.

"You will find in time that your gifts were given to you for a specific reason. All gifts are, you know."

"I suppose," I mumble and make my way to the blanket to lay down.

He lowers his voice. "I'll tell you a secret with formidable consequences should it ever be revealed to human kind. Perhaps it would ease your mind to know that you're not alone."

My heart quickens at his words and I sit up. I know there's more—that he's going to share something of profound significance. But he pauses as if weighing whether I can be trusted with his words.

"There are others like yourself."

I let his words sink in—far into the depths of my soul. The masses have always been looking for a single Favored One. "Are you sure? The masses have carried the legend down for generations of just one that would come."

"The ancients revealed just one Favored One would arise so that the masses would have hope and each of the Favored Ones could be protected. But there is not just one Favored One. There are more. The stars have aligned nine times—although I must say one of the alignments was somewhat off-center and slanted at an odd angle."

"You mean, there are eight other Favored Ones out there?"

"That is precisely what I'm telling you."

I have so many questions, and I don't know where to start. "Can they all speak to animals? Have you met them too? Do we all live near each other?"

Elder Elof holds his hands up and shakes his head. "Patience. Your questions will be answered when you meet with the Council."

"But I may not sleep tonight with all of my questions spinning in my head."

"Would the answers quiet your mind or raise still more questions?"

Elder Elof is right. My mind will churn all night and I would only keep both of us up. Better to try to sleep and meet with the Council as soon as possible.

"What can I expect tomorrow?"

The old man's eyes are soft—is it compassion or pity for the settler trying to find her place in the world?

"You will not get much time with the Council of Elders. There are twelve of us, each ranking in importance based upon our time serving in the Council. Make every word count and ask your questions directly to Elder Frode. He's the supreme ruler over the Council. You need to respect his authority."

"Much like respecting the King?"

"No, young Vixen. Elder Frode is wise and enlightened. He's the oldest of us all and has assumed the rulership of the

Council for the past nine years. But he's served in the Council for forty-seven years."

"What about you?"

He smiles. "I'm the least greatest in the Council. I have only served for nine years, when Elder Halvar expired in his sleep."

"Can I ask you a question?"

"Isn't that what you've been doing?"

I smile at the slight scoffing in his voice. "Just one more question and then I'll retire for the evening. I promise."

"Very well."

"Where do you all come from and are there any women?"

Elder Elof strokes his chin. "Don't think I haven't noticed how you tried to cleverly roll two questions into one. Nevertheless, I will answer both and then we'll both rest for the evening. All Elders are chosen from within our community."

He raises a warning hand as I open my mouth to blurt out another question. I have never heard of such a community. But the old man before me isn't going to divulge that information. At least not now.

"And yes," he continues, "there are four women in the Council of Elders."

"I'm happy to hear that," I mutter and lay back on the blanket. "I've always been told it's made up of men, but I always wondered about that."

I hear the soft scuffing of Elder Elof's wooden shoes as he softly blows out the lanterns. I close my eyes. The thought of other Favored Ones out there makes my toes tingle. My soul desperately cries out to find them—others who may have felt like an outsider all their lives. They will understand me as no one else can. Daybreak seems so far away, I think sleepily before succumbing to the darkness of the cave and the warmth of the blanket.

THERE ARE TWELVE THAT MAKE UP THE
Council of elders. Eight men and four women, ancient people from a lost time who view me with dim eyes as I stand before them, awaiting their guidance. They are a mixed multitude of races, held in unity by their old age.

From what I gather, the small community where the Elders live with their families is on the other side of the mountain, probably just as concealed and unreachable as this area. They allow outsiders to join their community when they've lived near them for a period of three years, joining in with their community gatherings and proving themselves worthy of being accepted into the tight-knit group.

Elder Elof had led me into their circle of the Council earlier. They meet in a large room just off from the cave, dug deeper into the mountain. It's an intimidating group with the Council arranged in order of importance. Elder Elof whispers for me to begin and takes his seat at the end of the row—the least important elder in attendance. No introduction. Just an expectation for me to begin talking.

I carefully remove the hood of my robe and look each elder in the eye before beginning. I relay my experiences with the animals and the elves' declaration that I was the favored One. I stare resolutely at the old man seated prominently at the head of the row—Elder Frode. He looks as though death is knocking very loudly at his door. His feeble hands stick out of his white linen robe and I can see a slight trembling from where I stand. His aging eyes stare at me without expression. Despite his bald head splotched with age spots, his gray beard is quite full and long, falling to his waist in a spirally mass.

At the end of my tale, I suck in a deep breath and raise a hand to quickly smooth back my hair. The Council of Elders is expressionless as they consider my words. If I thought I might have a softer, more empathetic ear with the four women, I am greatly disappointed. Their expressions are even more stoic than the men.

I shift uncomfortably in the silence and clasp my hands behind my back. Have I said something wrong?

"Do you understand why you were selected as the Favored One?" Elder Frode asks in a slow, croaky voice that reminds me of the wood frog's mating call in the middle of summer. I want to give him a drink of water.

"No, sire."

"Perhaps that is the question to start with."

I look at the elderly faces before me, all expecting *something* of me—perhaps looking for greatness that I don't possess? "Can you tell me why I was selected as one of the Favored Ones.?"

Elder Frode casts a disapproving glance at Elder Elof. "I see someone has already informed you of the other Favored Ones."

"I won't tell," I assure him. "The secret is safe with me. I've carried my own secret for five years."

"Yet you've started dropping hints to various people of your ability to communicate with animals."

"I can explain that. I was in a precarious situation when the animals actually listened to my commands. I had a couple of witnesses. What else was I to do?"

Elder Frode stares at me without responding. I can feel the sweat drip down my spine as I await his response.

"She's young and naïve," one of the women say softly.

"We don't know if she can be trusted," Elder Frode responds, his eyes never leaving my face.

"I'm coming to you for answers, not to have my integrity questioned," I say firmly.

I think I hear a groan from Elder Elof at the end of row. Several elders gasp at my audacity to speak so brazenly to the Council's ruler. But I hold Elder Frode's gaze without wavering. Finally, a smile lightens his face.

"You have a fire inside. You'll need that with the oppression that's headed for the lands."

"Are you referring to the King's proclamation?"

"That's only the beginning, young Vixen. But not to worry. Your battle with oppression will be won in ways that no one will expect."

"But why hasn't that happened yet? The masses are starving. The grain rations the King distributes to the settlers is not nearly enough. My grandmother and I rely upon the kindness of Kringles to feed us."

"It hasn't happened yet because you weren't aware of the wondrous gift of belief."

I frown at Elder Frode's reply. "What do you mean?"

"There is a power in believing in something greater than yourself. The animals singled you out as the Favored One and showed you a sign. But you haven't nurtured that gift."

"I didn't know it was something to be nurtured and I don't know how to do as you suggest. My grandmother kept me out of the forest since that time, away from the animals so that no one could find out."

He looks somberly at me and slowly nods his head. "She let fear keep you from becoming who you are meant to be. Now that you know, you can believe it into being."

I sigh, trying to quell the frustration welling up inside me. "Please speak plainly."

"It isn't just the animals that will do your bidding. You will speak health to a rotten tree and be amazed to see it blossom again. Instead of relying upon the King for food, your feet will whisper upon the ground to increase the produce wherever you trod."

How can his words be true? How can I believe in something as great as the elder is asserting? My head is spinning with the possibilities.

"I need help," I say resolutely. "I want to meet the other eight Favored Ones."

The elders exchange a look among themselves and lean in to whisper. I endure this for a few minutes before Elder Frode clears his throat.

"That is impossible. Each of the Favored Ones is protected by anonymity. Not all of them live within the boundaries of Klaus."

"How many live within Klaus?" Their indifferent expressions give me my answer. They won't reveal the others to me. "You talk about fear and belief and yet you would hide from me the identities of other Favored Ones? I will not let fear keep me from finding them, and I will believe that their locations will be provided by you."

Elder Frode rises slowly to his feet. I'm getting tired of his silent stare, his faded blue eyes drilling into me. Unexpected, he starts clapping.

"You are learning, young Vixen. Never give up, never retreat. We will give you the locations of the signs when the Favored Ones were born, but you will have to seek them out on your own."

I incline my head at his words. "I will do that. I'm accustomed to doing things on my own."

"She won't have to. I'll accompany her."

I whirl around at Hann's voice and see him standing at the entrance of the room. He's filthy and is wearing a look of utter exhaustion. He drops my wool blanket and supplies that he brought with him on the floor.

The elders don't seem surprised to see him. They remain seated, their eyes fixated on the young man who crosses to the middle of the room.

"Do you know how many people have successfully climbed the cliffs?" Elder Frode asks him.

Hann swipes his dirty hand on his equally dirty pants and shakes his head no. "Not many, I suppose. I'm Hann Havardr."

The elder shakes his hand without hesitation. "I've lived here all of eighty-seven years, and I've met nine men and three women who have had the fortitude to scale the cliffs. Two of them were Vixen's parents."

A gasp escapes my lips. "My parents?"

"They knew there was something different about you. They came to seek answers from us. They gave their life for more than rations of food that day, you know. They were seeking to break the yoke of the tyranny the King imposed upon the masses to control them in every way possible. You can't have a Kingdom without subjects. And the subjects rebelled. Thousands of them. Darkness fell upon the lands that day. They had their yoke removed, but it was only because they encountered death."

"I didn't know that. I was always told the rebellion happened because of the food rations."

"The masses must never forget," Elder Frode's whisper echoes in the stillness of the room.

"I'm prepared to lead another rebellion," Hann says fervently. "This time to victory."

Elder Frode's eyes soften as he takes in the passionate young man. "Zeal will only get you so far, lad."

"Then tell me what else I need to do to gain the support of the people. They cower in fear. My family has been ousted from our settlement because the settlers fear that I will cause another rebellion. They don't understand that many more will die in the sporting event the King has prepared during the Winter Solstice."

"Your words are true," Elder Frode concedes, "but you have to gain their trust before they will follow you."

"A leader is someone not afraid to lead by example," Hann says hotly.

"True, but a leader is also one that keeps his wits about him in the course of the war so everyone can trust him—or her," Elder Frode says, throwing a look my way.

Hann frowns. "Are you suggesting she would make a finer leader than I?"

"That is precisely what I'm saying. She will need a protector whom she can trust."

"I don't need a protector," I object, my voice booming in the room. "I can take care of myself, thank you very much."

"But a cord of two strands is better than one," the old man counters.

"What is this about cords?" I point to Hann. "He said the same thing."

"That's your confirmation then," Elder Frode says. "You two will only fulfill your destinies if you stay together. We don't want to lose a Favored One."

He rises to his feet and the rest of the Council follow suit. Without another word, they turn in unison and make their way out of the room. Only Elder Elof remains.

Hann turns to stare at me. "Did I hear correctly? You are the Favored One?"

I look at Elder Elof, hesitating to confirm his words. The elder smiles and nods permission for me to speak.

"I'm one of them, Hann. There are others that I want to find. Perhaps together, we will come up with a strategy to stop the sporting event."

Hann rubs his eyes and yawns. "I will offer you my protection."

"And she will accept it," Elder Elof says quickly before I can answer. "She will need your skills to find the others."

Hann's eyebrows raise in a silent question as he looks at me. I give a quick nod of acceptance. I'll accept his help—for now.

"I didn't get to ask all of my questions to the Council," I say to the elder.

Elder Elof shrugs. "Perhaps you received all you need to know for this part of your journey."

The old man crosses to a desk and retrieves a scroll, his frail fingers slowly unrolling the papyrus. He spreads it out and motions for us to join him. It's a map tracing the location of the other Favored Ones. Hann and I lean over to silently study it, mentally marking their positions because we won't be allowed to take the map with us.

A sudden chill engulfs my body, and I stand erect to face Elder Elof. "Impossible," I whisper.

His eyes gleam. "Not so impossible."

"What?" Hann asks, looking from the elder to me with confusion.

"A Favored One was born in the proximity of Oldenwald."

He whistles softly. "The forbidden premises."

"Someone of nobility?" I ask the elder.

"You will have to find out. Perhaps it's a lifelong servant in Oldenwald. If that's the case, that person's life would be in danger to live in the forbidden premises."

"But it's dangerous for us to enter there," I protest.

"Not during the Winter Solstice sporting event," Hann says with a grin.

He's right. The masses have an open invitation to the event. Some will attend to secure the bodies of their slain sons. Others will attend out of the same thirst for blood they share with the monarchy. It's our only chance of getting through the heavily guarded gates.

Hann watches me closely, waiting for my direction. I take a deep breath. "You ready, Hann?"

I think I see him smother a smile, but all I receive is a nod. I don't have a reindeer to carry me back down the cliffs. I'll have to climb down with Hann.

I can see why he would be only one of twelve people to scale the cliffs. He's very nimble on his feet, his hands and feet finding footholds that I wouldn't have even guessed were possible to grasp. He slings my wool blanket with supplies over his shoulders and motions for us to begin our descent.

Elder Elof had given us a rope to help with our descent. Hann uses that to tie around my waist and lower me down certain sections of the cliff, yelling to me to grab hold of almost inconspicuous crevices as he climbs down to join me.

We use this painstaking process until we reach the bottom of the cliffs at nightfall. We're both out of breath and I'm as filthy as Hann is. The solid ground is a welcomed sanctuary that we collapse upon, grateful to have conquered the climb down.

It's several minutes before Hann rises and starts gathering wood for a fire. I don't know how he has enough energy. I can't even move. I close my eyes to regather some physical strength and feel my wool blank lightly placed over me.

"I'll get up soon," I mumble. "I just need to rest for a minute."

"Stay there," Hann's voice quietly instructs. "I grabbed some wild greens on the cliffs and will make us something to eat."

I don't even have to question whether the wild greens are edible. All settlers learn about edible plants from an early age. It has kept us from dying of starvation during the cold season when the grain is dormant.

"Do you know how to read the stars?" Hann's question is unexpected and forces my eyes open.

"A little. My grandmother taught me what she knew—at least the basics of how to guide myself back to our settlement."

Hann nods his head and stirs the clay bowl crammed with the wild greens and water from a nearby stream. "That's a good start."

I raise to a sitting position and stare at his profile lighted by the glowing fire. "I have a feeling that you are pretty much an expert on navigation and climbing and living off the land. Did your father instruct you?"

He gives a small laugh. "My father? No. All my life he's been so consumed with the deaths of his brothers in the rebellion that he forgot about the sons he still had living at home."

"So you have brothers?"

"Two. One is married, and the other died from a fall when I was nine years old."

"How tragic," I whisper.

"He was trying to save me. It started off innocently enough, I suppose. A competition—who could climb to the highest point of the cliffs."

"These cliffs?" I ask, pointing to the sheer wall in front of us.

"No. We were visiting a friend of my father in a neighboring land. The cliffs weren't as steep as these. Though I was two years younger than my brother, I was quicker. I climbed and climbed without looking down. I reached a point where I couldn't go any higher. And when I looked down, I realized I was in a precarious situation—I needed help. My brother came to rescue me but slipped. I'll never forget seeing his body falling down the mountain."

"That's not your fault, you know. You were just a child."

"My father never forgave me."

We sit in silence for a minute, the air between us heavy with emotion as Hann relives the memory of his brother's death. Though I had never been fortunate enough to have siblings, I feel his aching heart. Almost subconsciously, I slide nearer him and place a hand on his arm as a gesture of comfort.

Hann's eyes travel to my hand and up to my face, searching. I give a small smile and remove my hand. I can't afford any awkwardness between us if Hann is to be my traveling companion.

"Am I not good enough for you, Vixen?"

My stomach tightens at his words. "What do you mean?"

"I have the feeling that you find me repulsive."

"What? No. Why would you say that?"

"Why did you pull away from me?"

"I was just expressing my sympathy for your loss—."

"But I sense from you that you don't hold me in high regard."

His words force me to my feet. "You have to earn my high regard, Hann. Just so we both understand expectations here. Elder Frode said our destinies were tied together—I'm not sure what that looks like, but I know it doesn't involve anything romantic."

"See? I repulse you."

"Not repulse, Hann. There isn't an attraction between us. And I like it that way if we're to continue on our journey together. If you had other expectations then we need to part ways."

Hann rises to his feet and steps uncomfortably close to me. "Careful, Vixen," he says in a low voice, "you may just fall in love with me."

I meet and hold his gaze. There is no chance of that— especially when my thoughts drift back to Stratton and how he made me feel in the short time I got to spend with him.

"To fall in love with a person means that you have to have feelings for them, right? Rest assured, we're both safe from that. Now, can we please stop this nonsense about feelings and come back to the reality of why we're together in the first place?"

A grin breaks out on Hann's face. It's crooked, but charming in its own way. I shake myself from that thought. Why had he spoiled everything by bringing up the subject of love?

"I like that about you, Vixen. Forget the foolishness of feelings—they'll only get in our way. You're right. Let's stay the course, find the others you seek, and defeat the monarchy. Sounds simple enough, right?"

I narrow my eyes as I consider him. "Are you mocking me?"

He laughs. "Of course. But there is an element of truth to it. I still don't know why you have to find the others. Do they speak to animals as well? Are we going to gather the animals together and take the sporting event by storm?"

"I don't see you being successful with rallying people together," I retort, "so I should think the animals would sound like a good option about now."

Hann draws in a deep breath from the sting of my words. "And you think you can do better—lead the people better than me?"

"Elder Frode thinks so."

"He's an old man—what does he know? He's part of an ancient people who have lost touch with the real world. What can they possibly know about the masses fighting for survival? How can they guide us on the best way to defeat the ruling class in Oldenwald?"

A fury ignites in the very core of my spirit, rising like a burning fire, consuming all thoughts of reasoning. I reach out and slap Hann's face—hard. I don't even feel the searing pain that shoots up my hand and into my arm. His head reels from the impact of my blow. Before he can recover, I dive straight into him, knocking him off balance. I succeed in delivering exactly four punches to his face before he can secure my hands.

"You're out of your mind," he yells, clasping my tightly woven fists in his hands.

But I don't give up so easily. I twist my arms around to free my hands, rolling swiftly off him while extending his arm above him. He pushes himself to a sitting position, allowing me to twist his arm behind his back and push up with all my strength.

I feel Hann relax, but I don't ease up on the pressure I exert. Suddenly, he starts laughing so that I can feel his body shaking. He leans his head to one side and spits out a string of blood.

"Do you think you've got me pinned, Vixen?"

"I don't think you're going to get loose any time soon. At least, not until you apologize."

"Why did you take personal offense at my observation of the Council of Elders?"

"You speak blasphemous words, Hann. The Council is our safeguard against tyranny. I refuse to allow you to speak against them."

"Our safeguard against tyranny? Please explain where they've been all these years while the masses die? How did they safeguard all those lost lives?"

"You know what I mean. We rely upon their wisdom."

"They aren't making it easy for the masses to reach them for that wisdom though, are they? How many would they have been able to save had they made themselves more available to us?"

I don't have a response. He speaks the truth, but it's hard to listen to him. I have been raised my whole life to hold the utmost respect for the Council of Elders. I never thought to question them just as I would never dare question the authority of the King. That is, until now.

Hann must have felt me ease up on the tension in his arm because he swiftly and unexpectedly swings his arm around, knocking me off balance so that I sprawl to the ground. He loses no time in twisting my own arms around my back with one arm and shoving my face into the ground with his other. I hold my breath as I try to move, but his weight upon me is too great. I sag against the ground in defeat.

Hann holds me in the position for several more seconds before he releases me and jumps to his feet. "I'm more capable than you give me credit, Vixen."

I sit up, feeling far more sore than before. I spit out the dirt from my mouth and throw him a scathing look. He laughs at me, obviously enjoying humbling me.

"Careful, I think you're falling in love with me," I say sarcastically.

His laugh rings out in the dark. "You're one of a kind, Vixen; that I'll grant. It just wouldn't work for me to fall in love with someone who can beat me up. Not my idea of romance."

I'm too fatigued to answer. I manage to crawl over to the wild greens still boiling in the clay pot. I'm so hungry that I reach in and grab a handful in my dirty hand, blowing it hurriedly before stuffing the bite in my mouth. Hann and I have come to an understanding. Fighting among ourselves will only lead to our demise.

And any nonsense about romantic notions between us is as remote as the location we're sitting in. As much as I try to tell myself that, I find myself sneaking glances at Hann as he settles down to close his eyes. I find his passionate demeanor somewhat captivating.

If I'm honest with myself, I've felt my heart skip a beat or two at the most unexpected moments. But it's an emotion that

I immediately dismiss—too much is at stake in the land of Klaus.

I WATCH THE SCENE IN FRONT OF ME WITH
great interest. Hann and I had arrived at a small settlement the
evening prior, spending the cold night huddled together under
my wool blanket. Our thin clothes are not suitable for the
freezing temperatures that are slowly creeping up on the lands.
I shiver beneath my robe and see Hann do the same. Though
he doesn't have the added protection of the brown robe, he
refuses to wear the blanket over his shoulders, insisting that I
cover myself with it instead. My own stubbornness won't give
in to his insistence, so we both remain colder without it.

According to the crude map Elder Elof showed us, the
settlement is in the vicinity of one of the Favored Ones. We
crossed two other settlements off our list as two full weeks of

our time spent there produced nothing of value. I don't know how I'm to find the person—I'm hopeful I'll just *know* who I'm seeking.

And so we sit in a small clearing of the settlement's village to watch two priests delivering a sermon in dry, monotone voices to a group of settlers gathered to hear a message of hope. Our attention is arrested when a very large, burly man with shaggy brown hair and a full red beard comes onto the scene. He's obviously one of the masses cloaked in the familiar brown robe.

"He's going to try to steal the loaf of bread the priest tucked in his pocket," Hann whispers in my ear.

I can't help the smile that creeps onto my face as I watch the very large man attempt to remove the loaf of bread that is tucked into one of the priests' robes. The priest had received it as a gift from one of the onlookers, and the large man aims to claim it as his own.

"Of course the priest will notice," I whisper back. "He's as large as an ox. No one can miss him."

The large man crowds closer to the priests, his hands clasped together as if in devout prayer. The priest who conceals the coveted bread loaf throws him a frown and keeps talking. At the precise instant the burly man gains the courage to move his hand into the pocket of the priest's robe, a woman screams, "Pervert!"

The burly man whirls around, his eyes wide with terror at being caught stealing. His large hand is caught in the priest's robe. When he attempts to extract it, the priest's robe raises in the air, revealing pale, skinny bare legs of the older man. He promptly slaps the burly man's face.

Hann and I are laughing outright by this time. Some men from the audience rush to assist the priest, clobbering the large, burly man with their fists. He yells at the men, still trying to wrangle his hand free from the confines of the robe's pocket. It's only when we hear shouts from two Cavaliers that the crowd breaks up.

The Cavaliers ride up on their horses. They're young knights, sitting proudly upon their steeds as they assume the authority given to them over the masses.

"What's going on?" one of them demands.

"He's a pervert!"

"He tried to accost the poor priest!"

I instinctively step forward to defend the poor man. "That's not true. He was just trying to steal the priest's loaf of bread."

Hann grabs my arm and yanks me back as the crowd gasps. At first, I don't understand why they are so shocked. Then it dawns on me. Stealing is a punishable crime according to the five laws that govern the land.

"No," the burly man shouts wildly, the nostrils of his bulbous nose flaring. "I wasn't trying to steal the bread. I was—I was accosting the priest."

"You were stealing," one of the Cavaliers says harshly.

"I wasn't," the burly man protests even louder. He gestures with his free hand to the priest who is by now trying to hold his robe closed as the large man's movements have loosened it to the point that it's draping over his frail body, revealing his nakedness beneath. "Look at this man, this priest. His white skin and skinny legs. He's a sight of beauty to behold!"

"I say you were stealing," the Cavalier insists and swings off his horse and draws the sword sheathed at his side. "That's punishable by losing a finger."

Hann moves swiftly to the front of the crowd. "He's a pervert. I can vouch for that. He's had his eyes on these priests since they started their sermon."

The burly man looks gratefully at Hann and nods his head. His eyes tear up and his bulging nose turns a peculiar shade of red. "That's right. Just like I said."

The Cavalier stares at Hann with a cocky grin, his attention suddenly diverted from the incident. "Well, who do we have here? We're looking for the likes of you. We've been commissioned to round up our opponents for the sporting event."

I see Hann's jaw tighten. He clenches his hands into tight fists and thrusts his chest out. Foolishly or courageously depending on one's perspective, Hann squares off with the knight—too headstrong to back down.

I push through the throng of people to reach him. "He's not eligible for the sporting event. He's my husband."

Hann turns to me and I quickly throw my arms around his neck. "What are you doing?" he asks in a low voice.

"Where's your marriage certificate?" the Cavalier challenges.

I glare at the knight. "We didn't realize we had to carry our certificate around with us."

"Well, now you do. We'll take him to the dungeon and you can claim him there with proof of marriage."

The only way to get a marriage certificate in Klaus is to perform the actual ceremony with one of the King's bishops, who meticulously records the union in the King's ledger. It's another measure for the King to control the masses.

I turn around to look at the crowd. "They are taking our husbands to the dungeon if we don't have our marriage certificates."

My words cause a great uproar from the people. The knight steps back in alarm and holds up his hands to try to quell the sudden agitation of the people.

"Are you trying to incite a rebellion?" he shouts at me.

I shake my head no and cling even closer to Hann. He's trying to push me from him but I persist in embracing him. I need his help in finding the others. Elder Frode said our destinies were intertwined and I'm not about to release him to the Cavaliers if I can help it.

The two young knights finally give up as the shouts of the people become louder and more intense. Settlers seem to come out of nowhere to join in the yelling. The masses aren't ready to relinquish their young men to their imminent death today. A loud, victorious shout fills the air as the Cavaliers finally gallop away.

I release Hann and he whirls on the crowd, his face flushed with excitement. "The monarchy is trying to kill us off. Many young men will die in the sporting event—young men who will never get the opportunity to grow up, have a family. If we are to defeat this act of tyranny, we must band together."

"What can we do? They have weapons and control that we don't have." shouts a father.

"Look what just happened," Hann yells. "When we came together, we chased them off."

"Mark my words," a woman yells from the crowd, balancing a toddler on her hip, "they'll be back. And they will bring reinforcements. Do we want another bloodbath on our hands like the rebellion that took our loved ones?"

Her cry creates a sudden deafness from the crowd. They look at each other, considering the weight of her words. Almost in unison, the people turn to start dispersing, shoulders sagging, spirits already defeated.

"Listen to me," Hann urges. "If we come together we can defeat them. The lives of you and your sons can be spared."

They ignore him, leaving as quickly as they had come together. A group of four boys, about fourteen or fifteen years old, approaches Hann with scared eyes. I stand back and watch as he quietly speaks to them. They listen intently to his words, nodding their heads in agreement. After a few minutes, he shakes hands with them and they depart, their steps somewhat lighter and more hopeful.

"What did you say to them?" I ask Hann when he crosses back to me.

"I told them there is strength in numbers and for them to spread the word to others to meet at the settlement by the river in a few days. We haven't much time since the Cavaliers have now been commissioned to gather the sporting event victims."

"And what then? So you get a group of fifty, a hundred recruits. How do you defeat the monarchy with them? There are thousands of Cavaliers. And those Juuls—more of those elves than anyone can possibly know. All awaiting the King's orders."

"Do you suggest we go in as lambs to be slaughtered?"

100

"No. Even if you were able to hide the boys until the sporting event is over——."

"Hide! Hide? I've never run from a fight in my life and I don't intend to now. I'm going to work with the boys on their fighting skills."

I shake my head at him. "Are you serious? You'll let these boys go into the ring?"

"They'll enter the ring with confidence."

"Are you sure the boys understand that you aren't going to help them escape the sporting event?"

"How can one person accomplish that, Vixen? The boys are scared. That fear will defeat them before their enemies will. I will show them how to overcome that fear and conquer their opponents."

"What do you know of fighting, Hann?"

"I studied with an old warrior for most of my youth. He lived in our settlement and taught me fighting skills only the most elite warriors know. I learned how to use only my body to overpower an opponent—no matter the weapon he wields against me."

I bite my lip, taking in his confident attitude. "And yet I was able to take you down. Imagine that, a mere girl."

A gleam enters Hann's eyes and he grins. Without warning, he pulls me to him. "Only because I let you. And what's this talk about me being your husband?"

"Don't flatter yourself," I retort, trying to free myself from his embrace. "I need your help—I can't afford to have you imprisoned right now."

"Really?" he drawls in a quiet voice. "Or was it wishful thinking?"

I pull myself free and place my hands on my hips defiantly. "Hann Havardr, behave yourself."

"Thank you," comes a voice behind me.

I turn to look at the large, burly man that has escaped punishment for trying to steal the loaf of bread. I don't know whether to feel compassion at his obvious hunger or anger at placing himself and others in danger by his actions.

"What's your name?" Hann asks.

"Rudolpho," the man replies, clumsily bending at his waist with a flourish of his hand.

"Rudolpho, that was utter foolishness," Hann chides.

The large man bows his head. "I know. I let the rumblings in my stomach get the better of me."

"You almost got some young men thrown in the dungeon," I tell him. "And what good would that have served? All for a loaf of bread that you didn't get after all."

Rudolpho smiles broadly and produces the loaf of bread from his pocket. "I don't think the priest even noticed that I got it."

"Of course not," I say. "The poor man was too busy trying to cover up his nakedness."

Rudolpho appears unfazed by my sharp rebuke. He breaks apart the bread with his thick, dirty hands and holds a piece out to Hann. After a slight hesitation, Hann accepts the bread. An audible gasp escapes my lips.

"Lighten up," Hann says with a wink and proceeds to sink his teeth into the bread.

"Don't you have any integrity? By eating that bread, you're as much a part of the thievery as this—this ox of a man."

Rudolpho lets loose a loud bellow—a laugh, if one can call it that. "It's only a loaf of bread. Those priests are well fed by the widows. Trust me. I've seen how good they eat."

"The priest you stole from looked like he needed that bread far more than you."

Rudolpho crams the last bite into his mouth before responding. "I can tell you don't hold me in high regard. That's all right. I don't need you to. I'm grateful to your husband for coming to my rescue."

"He's not my husband."

Rudolpho cocks his head to one side. "Not your husband? So you were lying? And you stand there accusing me of having no integrity. But I suppose lying is acceptable because it's not punishable by a law."

A hot flush sweeps over my body from his reprimand. The ox is right. "I'm sorry," I mumble.

"What's that?" Hann asks, raising a hand to his ear as though trying to hear me. "I don't believe I caught that. Is it possible the feisty Vixen St. Ridlington has been humbled by someone she was trying to demean?"

"I wasn't trying to demean him," I protest, but Hann holds up a hand to cut me off.

"Say no more. We forgive you, don't we, Rudolpho?"

"I'm not asking for *your* forgiveness, Hann. I didn't wrong you."

"Oh, but you did," Hann says softly, laughter dancing in his eyes. "You included me in your lie. Don't you think you owe me an apology too?"

"I saved your life," I say between clenched teeth.

"I don't need you to save me, Vixen. I'm quite capable of taking care of myself."

"Are you sure you're not married?" Rudolpho breaks in.

Hann and I pause to look at him. We both break out in laughter at Rudolpho's perplexed expression.

"We're not married," Hann says. "We're both too stubborn for our own good. Vixen needs someone soft—like one of those Cavaliers. Someone she can overpower."

My breath catches in my throat. A sudden memory of Stratton fills my thoughts. The memory of our short time together has faded now, but Hann's words bring back thoughts of our short interlude.

"What?" Hann asks, a small frown creasing his brow, almost as though he can read my thoughts.

"Nothing," I reply, moving away from them.

"Well, I must be off," Rudolpho says. "I've got to get back to the forest before dark."

"You live in the forest?" I hear Hann ask.

Rudolpho's next words make my ears perk up. "I do indeed. That's where my true friends are."

I turn my head to stare at him. "What friends?"

Rudolpho swipes at his red nose, hesitating before answering. "The animals. Sounds crazy, huh? I haven't been much of a people person, but the animals get me."

Hann and I exchange a look. Is it possible this man is one of the Favored Ones? I don't know what I'm expecting of the other eight I seek, but certainly not the large figure before me.

"They understand what you say?"

My question makes Rudolpho pause for a full minute before answering. "Now, don't you go around saying I'm crazy."

"I don't think you're crazy. I'm just curious."

He looks at Hann who gives him a slight nod. "Well, let's just say I have this special ability to communicate with animals. It's something you wouldn't understand——."

"She understands," Hann says quietly. "She has that ability too."

Rudolpho shifts his weight from one foot to the other as he looks at me. He scratches his head, his eyes full of confusion and questions. "By communicating, I mean, they help me."

"I know," I whisper. "They protect you."

A light enters Rudolpho's eyes and he nods vehemently. "That's right. They protect me. How did you know that?"

I gesture to Hann. "Like he said, I have that ability too. I've known since I was twelve years old."

Rudolpho gives a low whistle. "You're not jesting with me?"

"I've seen it for myself," Hann says.

"I've not met anyone else like me. I kind of thought I was special—maybe even the Favored One. You know that commanding animals is a sign of the Favored One. You just burst my bubble on that one."

"We need to talk," I tell him.

We lead Rudolpho to a secluded area so I can share my story with him. He's a rather boorish man with no manners, swiping at his bulbous, red nose as it drips from his allergic reaction to certain trees in the settlement.

The story of his childhood is one of loneliness and sadness. He was a young boy raised on the outskirts of a settlement because his family wasn't accepted into the settlers' fold. His father had been a Cavalier in his youth but had sustained a great injury during a war with a neighboring land, costing him the loss of one leg. Unable to continue his royal duties as a knight for the monarchy, he had been forced to join the masses who work off the land for their sustenance.

As an outcast, Rudolpho never enjoyed companionship with others. His family kept to themselves, working on their small piece of allotted land—forgotten by the monarchy and ignored by suspicious settlers.

Despite the poverty that Grandmullie and I have endured along with the rest of the masses, Rudolpho's memories bring me to tears—that is, until he gets to the point in his life where he's taken to stealing food to fill his enormous stomach. I cross my arms and frown with disapproval. He stops in his tracks and gnaws at his bottom lip.

"I suppose I shouldn't tell that part of the story with such glee?" he asks.

"I suppose not," I say shortly.

Hann tries to conceal a grin, but I catch it before he can look away. I know he can feel my glower even though he can't see me.

"We all make mistakes," Hann says to me as much as to Rudolpho.

I press my lips together and shake my head. "Choosing to steal is not a mistake."

"Neither is lying," Rudolpho says quickly.

"I'll have you know that I'm not in the habit of lying. I said one small fib—and that was an act of desperation to save Hann's life."

Hann turns back to me. "Look, we all need to get along. What's in the past stays in the past."

"I agree. If Rudolpho is to accompany us, he will need to stop stealing."

"But what if it will save one of our lives?" Rudolpho asks with wide eyes.

Hann groans and shakes his head. "Must we go on like this? Time is short. We'll react differently to each situation, right? No stealing or lying unless a life depends on it. Can we at least agree to that?"

Rudolpho and I nod our heads. I find him a distasteful individual and wonder why, out of all the people in the lands, Rudolpho was ever chosen to be a Favored One. My eagerness to find the others is diminished. The thought of being tied to the foul man before me is a most unpleasant thought.

Without warning, Rudolpho suddenly sneezes, delivering a spray of mucus within ten feet of where he's perched on an old log. I'm glad I'm standing far enough away.

"Sorry," Rudolpho sniffs, swiping at his nose.

I look away when I see a stream of slimy discharge strings down his chin. Hann clears his throat and makes a motion for him to wipe his beard.

"You're not sick, are you?" Hann asks.

"Just my allergies. I'm probably allergic to the tree log I'm sitting on."

"Are you sure it's just allergies? I mean, your nose—."

I look at Rudolpho's nose. It's the brightest red of any nose I believe I've ever seen. "With your nose so bright, won't you—."

Hann cuts me off at the fearful look in Rudolpho's eyes. "Nothing to worry about, I'm sure."

"Nothing to worry about," I gasp. "I've never seen someone's nose so red."

Rudolpho stands, covering his face with his hands. "Is it terrible to look at?"

"No," Hann says, looking at me. "It's just—how would you say?"

I look at him and shake my head. I can't answer his question. It's as bright as a lantern that would guide us. He grimaces and heaves a sigh.

"I've heard that large noses have the benefit of smelling scents no one else can pick up," Hann says. "It's quite a gift you have, Rudolpho."

The large man slowly lowers his hands and bears a grin. "A gift? I never thought of it like that. Much obliged, Hann."

There is something endearing in the humanity Hann displays in unexpected ways. I try to stifle my own smile—but it isn't directed at Rudolpho. That boy, Hann, has made me quite bewildered. I'm confident there's no one else like him in the lands.

Seven

THE BLACK SMOKE RISING IN THE DISTANCE
alerts us to the Cavaliers' presence in my settlement before we
reach it. A large group of the knights has been traveling from
settlement to settlement to imprison the boys for the sporting
event which is to take place in two weeks. They burn any
building that houses food or grain rations as a show of their
power so the settlers will submit to their authority out of fear.
Their strategy has worked in the first five settlements where
they've seized a multitude of boys.

My heart beats hard in my chest as we draw near. The black
smoke lingers in the rolling hills as a dark foreshadowing of the
evil about to embark upon the lands. Moaning from my

settlement enters our ears as we pass the small houses. Precious people to me, now heartbroken at the loss of sons and food.

Our best guess is that the Cavaliers had made their presence the day prior. I can only pray that Grandmullie was not hurt in the chaos of the Cavaliers' siege.

"I'm sure she's fine," Hann says softly.

I nod my head and blink back tears. Hann and Rudolpho have accompanied me for the past three weeks, seeking out the other Favored Ones. We've been unsuccessful with our search. Trying to fight discouragement, something inside hearkened my spirit, urging me to go back home.

"Which one is your home?"

Rudolpho's tone is somber as we pass the small houses, a few now smoldering embers. I can hear the moans come from the twins' home. Their mother must have been unsuccessful in finding them wives. Lila's house is quiet and still. I want to check on her, make sure they're all safe, but my grandmother is my first priority right now. It's only minutes before we arrive at my house, but it seems like hours from the impending anxiety that attacks my mental state.

When I see my small home in the distance, I break into a mad dash to get there faster. I fling open the door to find— emptiness. Grandmullie has not been there in a long while. I know this because the sparkling clean home I have been accustomed to living in is now cloaked in several weeks of dust.

"Grandmullie?" I cry out.

Only the silence greets my frantic voice. I look around the small home, trying to find clues to where Grandmullie may have gone. Surely, she would have left me a note—something to let me know she was fine.

"Nothing?" Hann asks quietly from the door.

I shake my head, my mind swirling with ugly thoughts of what may have happened to my treasured grandmother.

"Would she have gone to a neighbor's home?"

I shake my head no. "She's been gone for a while."

Rudolpho pokes his head through the door. "Well, this looks comfy, wouldn't you say?"

Hann pushes him back out the door and I follow, shading my eyes to look plaintively over the rolling hills. And then a thought occurs to me. Lady Sysselye. She's the one true friend that Grandmullie trusts. I would have to go into Kringle.

"I think I know where she may have gone," I say. "But you can't come with me."

"I'm not leaving you," Hann protests.

I turn to face him. "You will assuredly get captured, Hann. Rudolpho can accompany me."

"Where will you go?"

"Kringle."

Hann sighs and looks at me with guarded eyes. "We both know there is a danger in you going alone."

"They're looking for young men, not maidens. I need to make sure my grandmother is safe."

He heaves a great sigh and turns to look over the plains as I had done. His voice is tense when he finally speaks. "Keep your eyes out for St. Nicklaus. He will be looking for his own victims for Winter Solstice."

"Yes," Rudolpho interjects. "I hear he makes his list every year of those naughty and nice. You don't want to make it on his naughty list. Unspeakable things happen to people on that list."

"What kind of unspeakable things?" I ask.

"They're *unspeakable*," he says, drawing out the word as though it is a curse upon one's soul.

"We shall avoid that insidious man by all means," I say softly. "There is nothing about him that I trust."

Rudolpho crinkles his large nose at me. "Have you ever met him? Is he as foul as they say?"

"He is a revolting man who makes my stomach churn. I don't want to cross paths with him again."

Hann crosses to me and grabs my shoulders, staring hard into my eyes. I don't want to guess what the raw emotion in his eyes means—it scares me. "Stay safe, Vixen. Move as swiftly through the forest as you can. The Cavaliers will be scouting for victims. I don't want you to become one."

"I might say the same for you, Hann."

He gives me a wink. "If they capture me, it's only because I want them to."

I ease out of his grip and nod to Rudolpho. We need to be out of the forest before dark. The large man moves at a slower pace than me, so it will take twice as long to reach Kringle than if I went by myself.

"Wait," Hann says.

I watch him strip bark from a nearby tree. He approaches me and bends down, grabbing my foot to place the bark over my thin shoes. This is how the masses protect our feet in the winter. Thick bark wrapped with rags provide protection against snow. And snow is coming. The thick clouds are waiting in anticipation of a heavenly order to deposit it upon the lands.

When Hann's done securing the bark on my feet, I don't say a word. I start walking and don't look back at him. If I do, I may not leave without him. I'll have to trust that he will stay out of sight and be safe.

"All this walking is making me lose my trousers," Rudolpho says, huffing behind me and clutching at his pants to hold them up.

"Where's the rope Hann gave you?"

"I seem to have misplaced it."

I just shake my head in response. Rudolpho is a forgetful man. Somehow, he lost his brown robe along our journey. *How does one lose the clothing on their back?* Despite my misgivings about him—and his lack of personal hygeiene—I have to admit to a growing fondness for his bumbling.

"What do you know of true love?" he asks after a period of silence where the only sound we hear is the crashing of our, or rather, his, footsteps on the pine needles in the forest.

"Why do you ask, Rudolpho?"

"I think I found my one true love," he remarks unexpectedly.

I tense at his words and stop in my tracks, turning to face him with a scowl. "You better not be falling in love with me, Rudolpho."

The burly man's eyes bulge in his beefy face. "You? *You?* Please don't take offense, Vixen, but you scare me too much for me to ever fall in love with you. If I don't mind my manners, I fully expect you'll hit me over the head with a tree branch."

I frown. "I'm not that bad."

"You're not that good either," he mumbles, and then immediately shields his face with his arms when I take a step toward him.

"Oh, please," I sigh. "I'm not going to hit you."

He lowers his arms but still takes a step back from me. "Hann might enjoy your haughtiness, but you make the hairs stand up on my arms."

"I don't think anyone has ever told me that I have that effect on them. Thank you for sharing," I say with a huff, turning to walk away from him, quickening my pace so that he's forced to run to catch up. "And what do you know of Hann enjoying my haughtiness anyway?"

"I can read the enjoyment on his face when the two of you are—well, when you're having a titillating conversation. Look, I'm too big and too hungry to keep up this pace," he yells at my back.

"You brought it on yourself," I toss over my shoulder. "Titillating conversation indeed!"

"Don't you want me to tell you who my true love is?" he pants behind me.

It's several minutes before I stop to hear his answer. His face is flushed and beads of perspiration are rolling down his cheeks.

"You're a tough one," he gasps and leans over to draw in air.

"The brisk pace is good for you. I'll refrain from asking how you became fat when the rest of the masses are skinny from hunger."

Rudolpho stands to wipe the sweat from his eyes. "It's a bit complicated. I've always volunteered to work in sanctuaries throughout the land in exchange for food. That's how I know the bishops eat so well. They're usually so busy praying and fasting that they don't even realize the amount of food donated to them. Seeing how I usually end up in the kitchen to prepare meals and clean, I got first pick of the meals. It's worked out very nicely for the past several years—until the priests started catching on. Then I would be forced to leave one sanctuary for the next. I've pretty much run out of sanctuaries here in Klaus as the priests recognize me now."

"So the priest you stole the loaf of bread from that day knew you?"

Rudolpho grunts in reply. I can only shake my head at the disheveled man before me. His stomach may get both of us in trouble if he can't control his appetite.

"No more stealing, right?" I order sharply.

Rudolpho's face brightens. "Only if it's a life-threatening situation."

"Even so, I will have to approve it."

A sudden gunshot rings out behind us. Rudolpho ducks just as a bullet whizzes past us and strikes a tree. I dive to the ground with my large companion dropping beside me.

"Cavaliers," I whisper.

Rudolpho's body starts quivering and the color drains from his face. Fear is settling into his innermost parts, and he won't be able to run if we need to escape. I slap his face hard. My hand leaves an ugly red imprint against his ashen skin as his head whirls from my blow.

"Snap out of it," I command in a low voice.

Rudolpho swallows back the tears that fill his eyes. His tender heart will get us killed if he can't control himself.

"Show yourself," comes a harsh command several yards from us.

"Please don't shoot," I yell out. "We're coming out."

As soon as I raise up, another warning shot is fired. I duck back down as two Cavaliers' laughter fills the air. They sit on horses in their fine armor with rifles pointed in our direction. We're merely sport for them.

Rudolpho is curled into a ball on the ground with his fingers plugging his ears. I can't count on him to help me.

I crawl on my stomach in the direction of the Cavaliers, trying to stay low in the brush. When I'm just a couple of feet from them, I whisper for the horses to help me. They whinny softly, their ears perked up at my words. I persist in instructing them. Finally, one rears up wildly, forcing the Cavalier to drop his rifle. He clings to the horse as it charges through the forest.

The second knight's horse starts bucking the unfortunate Cavalier. His shouts to the horse go unheeded as the steed throws itself in the air. Just when it seems the knight can no longer hold on, the beast bursts into a full run to race after the other horse, removing the threat of the Cavalier from Rudolpho and me.

I stand and brush at the debris clinging to my brown robe. There would be other Cavaliers in the forest, scouting the area for young men who might try to hide themselves from being unwilling victims in the sporting event.

"Rudolpho, let's go!"

He slowly rises from the ground, still clearly shaken. "Are we safe?"

"Safe? No. We need to get out of this forest as quickly as possible. Follow me."

Rudolpho doesn't move. The imminent danger lurking in the forest is immobilizing the large man. I turn and stride off without him, hoping that will spur some action, but he doesn't budge. Finally, I turn back and cross to him.

"I can't walk," he says, his voice trembling like a child's when he's frightened.

"All right," I say quietly, soothingly. "Let's try to talk about something else for a bit. Like your true love. You never told me the maiden's name."

Rudolpho draws in a deep breath. "Her name is Mary Krist. I used to call her Mary kissed because I wanted my lips to touch hers softly. She's a winsome lady—was a winsome lady when I knew her."

"Is she dead?"

"No, no. She's alive. I met her twenty years ago. Her eyes met mine and I just knew she was the woman for me."

He pauses for several minutes and I wait for him to carry on the story. Finally, I can take his dreamy eyes no longer. "So what happened?"

"Well, nothing really happened. Just that look exchanged between us. I could never summon up the courage to speak to her, you know."

I blink at him in disbelief. "Are you telling me that you've never actually spoken to this woman you say is your true love?"

"That's right."

"Rudolpho, that's sad—actually, it's quite pathetic. It's been twenty years. Don't you think it's time you considered other possibilities? You're not getting any younger, you know."

"When you know you've found the one, you can't give your heart away to another."

"But she didn't even know that she was the one. Unless, of course, you did some kind of sign language to communicate that to her?"

"I never tried sign language. I think my fingers would have gotten tied into knots like my tongue. No telling what I would have said to her."

"Why don't you think about your Mary Krist as we continue. Think that may get your feet moving?"

Rudolpho starts shuffling his feet with a lopsided grin. "I think she'll make me dance my way out of here."

I have to laugh at the sight before me. "Dance? Is that what you're doing? I guess that's how a big ox like you *would* dance, Rudolpho."

We resume our trek through the forest. While Rudolpho is lighter on his feet with his thoughts preoccupied with a lost love, my own feet felt sluggish, weighed down with the reality of pending bloodshed soon to come upon Klaus.

We emerge from the forest without further mishap and push into Kringle at dusk. The elfin village is very quiet. The twinkle lights that have always greeted me at this hour have disappeared. Remains of charred homes that housed food rations greet us at every turn. The Kringles were adept at growing food, and I can only hope some of it survived the Cavaliers' assault.

Our steps are cautious as we make our way to Lady Sysselye's house, our footsteps echoing over the cobblestone path running through the village. The curtains are drawn tightly over the small windows of the earthen home. I lightly rap my knuckles on the door, but there is no answer.

"Lady Sysselye?" I whisper into the crack of the door.

It takes several more minutes of my frantic whispers before the door is suddenly flung open and I'm enveloped in the warm embrace of Grandmullie.

"Where have you been, Vixen? I've been sick with worry for you."

"I'm so sorry, Grandmullie. I was gone far longer than I ever expected."

"Come inside," she beckons, stopping short when she sees Rudolpho. "Oh, my. You have a traveling companion of sorts with you?"

"I have much to tell you, Grandmullie. This is my friend, Rudolpho."

She scans his large frame from top to bottom before responding. "Nice to make your acquaintance, Rudolpho. I would invite you in, but I'm afraid the quarters are a bit tight in here."

"Quite all right," Rudolpho says. "I'll perch myself on this wee little bench out here."

"Please try not to break anything, Rudolpho," I say in a stern voice and follow Grandmullie into the house, but Lady Sysselye is not there.

"She's gone to comfort some of the elfin mothers," my grandmother says softly. "The Cavaliers swept through the village four days ago and seized all the Kringles they could. The King expects a great turnout at the sporting event, so he needs to provide as many bodies as possible to satisfy the spectators' thirst for bloodshed."

"Do you know our settlement was attacked yesterday?"

Grandmullie sighs despondently. "I suspected they were headed that way. I can only imagine the devastation."

"The food rations are gone, Grandmullie."

"Whatever shall we do—what will *you* do? Did you make it to the Council of Elders?"

I nod my head. "There are multiple Favored Ones. Rudolpho is one as well."

Her eyes widen. "That large man outside?"

"I need to find the others. Our destinies are connected."

"You can't let anyone know or you will be killed," Grandmullie warns softly.

"I'm being very careful. There is a boy helping me find the others."

"You've been traveling alone with a boy?

I smile at her rebuke. "There's nothing to be concerned about, I assure you. No romantic feelings of any sort from either of us. He was very helpful in finding Rudolpho. I left him at our home so I could fetch you."

I avoid my grandmother's eyes. She reads me like no one else. She would find out my growing feelings for Hann, feelings that I won't even acknowledge to myself.

Thankfully, Grandmullie is too distracted to continue to probe. "We should be on our way to comfort and help our own settlement. The dangers at night are too great so we'll plan to leave at dawn."

A sudden knock on the door makes both of us jump. Grandmullie gasps and grips my arm. I pat her hand with a forced smile of reassurance and move to open the door. It's only Rudolpho.

"Beg your pardon for intruding on your conversation, but there's a Kringle out here who seeks Lady Sysselye."

I look past Rudolpho to see an old elf standing behind him, twisting a knitted cap in his hands. His long silver hair hangs in a braid down his back, and his eyes wear the graveness of the atmosphere around us.

"Lady Sysselye isn't here," I tell him.

"Do you know where I can find her?"

"She's somewhere in Kringle, comforting others."

He inclines his head. "Obliged, miss."

The Kringle crams his hat on his head and turns to leave. Something inside urges me to speak to him. "Wait. Is there something you needed—something we can help with?"

"The sadness in the lands only deepen," he says quietly. "I have word that the orphanage has been plundered."

Grandmullie gasps. "Poor innocent children. Who would do such a thing at a time like this?"

"Nicklaus," the small man says with a snarl and spits on the ground.

"What could the orphans possibly have that Nicklaus would want to steal?" I ask him.

"Their coal. The orphanage has been provided coal from the Kringles that work in the coal mines. They had a large storehouse that housed the coal—more than enough for the children to be kept warm during the winter months. Nicklaus took it all. And the gold coins that some benefactor gave to the children. They kept their coins safely stored in their small wooden shoes."

"How awful," I whisper.

The Kringle shakes his head and walks away without another word. We stand looking at each other, at a loss for words. Cruelty has no boundaries.

"Whatever can we do to help those poor children?" Grandmullie asks in a grave voice.

Rudolpho starts sniffling, his nose turning red and starting to run. "Oh, the tragedy of it all!"

"Blow your nose, Rudolpho, and stop being so dramatic," I order sharply. "All is not lost yet."

"What do you propose we do?"

I pause, my thoughts spinning. I can't help the grin that spreads across my face. "I have a plan, but it's going to require a visit to Nicklaus' sanctuary."

Rudolpho takes a step back, the color fading from his nose. "Not the sanctuary," he breathes. "Don't make me go to the sanctuary."

"What are you going to do?" Grandmullie asks.

"We'll take back what rightfully belongs to the children."

"You—you—you mean—*steal* the coal and money from Nicklaus?"

"Stealing would mean the coal and money belonged to him in the first place. No, we are going to retrieve the stolen goods from good ol' Nicklaus and give it back to the poor orphans."

My smile is erased when Rudolpho wheezes and collapses to the ground without warning. My large companion will need to toughen up. Too many years of hiding in the forest and allowing the animals to protect him has softened his manhood. The problem is, time isn't on my side for such a gargantuan task.

Eight

THE SANCTUARY IS MOST DREADFUL AT night. The moon peeks out from the clouds for mere seconds at a time before quickly drawing back into the misty darkness. I feel dampness on my face and realize the first flakes of snow are starting to drop, soft and unhurried. If only Klaus reflected the silent night, peaceful night amidst its turmoil.

Every hair on my body stands on end as we draw nearer the cold structure. Rudolpho is sweating so profusely by the time we reach the sanctuary that I'm fearful he'll have a seizure.

"I don't think I can do this," he whispers when we reach the stone steps.

"Just stick to the plan," I mutter under my breath.

I reach out and grasp the large, cold iron knocker in my hand. It's molded into the shape of a lion with a ring protruding from its mouth. It strikes the thick wooden door with a resounding clang, reverberating through the sanctuary.

And we wait. For almost an hour. Grandmullie told me to strike the knocker just once and wait as long as needed for the door to open. Other impatient people had suffered the dreaded consequence of the switch for knocking more than once.

We have almost given up hope of the door opening. After all, it's late and cold. Perhaps Nicklaus is tucked warmly into bed. And then the door creaks open and I see his beady eyes peer into the cold night. Evidently, evil knows no sleep.

"Who dares to interrupt me at this late hour?" Nicklaus' voice is slurred as though he has partaken of too much wine.

"Good evening, sire—."

"Saint," he corrects sharply. "It's Saint Nicklaus you're speaking to."

I take a deep breath and force myself to speak in a calm, controlled voice. "Of course, Saint—Saint—."

The words get stuck on my tongue. The reptile of a man standing before me is anything but a saint. He opens the door wider and thrusts a lantern in my face.

"Who are you?"

Rudolpho crouches behind me, quivering at the sound of the old man before us. Nicklaus' pungent breath fills the very atmosphere around us. I turn my head to the side in an attempt to suck in fresh air. Then I turn back to him and push back the hood of my robe. I hear him draw a breath.

"It's I, sire. I hope you remember me as you indicated our paths crossing were fate."

Nicklaus' eyes narrow and a devious smile crosses his lips as he opens the door wider. Very slowly, his hand reaches out to touch my hair with a crooked finger. "Ah, yes, I remember you. You've invaded my dreams for many a night. I knew you would come to me. I beckoned you in my dreams."

I swallow the sudden urge to vomit and force a smile to my lips. It's a fake smile and I'm sure Nicklaus realizes that. In his drunken state, he's willing to forgive my lack of enthusiasm.

"I'm sure that's why I'm here, sire," I manage to say.

His hand suddenly snakes out to clutch my head, his fingers spreading through my hair like a spider weaving a web of wickedness. Slowly, deliberately, he draws me closer to him. "What do you want of me, innocent maiden?"

"Sanctuary," I stutter. No matter how many times I practiced my speech in my head on the way over, all words have eluded me now that I'm pulled next to Nicklaus' bony frame.

"Yes," he whispers, his breath hot on my cheek. "I can provide you sanctuary."

"And for my friend too," I whisper, frantically reaching behind my back to clutch at Rudolpho.

"I think I'm fine," Rudolpho stammers. "I'm a big fellow—I can sleep out in the snow."

"Of course you can," Nicklaus says with a smile. His eyes never straying from my face.

"I shall not enter without my friend," I say firmly.

Nicklaus looks past me to Rudolpho with displeasure written on his face. He reluctantly releases my hair and opens the door fully, extending his arm in an invitation for us to enter the sanctuary.

I grab Rudolpho's arm and pull him behind me. His skin is cold—as much from meeting Nicklaus for the first time as from the cold outside.

A fire roars in the massive stone fireplace along one wall. A bundle of switches leans against the side of it like a trophy. Masses have long whispered about Nicklaus suddenly coming down the chimney to surprise unwitting visitors to the sanctuary. Too bad he never tried that when a fire was lit below. I think I may well enjoy seeing his backside in flames.

"A little wine to warm your spirit?" Nicklaus asks, crossing to the fire to pick up a jug of wine.

Rudolpho shakes his head no, but I see this as the perfect opportunity to lay my plan in motion. I cross to the sinister fellow with another forced smile.

"I've never had wine before, but it does sound warm and inviting."

Nicklaus can barely contain his glee at my words. He pours some wine in a goblet and holds it out to me. "We shall drink together tonight."

Rudolpho's groan reaches my ears, but I ignore him and take the goblet from Nicklaus. "My friend is very hungry, sire. Might he go to your kitchen for some food?"

"Yes, I can see his stomach delights in being filled," Nicklaus murmurs, raising his own goblet to his lips to empty the last swig of wine. He grabs the jug and sloshes some more of the red substance into his goblet while we wait.

At that moment, the sound of a cackle is heard behind us. I turn to see a Juul, his beady eyes glimmering in the firelight. "I wasn't aware we had visitors."

Rudolpho starts visibly shaking. He's never seen a Juul before either, and the frightful tales of the elves are more than the large man can bear.

"Take the fat man into the kitchen to find food," Nicklaus orders. "The maiden will share this evening with only me. And no peeking from you this time!"

The Juul motions for Rudolpho to follow him, but he's frozen again from fear. I desperately, silently nod my head in the direction of the Juul, but Rudolpho shakes his head no.

"My friend is rather cold this evening," I tell Nicklaus. "Perhaps a drink of wine will warm him."

I move to Rudolpho and hold out my goblet. His eyes are wide with fright and his hands tremble as he takes it out of my hand.

"I don't drink wine," Rudolpho whispers.

"Perhaps one drink will help you overcome your fear," I say quietly.

Dutifully, he takes the goblet from me and raises it to his lips to take a tentative sip. "Most tasty," he says with a grin.

"Are you coming or not?"

The Juul's scratchy voice jerks Rudolpho's head up, and a fresh wave of fear crosses his face. Rudolpho looks desperately from me to the Juul, and without another word, he raises the goblet to gulp the entire contents and hands the goblet back to me.

I cringe at his behavior but realize it's an act of desperation. Besides, he's taken care of the wine in the goblet, so all I have to do is pretend to drink. Hopefully, Nicklaus won't see my pretense.

"A young maiden like you must be accustomed to frolicking in the hills, am I correct?"

"Do you mean dancing?"

He laughs and pours more wine into his goblet. "If you wish to call it that. Drink up. There's much merriness to be had.

When we're done, we can retire to my room to frolic this cold evening."

I place my goblet on a nearby table and cross back to him, hurriedly pulling off the strips of bark from my feet. "I would like to frolic right now."

His head jerks up and he looks at me with a startled expression. "Right now?"

"Yes. I would like to frolic in front of this warm fire."

A low laugh emanates from him and he downs the remaining wine in his goblet, dropping it on the floor. He grabs a small twig broken from a tree and waves it at me as though coaxing me to come closer. "Have you ever seen a love plant before? It's called a mistletoe. Come to me, my sweet maiden."

I have a plan. I hope it works. I move to the man who has terrorized many of the masses and hold out my hand. He ignores my hand and reaches out to place his hands around my waist, holding the mistletoe above my head and puckering his lips.

"Sire, you move too quickly," I admonish. "The night is young."

"Yes," he whispers. "We have all night."

I twirl out of his grasp and hold out my hand to him. Grudgingly, he takes it. His fingers are soft. He's obviously never worked manual labor in his life.

I start humming and swaying back and forth, trying to still my chattering teeth from the cold floor on my thin shoes. He stands like a statue, watching me through his wine-dazed eyes.

"Dance with me," I urge.

"Take off that hideous robe," he says suddenly. "It hides your beauty."

"But I have trousers on. They're far less flattering than the robe."

"That will never do," he mumbles.

Nicklaus releases my hand and puts his fingers to his lips to produce a shrill whistle. Within seconds, two Juuls appear in the room.

"Fetch the maiden a dress. Something lovely—something the monarchy would wear."

The dark elves silently eye me up and down before departing. Nicklaus turns back to the wine and empties the remaining liquid from the jug.

"Bring more wine," he shouts.

Within minutes, the Juuls' reappear. One carries another jug of wine; the other has a gown draped over his arm. He holds it up for Nicklaus to approve. The bodice is made of a gold material, close-fitting with long sleeves lined with small pearls. The long flaring skirt is made of a sheer, cream-colored material. It's the most beautiful dress I've ever laid eyes on.

"Yes," Nicklaus croons, "the dress is perfect."

I carefully take the dress from the Juul and look around the room for a place to change into the glorious gown. The Juul silently point down the hall.

"Thank you," I say and start making my way in that direction.

"No need to leave," Nicklaus' loud voice booms. "You can change here. The elves can leave."

The Juuls scowl. One steps forward, eyes flashing. His forked tongue snakes out to lick his thin lips. "We want to see too."

"No. You're invading on my private time. Away with you!" He waves his hand at the Juuls to shoo them away.

With a last look at me, they depart, leaving Nicklaus alone with me once again. The suggestive look in his eyes makes my stomach feel sour—like when I ate some curds that had developed mold.

"While I change into this lovely gown, sire, may I be bold and ask that you put on the scarlet cape you wore when declaring the proclamation for the sporting event? I fancy my hands will enjoy being tickled by the snow-angel jack rabbit fur."

"The fur strikes your fancy, does it? Perhaps that's the only article of clothing you want me in?" he asks suggestively.

I turn my head so he can't see how horrified I am at the prospect of seeing him in only a cloak. "All good things take time, sire. I would blush to see you in only the cloak and fear I wouldn't feel like frolicking any longer. No, the cloak over your clothes is fine—and perhaps more wine."

"More wine. Of course. I'll have it waiting for you when you come back to me."

I quickly dart into the first room I see, slamming the door behind me. It's an old library filled with the scent of musty books. A thick layer of dust covers the books. I wonder why Nicklaus has them in his possession if he doesn't read them.

Hurriedly, I shove a chair in front of the door and make haste in undressing. The room is cold, but my hands tremble more with excitement at the prospect of sliding a dress over my body. I've never had the privilege to don one before, and I tingle as the rich fabric brushes my skin. The Juuls have selected well. The gown is a perfect fit. I close my eyes to relish wearing such a fine article of clothing. Lila would be so envious.

Heavy, faded velvet drapes conceal a window in the room. This may be my only opportunity to see myself in such fine attire. The dust and cobwebs clinging to the drapes shoot in the air at my disturbance. In the dim light of the room, I can see my reflection in the window. The bodice of the dress hugs my small waist and flows out. My long braid looks out of place with the dress. I should have my long curly locks flowing down my back to complement the dress.

"Be brave," I whisper to my reflection, trying to mask the fear that threatens to overtake me.

My enjoyment of the dress is cut short by Nicklaus, shouting for me to return. A deep breath, straightening of my shoulders, and I'm ready to continue with my plan.

Nicklaus has given up any pretense of being a gentleman. He's swigging straight from the wine jug when I rejoin him. He takes a drunken step back when he sees me, almost tripping on the scarlet cloak.

"Where have you been all my life?" he asks, his words thick and slurred.

"Shall we dance?" I ask brightly.

"No more dancing," he declares with a loud belch. "I don't think I can stand up straight."

"Nonsense. The dancing will wake you up. Take one more teeny tiny sip and sweep me in your arms, sire."

I don't have to tell him twice. He takes a long gulp from the jug and tries to set it on the table, but his hand slips and it crashes to the floor.

Before he can wail about the spilled wine, I sashay to him and grab his hand, twirling myself under his arm. Clumsily, he grasps my waist and all but clings to me as I forcefully lead him across the floor in a waltz, humming all the while. It's the only dance I know. Lila's mother taught it to both of us several years ago in preparation for us marrying one day.

"Slow down," he gasps.

I purposefully increase the pace of my steps and hum louder, whirling him around as he stumbles to keep up. He's not too heavy, and with a little effort, I'm able to keep him moving. I tell myself that the pain my feet incur every time he steps on me will be worth it in the end.

When his eyes start rolling back in his head, I release my tight grip, sending him sprawling to the stone floor. He's not even aware of the hard conk his forehead takes when it strikes the hard surface. The cape fans out around him, swirling on the floor like a pool of blood. Too bad it's really not his blood being spilled.

Quickly, I wrap the bark around my shoes again, enjoying the sweet taste of victory at the unconscious state of the foul man laying so very still on the floor. With him out of the way, I now just need to find Rudolpho and complete our mission.

"What did you do?"

I whirl at the voice of the Juul, my mind frantically searching for words. Finally, all I can say is, "Saint Nicklaus is drunk."

He can't ignore the evidence. His beady eyes dart around the room, taking in the broken wine jug on the floor and Nicklaus' scarlet cape.

"What do you have to say for yourself?"

"I was merely frolicking with him."

"Frolicking? With *him?*" the Juul's laugh pierces the room. "Now you can frolic with me!"

Without warning, he rushes toward me and pounces, straddling me much like the baby desert monkeys cling to their mothers. His black, forked tongue reaches out to sneak a lick of my face. It's slimy and cold as it extends along the length of my cheek.

Purely by instinct, I spit in his face. He loosens his grip for a split second—just enough time for me to grab that elf and fling him across the room. The small man lands with a dull thud against the stone fireplace. I rush to him, taking advantage of his dazed state by grabbing a switch from the pile and holding it over his head threateningly. He screams as if in agony.

"Not the switch! Not the switch!"

"Where did my friend go?"

He points in the direction Rudolpho had disappeared. "That way."

"Show me," I order, yanking him to his feet and kicking his bottom with my foot.

The Juul holds up his hands defensively and starts scurrying in the direction he pointed, his hands shielding his buttocks— whether from the switch or my foot, I can't be sure.

The kitchen is dark and cold. In the dim light, I can barely make out the large figure of Rudolpho slumped over the sink.

"Light me a candle," I command the Juul, holding the switch over his head as a warning.

He grabs a candle from a nearby counter and lights it. I take it out of his hand and make my way to Rudolpho, ignoring the frightened Juul's quick disappearance from the kitchen.

"Rudolpho," I whisper, frantically shaking his shoulder.

His body jerks and he raises his head, rubbing his red eyes. "What happened? Where am I?"

"We're at the sanctuary," I tell him. "I'm afraid we'll have to get out of here in a hurry. The Juuls will be coming for us any minute."

As realization of where we are strikes Rudolpho, I turn at the sound of small footsteps moving in our direction. The little men are swift on their feet. I scramble to the kitchen window to fling it open, but curiously, it's already unfastened. That explains why the kitchen feels so cold.

"Through here!" I yell.

Rudolpho dives through the window without thinking. A group of five or more Juuls enter the kitchen just as I let myself out, landing with a thud on the frozen ground as I try to protect the candle from extinguishing.

"Run!" I scream at Rudolpho.

We move quickly from the sanctuary into the cold night. I don't know what it is, perhaps the effect of the wine he drank, but Rudolpho pushes past me, his large footsteps bounding over the snow-clad ground stretching out before us.

When we're far enough away from the sanctuary, and I'm confident the Juuls haven't followed us, I yell for Rudolpho to stop. His eyes are wide when he approaches me, and his nostrils flare from breathing in the cold air.

I hold the candle up to him. Remarkably, it has stayed lit as I ran through the softly falling snow. "Are you alright?"

He falls to his knees, breathing harder than he's probably ever been forced to breathe in his life. "I think I'll live."

"We have to go back, Rudolpho."

He vehemently shakes his head no. "I won't go back there if my life depended on it."

"The children will freeze without the coal to warm them."

Rudolpho slowly rises to his feet. He pulls up a large bag from the ground. "I don't think so."

"What's that?"

"The coal I took from the sanctuary. It was a bit tricky with the elf's little eyes watching my every move. I told him I needed some fresh air and opened the window. His wee little body got cold so he left me alone. Let me tell you, it's not easy for a large man like me to be sneaky. Trying to tiptoe around the sanctuary is like a bear trying to tiptoe in the forest. I found the coal in a small room behind the kitchen. There was a bag of money in there, too."

I'm dumbfounded and can only stare at him in amazement. "But how—how did I not see you running with that large bag?"

"Well, it is dark out here and it's not like you were paying too close of attention to me while trying to save your own hide."

"I'm impressed by your effort, Rudolpho," I say with a smile and curtsy.

Unfortunately, that small action causes the candle wick to be extinguished, plunging us into darkness. I look to the heavens but the ominous clouds conceal the luminaries.

"Do you know where we go from here?" Rudolpho asks.

"We're not far from the orphanage. Let's get the coal and money delivered before day breaks."

Rudolpho slings the large bag over his shoulder and follows me. The snow collected on the ground is already penetrating my thin shoes. If we allow ourselves to stop, Rudolpho and I may well meet our demise.

While the snow may have been met with excitement at first, the snowflakes become more intense. Our visibility is dim to the point where we have to hold hands to ensure we stay together.

I don't complain as Rudolpho's large fingers squeeze my hand. He wouldn't hear me anyway. Besides, my fingers would probably be numb from the cold anyway—especially when the wind picks up, howling at us for daring to venture into the snowy night.

"The orphanage is up ahead," I shout to Rudolpho.

He squeezes my hand even harder in reply. His footsteps have slowed considerably by the time we see the dim candlelight from the orphanage beckoning us. I reach over to push the heavy bag back up his shoulder. Fatigue is wearing the large man to the point where he is stooped over, forcing one step in front of the other.

Rudolpho heaves a huge sigh of relief when we reach the courtyard leading into the orphanage. He throws the heavy bag on the ground and stretches his arms over his head.

"What now?" he asks. "Should we just knock on the door?"

"We'll just leave the bag and money by the door and knock so someone finds it."

"Can't we just go inside and warm up?"

I click my tongue at him. "Don't you know you're supposed to give in secret? You'll lose your blessing if you let yourself be known."

"What blessing?" he asks with a sudden spark.

I shrug. "I don't know. But good deeds done in private always receive a reward somehow."

"When?"

"I don't know, Rudolpho," I reply, hearing the exasperation in my voice. "Grandmullie says a good deed is always repaid with a blessing. Okay?"

"I suppose," he mumbles. "I'm just saying that my toes are a bit frozen and could use some warmth from a toasty fire."

"The orphanage doesn't have a fire to toast your toes," I snap. "Their coal was stolen from them, remember? Stop delaying and place the bag by the door and knock. Don't let anyone see you."

I stand outside the courtyard, breathing into my cold hands and peeking through the iron gate to watch Rudolpho lug the bag of coal and money up to the door. Unfortunately, the path to the door is lined with cedar trees—the trees that affect Rudolpho's allergies the strongest. I can hear his sudden sniffles from where I stand fifty feet away. It's a matter of seconds before the itching to his nostrils takes hold of him and he releases a rapid-fire of sneezes into the cold night.

Light from a candle flickers from a window of a neighboring house. The shutters are thrown open and a man sticks his head out to watch Rudolpho.

From within the orphanage, I see the shadow of a woman in a long white nightgown cross by the window. All of a sudden, Rudolpho audibly gasps—loud enough for me to hear him.

"It's her," he whispers loudly to me.

"What are you talking about, Rudolpho?" I ask in a loud whisper. "Just leave the bag and let's go."

"It's Mary," he says louder. "Mary Kissed—er, I mean, Krist."

"Your true love?"

"Who goes there?" the man asks from the open window.

Rudolpho again sneezes loudly. I can only imagine all of the snotty mucus that must have flown out of his nose at the force of that one.

"Drop the bag, Rudolpho," I order, my whisper as loud as I can force without shouting at him.

"What business do you have at the orphanage at this hour?" the man persists. Another man joins him at the window to curiously poke his head out as well.

"Is someone robbing the children?"

"No," Rudolpho says to them. He turns back to me, sniffling. "It's fate that brought us here, Vixen."

It's not clear if he is tearing up from his allergies or seeing his love for the first time in many years. There is no time for Rudolpho's sniffling, however. The two men have disappeared from their window, and I suspect they're on their way over to the orphanage.

"Leave the bag, Rudolpho," I call out in a loud voice.

"I can't just leave," he belts out between sneezes.

The two men leap over the courtyard fence to face Rudolpho. Both men freeze. Rudolpho's size is enough to make them hesitate to jump him. Their scrawny figures look as though they haven't eaten a meal in a week.

"Who are you here to see?" one of them demands.

"Leave the bag," I call out again.

Rudolpho looks at them with wide eyes and sneezes again. "M—M—Mary Kissed, no Mary Krist—must go!"

Rudolpho drops the bag on the ground and turns to run toward me.

"What did he say?" one of the men ask.

"He said merry krist, mass."

"Merry krist? Perhaps he thinks your name is Krist."

"Why would he think that? I never introduced myself."

"Maybe it's a secret code word," the skinny one breathes out with wide eyes. "Let's look at the goodies he left. He must be talking about the masses being merry."

"Merry? On a night like this?" the other man asks in a bewildered voice. They seize the bag from the ground and open it.

"It's coal," I hear one of them remark.

"That's for the orphans," I yell to them.

He raises his hand in a wave. "Much obliged. The children will be needing this as their coal was stolen."

As Rudolpho struggles to climb back over the fence, I see them extract the small bag of money. A big smile breaks out over both of their faces.

"The large fellow wants the masses to be merry," I hear one of them say.

"That's for the orphans," I yell again, clutching at Rudolpho's pants to help him land with a mighty heap on the ground.

"You can't be merry without wine, my friend."

"The large fellow wants us to buy wine."

"Let's go," Rudolpho says, clamoring to his feet and striding away.

"It's all for the children," I yell to the men one last time and turn to chase after Rudolpho.

"The children will sleep warm tonight," the man yells back. "And so will we."

I hear a hearty laugh from his friend echoing after me. "Thank you and a merry krist, mass!"

A merry krist, mass, indeed! With Rudolpho's large figure disappearing into the snowy darkness, I don't have time to go back to the men. I console myself with the thought that the children *will* sleep warm tonight. As will two poor souls who will drink their sorrows away for at least one cold evening.

Nine

THE CONSTELLATIONS WHISPER TO ME THAT
Hann has been captured before we even return to my home. I
can feel tension mounting as we enter our settlement.

We trudge through the hard packed snow past Lila's house.
It looks forlorn, smothered in thick layers of white. I haven't
spoken to my friend in far too long. We used to share
everything on a daily basis. But that seems so long ago now. I
wonder if she and George married after all. I had told her I
would attend the wedding, but the ominous threat enveloping
the land pushed that promise to the back of my mind. I feel a
tinge of guilt and try to move at a faster pace. But it's too late.
Lila throws open the door and rushes out to meet me in
nothing but a long cotton nightgown and bare feet.

"Vixen! Vixen!" she shouts, running full force toward me.

I turn to meet her. She looks as lovely as ever with her honey gold hair twisted in a high bun atop her head.

"Lila! I missed you so!"

We grab each other and hug tightly. Then she starts hopping from one foot to the other in an attempt to protect her feet from the cold.

"Go back inside before you catch a chill," I chide her.

"You were going to pass by without saying hello," she pouts.

"Only because it's so cold."

"Come inside for some hot tea. I just baked a pie yesterday."

Behind me, I can hear Rudolpho's disappointed sigh when I shake my head no. "We must keep moving. I need to get Grandmullie home."

"But I have so much to tell you. George and I got married—of course, you would have known that if you had come to the wedding."

"I'm so sorry, Lila, but I was away."

She playfully sticks her tongue out at me to let me know she's not truly offended. "Yes, well, you're the third person to know that we're already expecting."

I take a step back. "Expecting? As in a baby? You just got married—I mean, isn't it too early to know for sure?"

"Grandmother was sipping on tea three days ago, and two tea leaves floated right up to the top before she even took a sip. She thinks it's a sign that I'm pregnant with twins."

I blink hard and try not to laugh. Was she serious? She and I had always giggled secretly at her grandmother's silly superstitions. I'm supposed to congratulate her, but news of her pregnancy—if it's true—actually fills me with dread. Our settlement will start applying pressure on me to get married and have children. But the sad reality is that all the eligible young men will probably be dead before that happens.

"Are you happy?" I manage to ask.

Lila frowns. "Of course. It's what I've wanted—what George and I want."

I look toward her small house and see George's shadow in the window, watching us. Without a home of his own to provide for his wife, he moved in with Lila and her parents. It's too surreal. I grew up with George and to imagine him taking on the role of husband and father is a stretch to my imagination.

"I'm filled with joy for you," I say with a big smile—the biggest I can muster. "Now go inside so you don't get sick. You have little ones to protect now."

Lila squeezes my hand gratefully. With a last wave, she darts back to the warmth of her home, leaving us to push onward through the snow toward our own home.

I stand in the doorway of my small home for several minutes, watching Grandmullie busy herself with sweeping out the dust. It's a lonely house to me now. Not even Rudolpho's large presence can fill the corners of loneliness. "He was supposed to meet us back here," Rudolpho says, his voice sounding offended.

"He was captured," I reply in a low voice.

Grandmullie looks at me, her eyes squinting from the stream of sunlight that dares to peek through the dark clouds covering Klaus. "You don't know that, Vixen."

"I do, Grandmullie. The signs in the heavens told me so. For all I know, he may have turned himself in."

"Turned himself in?" Rudolpho's voice is shrill in the small house. "Are you a bit daft? No sane person would willingly participate in the sporting event."

I have to laugh despite the feeling of sadness welling up inside. "Hann is not one to play it safe."

"Vixen, you will find people that briefly cross your paths at various periods in your life—like ships that greet each other for a short time on the open waters of the sea," Grandmullie muses quietly.

"Or like a bowl of stew where you have the vegetables touching, and then they get pushed back by your spoon scooping in to eat them all up," Rudolpho says.

In unison, Grandmullie and I look at him with a frown. Rudolpho scrunches his face and gives us a weak smile and a slight shrug of his shoulders. The fellow is always thinking of food.

"With the food rations destroyed, the masses will again experience starvation," Grandmullie says.

I don't respond. Her words actually make my head start spinning. What was it Elder Frode had said to me—'Instead of relying upon the King for food, your feet will whisper upon the ground to increase the produce wherever you trod.'

I silently leave my house and walk outside, staring around the rolling hills now covered with snow. Is it possible? Can I speak life to the dormant vegetation buried under the snow?

Perhaps there's some kind of ritual I should be performing, but the only thought that comes into my mind to test the elder's words is to get down on my hands and knees in the snow. I push back the ice-white powder to reach the dead grass. It's already faded from brown to a milky white, sleeping until spring will bring it back to its vibrant green color.

I move my hands over the grass and close my eyes, imagining it growing greener as my hands lightly touch its frozen strands. I peek open an eye, expecting to see it green and standing proud, but the same frozen grass greets me.

"It's time to wake up," I whisper. "Just for a brief time and then you can sleep."

Nothing.

Had I misunderstood the elder's words? I ponder the grass, whispering Elder Frode's words and then it clicks. I'm missing belief. The belief that comes from prayer to the Creator of the universe with an expectation that what I speak will come to pass.

And so I pray. Not for myself, but for the masses to be fed.

Before my eyes, the small patch of grass receives strength from my prayer and slowly rises, returning to its shade of green. It's a sign of hope for Klaus.

"How did you do that?" Grandmullie whispers behind me.

I wasn't aware that she and Rudolpho had followed me, watching the miracle that just occurred. They stare at me with a mixture of awe and fear.

"The Council of Elders," I try to explain, "they said I would be able to do this. Not me, but belief."

"Maybe I can do that too," Rudolpho says, his breath swirling in the cold air. "Tell me how—show me."

"I can't show you, Rudolpho. It's an unspoken belief. And prayer. If we can tap into this belief, we may be able to bring food to the masses."

"We'll be heroes," Rudolpho breathes, his eyes gleaming.

"We do it in secret, Rudolpho," I snap. "No one must ever know or suspect we can do this."

"Why not?" he asks innocently. "My true love may finally take notice of me."

I look at him and slowly draw a line across my throat with my finger as though it's been slit. I hang my head with my tongue sticking out, making Rudolpho winces. "Get it?"

He nods. "Say no more."

"Do it again," Grandmullie says, her eyes still wide.

I bow my head and begin to pray again. This time I feel a tingling running through my veins. I pray harder, desperately seeking the Creator of all things to breathe life back into the dormant land stretched out before us.

My breath catches in my throat and I try to open my eyes, but they're sealed shut by a power outside myself. The tremor in my veins moves forcefully through my body, enveloping it in such a state of shaking that I fall to the ground.

Faintly, I can hear Grandmullie scream as though she is in a deep tunnel far away from me. I try to call out to her, but my tongue is stuck to the roof of my mouth.

A shock of cold hits my face and I open my eyes. Grandmullie and Rudolpho are crouched over me, dread written upon their faces.

"No more snow," Grandmullie warns Rudolpho when he's about to rub a handful over my face.

The cold of the snow had revived me. I try to sit up, but my grandmother lays a hand on me.

"What happened?" I whisper.

"You had a seizure, I think," she says softly, stroking my hair. "Stay still and take some deep breaths."

I suck in the cold air, relishing the burn in my chest. It reminds me that I'm alive. "I'm sorry, Grandmullie. I was just praying and then I was helpless. I couldn't control myself. I'm so sorry. I failed."

"Failed? Nonsense, dear child. Look around you."

She helps me sit up, and I look around, my head thick and eyes blurry as if in a fog of confusion. Before me stretches grass—green grass—over the gently sloping hill, proudly standing erect in the brisk air. It's a stark contrast to the blanket of snow surrounding it.

"I wouldn't have believed it if I hadn't seen it with my own eyes," Rudolpho says loudly.

"Shh," Grandmullie whispers.

And well she should shush him. Something is happening in the air. Swirls of the cold mist hover expectantly over the ground, waiting to release its onslaught of death over the new growth that defies the elements. It is almost as if an unseen force holds the frigid temperatures at bay so the ground can reproduce earlier than its duly appointed season.

And then the ground starts trembling, a low rumble at first and then steadily growing more forceful. I recognize the tremble. A stampede of animals is headed our way. All thoughts of re-producing food are pushed back in an instant.

"Get Grandmullie to the house," I yell to Rudolpho.

Without thinking, he grabs my grandmother with his beefy hands and starts running with her frail body tucked under one arm. She doesn't even have time to protest.

The animals are upon me in less than a minute. I'm too weak to stand and run. Perhaps I should yell at them to try to stop their mad dash that comes from seemingly nowhere.

A calm overshadows me. The kind of calm that brings peace in the midst of a storm. I close my eyes, waiting for the inevitable.

Suddenly, I'm knocked to the ground by the force of a body. It's not an animal. It's a young man—a Cavalier. It's Stratton.

"Stay down," he shouts, using his shield to protect my body from the blows of animals leaping over us—a mix of lions and bears, their eyes wild with the frantic desire to escape.

And then they disappear out of sight.

"Stratton?" I can hear the fear in my voice.

"It's all right. They're gone," he whispers, slowly rolling off me. "What are you doing out here? On the ground?"

"I don't feel so well."

Stratton reaches down and places his hands under my arms, helping me stand. Out of the corner of my eye, I see a couple of other Cavaliers, about the same age as Stratton, atop their large horses, lingering back from the others to eye us suspiciously.

"Get into your house. You're not safe out here," Stratton orders in a low voice.

"What's going on, Stratton? What are the animals for?"

"Just go, Vixen."

"Tell me," I insist. "You disappear and I think I won't ever see you again, but then—you're here. Saving me."

"I come by often and wait for a glimpse of you, Vixen. But you're never here. What makes you leave your home?"

I don't offer an explanation. I'm still taken aback at the prospect of Stratton checking on me. Was he spying on me or trying to make sure I was safe?

"Why are you chasing the animals?"

Stratton tries to mask the sudden hurt that springs into his eyes, but I catch a glimpse of it. And it confuses me. I don't know how I feel about Stratton. Too much has happened since I last laid eyes on him—too much for me to have the innocent emotions I felt when I first encountered him.

"Aren't you going to ask how I've been? You seem concerned about the animals, but what about me?"

I look away from him to stare at the ground, chewing on the inside of my mouth. "Are you going to fight the young boys, Stratton?"

Stratton expels a breath. I can feel his eyes poring into me, but he avoids my question. "The animals were captured for the sporting event," he says instead. "We were transporting them to the stadium, but somehow they escaped out of the wagons."

I had seen the wagons on our way back home. I hadn't realized that they held animals prisoner or I would have taken matters into my own hands and helped them escape. Thankfully, someone else had taken action. And the Cavaliers would be looking for a scapegoat.

"You need to get into your house," Stratton suddenly orders again, his voice more insistent.

The other Cavaliers are approaching us. After my encounter with the Cavalier in the forest, I don't want to experience their cruelty again. I whirl and half limp, half run toward my house. Stratton will take care the Cavaliers don't bother me. But he'll have to answer for why he helped me.

Grandmullie seizes me in her arms when I enter the house. "Child, what were you thinking? You could have been killed. If it hadn't been for Stratton showing up, I shudder to think of the harm that could have come to you."

"I'm fine, Grandmullie," I say, brushing past her. "Stratton was paying me back for saving him."

"What is it? There's something happening, isn't there?"

My grandmother can read me as no one else can. I sigh and sink onto my cot, covering my eyes with my hand.

"The sporting event has become very real," I say softly. "They're bringing large animals into the ring to tear the poor boys to shreds."

My grandmother's eyes mist with sudden tears. She's visibly shaken and sits down on the edge of my cot. Rudolpho hangs his head, not knowing how to take the news.

"We may be able to protect the boys from the animals if we can get close enough to the ring," I say quietly.

"I don't think I can go," Rudolpho protests. "You know me—how I get when I'm scared. Just the sight of the Cavaliers out there scared the holly jolly out of me. I couldn't have saved you, Vixen. I had to watch helplessly from the safety of your house."

"That's nonsense, Rudolpho. Look how you saved Grandmullie. If you don't think about it, you can do great things. You have to go with me, Rudolpho. It's the only way. Together, we can confuse the animals, order them to stop."

"But we'll be caught and hung in the gallows."

"The sporting event will be attended by many of the masses. What do we all have in common?"

Rudolpho looks at me, perplexed. "That we're all poor and starving?"

"Think, Rudolpho. We all wear brown robes. And just like previous Kings, we'll be ordered to wear our hoods over our heads."

The monarchy takes great pride in displaying their bright clothing. Our hooded, drab robes make them feel superior somehow. They enjoy watching us walk past with our hoods pulled over our pathetic hanging heads—the lowly position we are ordered to assume around them. And they always take pleasure in counting the number of slaves they see gathered on rare occasions.

"I just don't understand," Rudolpho says, staring at me with a blank expression on his face.

"For goodness sakes, use your noggin," Grandmullie says in an exasperated voice. "If everyone is wearing a hood, they'll never know who is ordering the animals."

"You don't say," Rudolpho says. A slow smile spreads across his face. "You can hold my hand and we'll do it together."

I shake my head no. "We'll have to be on opposite sides of the ring. We won't know where the animals will be and we'll have a much better chance of communicating with them."

"I can't go in there alone."

I stare up at him, fighting exasperation. Just as I'm contemplating how to make the idea sound attractive to him, Grandmullie speaks.

"I'll go with you."

"No," I say vehemently. "You will not go near that evil place. I don't want anything to happen to you."

My grandmother's eyes soften as she looks at me. "What can happen, Vixen? Look at this big fellow. He looks threatening, but his heart is soft. He needs some kind of support. It's the only way."

Of course I know she's right. But an uneasiness settles into the pit of my stomach. A thousand things can go wrong. But the risk of Rudolpho freezing up out of fear is too great. Grandmullie will have to go with him.

Rudolpho drops to his knees and grabs my grandmother's hands, planting slobbery kisses all over them. She pulls them away from him with a frown.

"Enough of your nonsense. I'm not going with you unless we have a plan."

"We need to get a peek at the stadium so we know where to go in," I say.

Grandmullie's eyes narrow and she suddenly grins. " I know some wee little people who can help with that."

The Kringles. They helped build the stadium. The King had commissioned their artisan skills for the four years it took to build the stadium. No one in all the lands can create the solid, handcrafted buildings that bring the small people their notoriety. Unfortunately, their hard labor received only the reward of a few bags of beans. But the Kringles are smart. They planted the beans and produced a massive crop that fed hundreds of people and the orphanage. That is, until the King got wind of their success and ordered the burning of four of their six fields. I still recall the thick black cloud that hung over the lands for several days.

I may be able to use their intimate knowledge of the stadium. Perhaps they can draw us a sketch of what it looks like, where the animals will be released in the ring. That information will help us know where to position ourselves.

"I'll let you take care of that, Grandmullie. I'll come up with a plan to get us closer to the ring."

With the masses packed into the stadium in the limited seating the monarchy allows us, it will be difficult at best to find a seat close to the ring. But I have a plan. And this plan involves me making contact with the monarchy.

Ten

OLDENWALD. THE FORBIDDEN PREMISES.

I have only imagined visiting the place the monarchy calls home. In my dreams, I have envisioned the forbidden premises to be a place of opulence. I am not disappointed.

The heavy iron gates are pushed back for the first time in history to allow the masses entry into Oldenwald. I slowly walk with Rudolpho and Grandmullie in a straight line. To sneak a peek at the forbidden premises, I have to look past the Cavaliers, dressed in their shiny black and silver uniforms, standing erect along the pathway to the stadium—positioned to keep any of the poor masses from altering their course out of curiosity about the shrouded city.

The streets are lined perfectly with polished bricks. What buildings I can see are towering and constructed of the finest wood from the acacia trees and stone and brick. We're a long way away from the humble earth bag houses in our settlement.

The bells from the sanctuary ring in the far distance, announcing the assured death of many men today. I briefly get a vision of several sadistic Juuls standing in the bell tower with the heavy rope attached to the bell clapper wrapped around their small frames to aid their efforts.

From my perspective, the imposing stadium seems to stretch to the sky. Its massive stone columns are surrounded by intricately carved ivory statues of hybrid creatures—swine bodies with mice ears, elephant torsos with elk heads, human forms with giraffe necks.

A very curious tall fir tree can be seen just inside the stadium doors. Large silver and gold balls adorn the tree, and small candles are balanced precariously on its branches.

Massive fires with specially selected yule logs are contained in large iron barrels. The heat is welcome this cold morning, but the fires attract curious children who inevitable scorch tiny fingers on the red-hot iron. I learn quickly to shut my ears to their tender cries.

The masses come in droves to the stadium for the sporting event that will claim the lives of many of our young men. It's utter pandemonium, bodies smashed tightly together in the frigid winter air as we all await permission to enter.

The Cavaliers take delight in selecting the fortunate—or unfortunate—souls that are allowed entry. All wailing women are detained at the colossal wooden doors. They're too much of a distraction for the monarchy's guests from neighboring lands. If I'd had the luxury of time, I would have been far more curious about the foreign guests and their strange clothing and modes of transportation. Right now, my focus is solely on gaining entry into the stadium and positioning myself near the ring.

By the time, I'm pressed toward the stadium's entrance, I feel like I've participated in an obstacle course. By his sheer size, Rudolpho has managed to stay close behind me and keep my grandmother somewhat protected from the crowd.

I approach a Cavalier who is stationed at the entrance. He has a sadistic grin curling his lips as he views the sorrowful masses trying to enter.

"Pardon me, sire," I say loudly and curtsy before him.

"Back away from me, filthy wench," he snarls and reaches out to strike my mouth without warning.

I can taste the blood in my mouth but I don't cower. "I've come to help, sire."

He snorts at my words, his brutish laugh ringing loudly in my ears. "Help? Do we look like we need help?"

"Inside, sire," I persist. "My companion can help control the masses when the event starts so the masses don't get out of control."

The Cavalier looks past me at Rudolpho. Rudolpho stares straight ahead as I've instructed. If he makes eye contact with the knight, he'll crumble.

My words have piqued his interest. "How do you propose to keep control of the masses?"

"My large friend has killed two bears, a lion, and multiple deer with his bare hands. No one will get past him if you position us near the ring. The masses will listen to him, I assure you."

The knight looks Rudolpho up and down. I can see the vein in Rudolpho's temple start pulsing rapidly, but other than that tell-tale sign, he looks remarkably calm.

"Why would you want to help? What do you get out of it?"

"Front row seats to the event, sire," I say with a forced smile—the kind of smile that fools use when they think they're being wise. The kind I've seen from the Cavaliers.

He grunts and spits at my feet. After a minute of looking from Rudolpho to me, he nods his head and whistles to another knight to let us in.

"Not the old lady," the other knight says sharply as we three pause at the doors.

"She won't be a bother," I say quickly. "Her dying wish has always been to see the stadium. Please, sire. She'll stay near us."

The pressing crowd is growing anxious. Yells from the back of the crowd arrest the Cavalier's attention. He gives a curt nod and moves aside for us to enter.

Inside, the atmosphere is loud and thick with sorrow. And the thirst for blood. Anxious parents wring their hands as they try to contain their emotions. One last chance to see their son alive is all they seek.

The stadium is massive in size. Stone bleachers line the outside, all leading down to the ring below. Above, there are private balconies overlooking the ring—most likely reserved for the monarchy as they're choice seats from where to view the action in the ring.

I duck my head and fight the sudden tears that threaten to get me booted from the stadium. There are so many people that I worry how we're going to be able to make it down to the ring. The masses are already crammed so closely inside that it makes sitting on the bleachers virtually impossible.

The stone steps are steep to the ring, and we're jostled constantly as we make our way down. Rudolpho keeps a protective arm around Grandmullie, but I catch more than a couple of rough nudges delivered to her frail body before we reach the Cavalier waiting for us at the bottom

"You can stand here," the Cavalier shouts over the noise. He turns and thrusts his finger in Rudolpho's chest. "No one gets into the ring from this side, do you hear? Otherwise, you will bear the brunt of punishment upon your shoulders."

I quickly step in front of Rudolpho. "You don't have to worry about this side of the ring."

The knight gives me a hard look but leaves us without further questioning. I look at the large ring taking up a quarter of the stadium. There's plenty of room to run from one's opponent—almost too much as someone not accustomed to the exercise may well find himself exhausted after a length of time. Perhaps that will work in the young men's favor as they're used to the rigors of working the lands.

The floor of the ring is nothing more than dirt which will receive innocent blood this day. Iron bars surround it to ensure no one can leave. It will be a fight to the death. The only way to leave the ring is to escape death by defeat.

It's easy for me to see that Rudolpho is nervous. The sweat on his brow gives it away. I punch his arm. It's enough of a jolt to shake his fear. At least for the moment.

"I know you," comes a voice from behind.

We turn to face two men with lopsided grins looking intently at Rudolpho.

"I don't think so," Rudolpho says, turning back around dismissively.

"Yes," one of the men insists. "You came to the orphanage and gave the children some coal. A right fella, you are."

Rudolpho turns his head to give a polite smile. "I'm sure you're thinking of someone else."

"It's you," the man persists. "Not too many fellas are as big as you are. Your stature alone would give you away."

"That's right," the other man chimes in. "Me and my friend would like to personally thank you for the extra special gift you brought. A merry krist, huh mass?"

He elbows his friend who gives a boisterous laugh at their private humor.

"That's right. Merry krist, mass."

"I don't know what you're talking about."

The men look at each other and wink. "We get where you're going with this, but charity isn't dead and we're going to let everyone know about it."

"Please don't," I say firmly. "You're never to speak of charity or people will lose their blessing."

The men's eyes widen and they gasp. "Well, it'll be between the three of us—the four of us then. We'll just use our secret words."

"What words?" I ask.

"Merry krist, mass."

Rudolpho looks appalled and appeals to me with his eyes. I pat his shoulder.

"You worry too much, Rudolpho. It won't go any further than here."

"All right," he says with a gulp. "I just never want Mary Krist to hear of this."

"It will be fine. I need to get to the other side of the ring. Keep an eye on Grandmullie."

I give my grandmother a swift hug before leaving them to begin the laborious process of fighting my way through the masses to reach the other side of the ring. The side where the gypsies have planted themselves.

They're a wild bunch—probably about a hundred have shown up to the event loudly scoffing and opening drinking ale from leather skins. Their olive skin and dark hair stand out among the masses. They defy the monarchy and refuse to wear the brown robes. Why the King allows this is a mystery. Instead, they wear brightly colored garments made of dyed yarns and threads. Even in the cold air, some of the men brazenly reveal their bare chests. Does it make them feel stronger?

The gypsies' dark eyes flash at me when I push through them to reach the ringside. I look out of place among them— a drab commoner among the colorful people who have a reputation for stealing and killing to make their living.

Since my youth, Grandmullie has warned me never to join with a gypsy clan as I would surely encounter danger all the days of my life—that and wander aimlessly with a rowdy group that seemingly has no respect for anyone outside their clans.

"What are you doing here?" a young man challenges.

I stare into his dark eyes, foreboding and peering at me through thick eyelashes. His black hair is gathered into a ponytail and gold hoops pierce his ear lobes and nose. Others gather around him, silently challenging me as well.

"I might ask you the same question," I say pointedly, ignoring my racing heartbeat pulsating in my chest. "Why do you have the privilege of sitting outside the ring while boys your age are locked inside, preparing to meet their death in the ring?"

His eyes register a slight surprise at my provocative words. "The gypsies weren't summoned to the sporting event as participants. We're merely spectators."

"You should be ashamed of yourselves," I spit out contemptuously, looking at the faces before me. "There are parents who can't get in to see their boys one last time. And look at you—all fat and giddy with the prospect of seeing young men die for the King's pleasure. Make room for those of us who have loved ones fighting."

The young man moves toward me with clenched fists, but an older man with a long braided beard places a hand of caution on his arm. "No time for this, Gallius. Take a seat."

Dutifully, Gallius backs away from me, his eyes never leaving my face. I stubbornly lock eyes with him. It's only when I'm abruptly bumped by a girl that I break contact. Her face registers jealousy.

"You take a seat too," she says with a thick accent.

I'm struck by the girl's beauty. She's about my age with thick flowing locks of jet-black hair that flows freely down her green peasant top made of finest linen. Full, red lips are parted angrily as the girl plants her hands on her generous hips and thrusts her bosom out. Her dark eyes are hard, as though she's lived a tough life and learned to fend for herself at an early age. In contrast, I have been carefully sheltered by my grandmother.

The girl points toward the outer crowd of the gypsies as though expecting me to climb to the outward level. I stubbornly shake my head no.

"I must stand by the ring."

"You will only make this bad for us," she says. "Other settlers will think they can take our place if they see you."

I can't afford to be cast away from this side of the ring. It's the only place I can position myself opposite Rudolpho. And it's the closest to the structure from which the animals will emerge.

Without thinking, I hurriedly remove the brown robe. Under it, I'm wearing a thick cotton shirt that has turned a dirty gray shade from numerous washings. My black trousers suddenly seem too tight as they hug my hips. Self-consciously, I try to smooth the frays of hair sticking out from my braid.

"Beautiful hair," an older gypsy woman standing by me murmurs and reaches out to stroke my braid.

The girl takes in my modest apparel with a sardonic smile. I can't compete with her beauty and she knows it. "Why must you stand by the ring? Is your love going to be fighting?"

I think of Hann and feel the heat rising in my cheeks. She gives a low, knowing laugh. I raise my head and stare fully into her face.

"Several noble young men that I know are fighting. I'm here to help any way I can."

Curiously, she doesn't laugh at my remark. Instead, her eyes narrow and she says something in her native dialect. The older woman immediately whips out a blue cloth and holds it out to me.

"For your head," the girl explains. "Your red hair stands out in our group. I'm Cupid, by the way."

I take the cloth in my hands and wrap it around my head. My long braid still sticks out, but from a distance, I blend in better—if one disregards my pale skin.

"I'm Vixen."

"You have a gypsy's name," the older woman remarks. "One of your parents a gypsy?"

I shake my head no and turn around to take in the crowds of people gathered. The monarchy and foreign guests sit in the private balconies above us. I catch a glimpse of an occasional curious guest leaning over the railing to take in the crowd gathered below. I wonder what they think of the mayhem in the land of Klaus?

Faintly, I start hearing a chant that seems to grow in the stadium. I can't make out what the masses are saying and strain to catch the words.

The gypsies stand on the bleaches to look out over the crowd. The chant becomes stronger, louder and I can't believe the words when I can make them out.

Merry krist, mass… Merry krist, mass… Merry krist, mass."

I look across the large ring to see how Rudolpho is holding up. He's standing with his head buried in his arm—a stance of humiliation.

"What does that mean—merry krist, mass?" the woman asks curiously.

I shrug. "I'm not sure what they're chanting."

The chanting lasts for longer than an hour, ebbing the tension in the room. Then exhaustion from standing so long sends the masses to sit on the bleachers, and the noise level slowly lowers before solemnly becoming eerily silent.

I take a seat on the ground by the ring, perching on my brown robe for a measure of comfort. I'm joined by the older woman who fans herself with her hand. The multitude of bodies pressed into the stadium has caused the temperature to rise. I can feel beads of perspiration break out on my upper lip and a trickle of wetness drip from my nose.

"Your nose is bleeding," the older woman says, concern written on her face as she produces a scarlet cloth from beneath the layers of clothing she wears.

I take the cloth and swipe at the blood that darkens the material. "I must be overheated."

The woman leans in to speak into my ear. "I can read you. You have much stress inside. Your blood is preparing for the slaughter that is about to take place."

Her words make me shudder. I don't think I can watch innocent lives being taken so brutally right before my eyes. Holding the cloth to my nose, I stand back to my feet and look across the ring to make sure Rudolpho and Grandmullie are still there. They are, but Rudolpho's eyes are tightly shut and I can see my grandmother whispering into his ear.

A low tinkling of bells can be heard from inside the structure that houses the animals and humans that will war against each other this day. The bells get louder, and the crowd seems to hold its breath as the large door parts and a golden chariot emerges from the structure, bearing the new King.

It's the first time I've laid eyes on him. I crane my head to look through the bars, trying to catch a glimpse of the man that held the keys of power in the land of Klaus.

King Lawrence Oxneed Sinter is middle-aged with salt and pepper hair falling to his shoulders. His face is void of a beard, as are the rest of the royal males. His lavish red silk suit is adorned with the Kingdom's crest on the back, which he proudly turns in every direction to make sure everyone sees the embroidered gold lions surrounding a green fir tree. His prized possession, however, is the ruby and diamond crown atop his head.

"All hail King Lawrence Oxneed Sinter!" a voice booms from the balcony over us.

A polite clapping emanates from the crowd. From the sheer number of the masses, the applause sounds much more impressive than it really is.

"All hail King Lawrence Oxneed Sinter!" the voice booms again. This time, we know it's an order for us to honor the dictator before us.

The clapping suddenly stops as though on cue. The masses will not applaud this man and his activity—not while the lives of our boys are in his hands. Instead, we take the action our ancestors did on that day they rebelled. In unison, we start rubbing our hands together. The noise inside the stadium sounds like the sea's billowy wave, unpredictable and filled with anguish.

From my vantage point, I can see the King is greatly displeased by the masses' action. In his fury, he opens his mouth into a full smile, displaying his teeth for all to see as a sign of his dictatorship. For the past nine dynasties, newly appointed Kings in Klaus have crowned their teeth in pure gold with small diamonds embedded into the two front teeth. There is something powerful in that action. The torch lights surrounding the ring illuminate the diamonds, sending streams of radiance bouncing throughout the stadium.

The crowd is subdued. The King is all-powerful.

With only the sound of the chariot bells jingling, the King rides around the large ring several times before disappearing back into the structure.

"Shameful," the woman next me mutters.

A loud trumpet blares in the silence and a Juul steps from the structure with a stool. He's wearing a green suit with a pointed green hat that looks ready to fall off his small head.

With a scowl, the Juul places the stool on the ground in the center of the ring and climbs on it. "And now, St. Nicklaus will pray for the souls of the deceased—er, the soon to be deceased."

The small elf climbs down when St. Nicklaus appears. The old man wears a somber expression as he strolls to the center ring, but I can tell that he can barely contain his glee. He's the center of attention, and it's apparent to me that he relishes all eyes upon him.

"He has no heart in his body," the older woman whispers with a fierce tone.

I understand her words. Nicklaus has no compassion or love for people. While his suit is the same red silk as the King's, it's the famed cape about his shoulders that tell the truth about his black heart. All of the masses know him by his scarlet cape lined with white fur.

"Pious ones," he calls out to the crowd. "Have your children been naughty or have they been nice?"

The masses look around. His words make all of us squirm. There is no doubt that many in attendance this day have felt the sting of a switch across their bare skin for being labeled as naughty.

"If your children have been naughty," Nicklaus continues, "then you already know what will become of them this day. If they've been nice," he pauses again, shrugs suggestively and smiles. The masses hold their breath for a chance of hope—perhaps the nice boys would be released.

It's an agonizing pause, and the old man enjoys the added tension he's been able to stir up. Finally, he speaks. "If they've been nice, let's just say they have a fighting chance."

The masses start to murmur, but Nicklaus quickly raises his hands in the air and looks toward the heavens before the noise grows too loud to mask his prayer.

"Oh, woe to the wicked and woe to the enemies of the King," he shouts. "Woe to those that don't keep their places in this world that was appointed to them from the beginning of time. Accept the souls of those prepared for destruction this day. And we will all rejoice and declare the doom of those who oppose the King. And the land of Klaus will again rest in peace."

Nicklaus ends his evocation with a low guttural chuckle. His words are twisted and confused, ramblings of a mad man. The masses don't know how to react.

Nicklaus gives another sadistic chuckle and claps his hands. A group of Juuls strides forth from the structure, all wearing the green attire as the first one. They carry boxes wrapped in gold and silver paper.

Joyfully, Nicklaus takes one of the boxes and holds it in the air. "These are gifts for the victors—not victims. All who win their battle will receive a token of victory. All who lose—well, they won't care about the gift anyway. You may very well ask what the gifts contain. I'll let you in on a secret and show you. If I could have one *very* nice child come and open a gift."

The masses look around nervously. No one wants to send a child to Nicklaus. Especially today.

"Come now," the old man shouts. "Surely not all the children present are naughty. There must be one nice child to be found in the lot of you!"

The Juuls drop their packages and run to the bars of the ring, peering out at the crowd to find a child, their beady eyes scouring for little ones that the parents try to conceal. It's an unexpected request and parents might not have brought their younger children had they known. Nicklaus has a reputation for doing the unexpected—and someone usually ends up hurt or in tears. No one offers up a child, and it doesn't look good for the masses to defy the bishop. That action will make the foreign guests feel the Kingship is weak.

Finally, a Cavalier brings a weeping boy, no more than five years old, to the gate of the ring and forces the child to enter. The child crumples to the ground, sobbing uncontrollably while his mother looks on helplessly outside the ring.

Nicklaus motions to a Juul holding a silver trumpet. The evil little elf darts to the boy and blows the trumpet into his face. The child cowers even lower on the ground, screaming.

"Bring me another child," Nicklaus yells. "One that will appreciate a fine gift."

A Cavalier pushes through to the ring, his hand gripping the shoulder of a boy a few years older than the first child. This boy isn't crumpling at the presence of the bishop. He bravely fights back tears and walks right up to the old man.

"I will open the gift," he says loudly.

Nicklaus smiles—a cold smile—and hands the gift to the boy. I catch my breath, praying for the boy. Will the box contain something to harm him? Will the contents be so grotesque that it would scar the child for the remainder of his days?

Carefully, the boy unwraps the gold paper held on the box with a string of twine. I can see him take a deep breath before he opens it. There is a pregnant pause. I strain to see what the contents are. Finally, the boy pulls out a basket. I can't make out what it's filled with as the boy's back is to me. He holds it in the air.

"It's filled with fruit and nuts," the child yells out.

Nicklaus' booming laugh can be heard over the relieved gasps from the crowd. He crosses to the younger child still crying on the ground and delivers a swift kick to his buttocks. Then he turns to the crowd, his arms outstretched as though he were royalty himself.

"See what you get when you're nice?" the old man all but purrs. "And there's a hidden treat in there. Chocolat. How many of you poor settlers have tasted chocolat before?"

I would venture to guess none of the masses have tasted the creamy substance before. We've heard stories about how it melts on the tongue, leaving a smooth, sweet taste even after it's long gone.

Nicklaus holds a brown bar out to the young lad. Carefully, the boy leans in and takes a bite. Greedily, he moves to take another, but Nicklaus pulls it away from him.

"You'll have to fight and win if you want any more," he tells the boy. "Out with you. We must be on with the festivities. And a merry krist, masses!"

A Juul pushes the boy out of the ring as the masses greet Nicklaus' comment with boos to show their disapproval. They say the words as though there is hope. Nicklaus has taken the masses chanting and twisted the words to become a taunt.

Somehow, the other small child has disappeared from the ground—back to his mother's arms, I suppose. My attention had been diverted so I can't recall seeing him leave.

"Foolish settlers," I hear the girl scoff behind me. "They'll fight to their death over a piece of chocolat."

I turn to face her. "They won't fight for chocolat. They'll fight to save their lives. No boy wanted to be part of this."

She doesn't respond. She turns her gaze back to the ring. The Cavaliers have started filing into the ring, their silver shields glinting in the light. They're a mixture of fresh young men new to their knightly mission and mature men who have already seen war face to face. Today, they are all commissioned to enter the ring with helpless young men who wield no weapon. Today they will kill simply for the sake of sport.

I strain to catch a glimpse of Stratton. It takes a few minutes but I make out his figure on the opposite side of the ring. He stands as erect as the other knights. He's come to do his duty, to fulfill the King's orders. I feel nausea rise in my throat.

"You want some chocolat?"

I turn to the older woman beside me. She's holding out a brown bar like the young boy had eaten from.

"What? Where did you get that?"

"I made it," she says with a smile. For the first time, I notice she's missing two front teeth. I wonder if the chocolat has something to do with that.

"No, thank you," I say, trying to pull my eyes from her teeth, or lack thereof.

"We make the chocolat for Oldenwald," she says. "Take the bar. You can share it with your loved ones."

She wraps the bar back into a gingham cloth and hands it to me. I'm not sure if I will eat the chocolat. I don't know if the gypsies can be trusted. Perhaps the chocolat is poisoned. Why else would she give it to me? Gypsies aren't known for sharing.

As though sensing my hesitation, the woman breaks off a piece from the corner of the bar and pops it in her mouth. "See? It's good. Merry krist, mass."

I nod to her and turn my attention back to the ring. I don't want to experience my first bite of chocolat now, so I tuck it into the inside pocket on my brown robe. Besides, I'm eager to share the chocolat with Rudolpho and Grandmullie. And, of course, Lila.

And then I think of the masses that are starving. What right do I have to enjoy chocolat when so many are going to bed hungry? I've already started secretly moving through the settlements to try to prepare the ground to plant food. It's difficult, though, and drains my energy. But I know I must continue my efforts so the masses are able to withstand the winter in Klaus.

The knights have started moving in the ring, advancing closer to the outside bars. These men belong to the Oldenwald. The King is showing off his possessions.

I hold my breath, hoping to catch Stratton's eye if he comes close to me. Just when he's within two feet of me, the trumpet is blown to call the Cavaliers back into the structure. My eyes graze the Cavaliers as they pass and I gasp. Meeting my eyes is Hugh, one of the boys I grew up with from my settlement. He did enter the King's army after all. I don't think he recognizes me as his face registers no emotion. He will partake in the fighting the young settlers, but he'll have the advantage of a wielding a weapon.

I look over the masses. They're growing increasingly concerned. Any time now, blood will be shed.

Eleven

A HUSH FALLS OVER THE CROWD WHEN A
Kringle slowly makes his way to the center of the ring. He is
an older man with silver wisps of hair lightly blowing in the air.
The monarchy have dressed him in white linen. Better to see
the blood. He will most assuredly die as the Kringles are a
peaceful people. They feel that to take the life of another
human will not grant them resurrection in the afterlife.

His opponent emerges from the ring. He's a young knight.
It's probably his first time shedding blood. What better
opponent could he have than one who will not fight back?

The King has seated himself on his throne above the
structure leading into the ring. It's a royal platform, adorned
with candles and vines of holly trellising the large columns. The

platform offers the King close proximity to the fighting in the ring without being in danger himself.

He's accompanied by a small number of people who may be his family and perhaps choice guests. I assume the woman seated on the throne beside him is the queen. We never hear anything about the queen. She's beautiful from what I can tell—hair pulled back into a severe bun and delicate features. Her face is void of any expression as she looks out over the ring, wrapping her white fur coat snugly about her frame.

"Hear ye! Hear ye!" a Juul shouts. "A warm up for the distinguished guests of the King who traveled from far away to attend this event to honor Winter Solstice. For your pleasure, you'll gaze upon the worthy knight slaying his first victim. The sporting will commence!"

The young knight withdraws his sword and raises it in the air with a grin. I can hear the applause from the balconies. Many of the masses close their eyes, praying for the Kringle, soon to be sacrificed for the King's good pleasure.

The Kringle sinks to his knees and clasps his hands to deliver his own prayer. He doesn't close his eyes as the young Cavalier circles him, holding the sword out threateningly. The knight pokes at the elf with the sword's end as though trying to provoke him to action. But the Kringle remains silent and seated.

The knight strikes the elf's shoulder with the sword and blood soaks his linen shirt. But the small man remains still, not even showing pain.

After several more minutes of the knight yelling at the elf and slicing him in various parts of his body, the King stands up. It's his signal for the knight to complete the task.

And so the young knight does as the King beckons. He takes the sword and plunges it into the Kringle's chest. A cry rises from the masses. This is what we have to look forward to for the remainder of the sporting event.

I feel sick to my stomach as the body of the Kringle is carried out of the ring. The other Kringles will collect their dead outside the forbidden premises. They refuse to be witness to the slaughter and are not in attendance at the sporting event.

Three more Kringles are killed by fresh, young Cavaliers eager to experience their first taste of blood. What sport is there in killing the peaceful men who put up no fight? The King gets bored—he can barely contain his yawns between the matches. He's eager to show his guests some action.

Two wild tigers are released into the ring. They are scrawny as though they've been starved for many days. Starved so they will be sure to pounce upon their next meal—the young men that will be let loose in the ring against them.

And then a most unexpected turn of events occurs right before our eyes. As the tigers restlessly circle the ring, a young man from the King's entourage is lowered from the platform into the ring. He looks to be in his mid-twenties, a man of slight build wearing the same crest emblazoned red silk suit to identify himself with the King.

"My nephew," the King shouts, "Lord Donder van Rycke Sinter, the Favored One."

An audible gasp can be heard from the masses. Is it possible the Favored One is from the royal lineage? The masses aren't aware of multiple ones, and I'm not sure if the King is either.

Donder extends his arms toward the tigers and they snarl at him, advancing. Calmly, the man utters a sharp command. The tigers stop and snarl at him again. When Donder points to the ground, the tigers reluctantly, but obediently, sit.

Confused shouts are hurled at the young man. "If you're the Favored One, why are you killing our young men?" "The Favored One is for the masses!" "You can't be the One!"

The King stands again and lifts his hands. From his vantage point, his words ring through the entire stadium. "I assure you this is the Favored One. It's only fitting that this special person is born into the royal family. Now you have a witness that the Sinters rightfully rule the land of Klaus."

"The Favored One is supposed to be for *us*!" a man shouts from the crowd.

The King turns in the direction of the words. He gives a slow smile that shows his crowns of gold. "The Favored One is for you—all of you. One day, he will assume the throne and rule over you. But today—today belongs to me. The sporting event will resume, and I will see your blood spilled and mingled in the dirt of this ring!"

His words bring cries of anguish and hopelessness. What hope is there for Klaus with such a villain reining? The King allows the noise for a few minutes as his nephew is raised back to him and then he claps his hands for the sporting event to continue.

The time is at hand—why we've all gathered at Oldenwald—to say farewell to the young settlers who will die. No one expects any of the young men to be victorious against the knights. After seeing the bloodshed of the Kringles, all hope is gone. The young boys may be able to put up some sort of fight, but the sword will eventually overpower them.

The sunlight peeks from beneath the dark clouds when the next victim is released from the structure. My heart stops when I realize it's Hann, wearing the white linen clothing provided to the captives. Of course it's Hann. As the most vocal settler who no doubt was as bold in his ridicule of the monarchy in captivity, the Cavaliers would want to make him an example so the other boys will see they're defeated before they even begin fighting.

Hann is angry. I can tell by his clenched fists. He blinks in the sudden brightness and is pushed from behind by a Juul. He runs into the ring, yelling to the masses. I can't hear his words from the thunderous applause from the masses. I try to yell to him, but my own voice is drowned out.

The King leans forward, his attention arrested by the fiery young man in the ring. Hann has an intense fight within him, and this promises to be more of a show than the peaceful Kringles provided.

A Cavalier emerges from the structure. He's a large man with bulging muscles that threaten to rip apart his uniform. He swings a heavy sword in his hands. Hann's fire seems to ignite a fury within the large knight. He roars at Hann, the veins in his neck protruding.

The masses gradually quiet. It's more out of respect to Hann. He'll need to have his wits about him to fight such a large opponent.

The large Cavalier circles Hann warily, his sword positioned offensively in his hand, ready to strike his young opponent with a deadly blow. He thrusts the sword at Hann, who easily steps aside.

For several minutes, the two face off, the knight thrusting his sword and the young man, light on his feet, evading him. I notice that Hann keeps moving further through the ring, making full use of the large space. He's tiring the older man.

The longer the match drones on, the heavier the sword becomes in the Cavalier's hand. He's wasted precious energy by following Hann's lead and chasing him around the ring.

The large man pauses near the side of the ring where Rudolpho and Grandmullie are positioned. He stands heaving, closely watching Hann approach him. As soon as Hann is within striking distance, the Cavalier roars and makes one final, desperate lunge toward Hann. The young man leaps in the air and delivers a swift kick right into the large man's face. It's enough to take the knight down. Slowly, like a giant tree, his unconscious body topples to the dirt.

The masses emit a prolonged cry of victory as Hann raises his hands and jogs around the ring, playing to the crowd. It's an ear-splitting noise, but I don't care. I join in and yell until my throat feels hoarse.

Then a gunshot rings out, and the crowd is instantly silenced by fear. Guns are only used for hunting. The ammunition is too precious to come by to waste on the masses. The knights have been effective in keeping us subdued by the sheer force of their presence.

The King slowly, deliberately rises from his throne. He stares at the sight of the unconscious man below and Hann, the unexpected victor. A cruel smile twists his lips.

"Fight to the death!" he shouts.

The Juuls scurry to the ring with a bucket of water which they toss on the large man. He promptly sits up, sputtering.

Not even the booing of the masses will impact the King's command. Hann stares somberly at his large opponent rising from the ground. One of them will have to die. It's not a choice that Hann gets to make.

Again, Hann moves swiftly from one side of the ring to the next until the Cavalier cannot stand. The large man sinks to his knees, face red, body shutting down as he drops his sword. He clutches his chest and lets out a shout that lifts to the upper balconies. Then he slumps over. He is finished. I don't know if the knight has died from exhaustion or became an invalid in the ring, but he is powerless to move.

Hann doesn't approach him. Instead, he looks up at the King defiantly. "Go tell it on the mountain. This man's blood will not spill today!"

It isn't supposed to be like this. The King's knights are accustomed to fighting battles. The difference in the ring is that the Cavaliers have no horse to carry them. They aren't accustomed to having to run around a ring.

The King stands, his face twisted with fury. "*Your* blood will spill this day! Bring another opponent."

He claps his hands and the Juuls standing at the entrance of the structure go inside. A younger knight soon emerges, one that can go the distance with Hann. The Cavalier holds his sword out with an arrogant grin, sauntering toward him.

It is as expected. The King will not allow any young man to be the victor in the ring.

I wipe the tears that spill onto my cheeks as Hann bravely faces the young knight. He isn't a novice like those who had slain the Kringles. This Cavalier is confident, very confident in his ability with brandishing a sword.

With a sudden movement, he leaps toward Hann, swinging his sword. Hann dodges to the right, but the knight is light on his feet and easily adjusts his footing. His blade grazes Hann's arm and I see a streak of blood spill out onto the white linen.

Hann ignores the cut and lowers his head, eyes fully focused—not on the knight but on his sword. Each thrust of the sword gets closer to my friend. A final, hard swing from the knight strikes Hann full force in the shoulder. But Hann doesn't flinch. Instead, he takes that relaxed second of victory the knight feels and uses it to his advantage. He swings full circle and raises his legs to deliver repeated kicks straight into the knight's face. The Cavalier stills stand, stunned but conscious. The sword hangs limply at his side.

I realize I'm holding my breath, wondering if Hann will see death as the blood oozes onto the white linen, rapidly staining his shirt.

Hann moves in closer to the young knight and drives his elbow in a crushing blow straight into his face. The Cavalier can't recover. His own blood spurts from his nose and his eyes cross before he falls forward in an unconscious state.

The crowd can barely contain its exultation. Both victories for Hann have increased their hope that their sons will also defeat their opponents in the ring.

But the King is not finished with Hann. As the young man holds his bleeding arm, the body of the knight is dragged from the ring by two Juuls who struggle under his weight. Another one snatches the Cavalier's sword, discarded on the ground, lest Hann decide to arm himself. He chases after the others to get out of the ring.

"Bring out the tigers," the King bellows.

A cold silence overtakes the settlers. Our hero will surely meet his death now. No one wants to witness Hann ripped to shreds in such a gruesome manner. Unfortunately, he's on the other side of the ring where Rudolpho and Grandmullie stand, and I can't tell if my large friend is too scared to command the animals.

"Stand back," Cupid says, pushing me back with her hips to position herself as close to the ring as possible.

"How dare you?" I mutter between clenched teeth. "Take your thirst for blood away from here—."

The girl grunts in my face and turns back to the ring. I lick my dry lips, a million thoughts running frantically through my mind. I can't help Hann unless I'm able to get close enough for the animals to hear me.

With a deep breath, I use my elbow to sink into the gypsy girl's ribcage just as the tigers lunge into the ring. They stop upon seeing Hann, bleeding and barely able to stand. I resume my place, ignoring the yank on my braid from the girl.

"I can help," Cupid hisses in my ear.

"How?"

"Stand back and see," she orders. I move sideways so she can join me.

"What are you planning?" I ask.

"Just watch."

The tigers crouch, making low vocalizations. The noise inside the stadium makes them nervous, unsure. In unison, they start advancing toward Hann.

I yell, along with everyone else. My voice is again drowned out in the sea of noise filling the stadium. Rudolpho's mouth appears to be moving, but he's having no effect on the tigers.

Suddenly, the gypsy girl puts her fingers in her mouth and gives a shrill whistle. The tigers pause within five feet of Hann. She whistles again and they turn in our direction.

"Down," the gypsy girl yells, pointing a finger to the ground.

The tigers snarl in response, not taking their eyes from her. I see the King peering in our direction, but the other gypsies have gathered around her, shielding her from their eyes with their wild jumping and hollering. Too much commotion makes it impossible to see who is commanding the animals.

The noise level of the masses is lowered at the animals' behavior. Heads crane to see who or what is controlling the tigers.

I don't have time to talk to the girl about her being a Favored One. Hann is losing so much blood that he sinks to the ground. I grab my brown robe and shakily put it back on, pulling the hood over my head.

"Can you get me over the bars?" I ask Gallius.

He nods and holds out his hands. I step on them and gratefully accept his support as he helps me hoist myself to the top of the bars and over, dropping into the ring.

King Lawrence rises and yanks Donder to his feet. The boy stands and yells to the tigers, but he can't be heard from the masses' uproar. He's lowered by a rope back into the ring as I rush to Hann's side.

"Vixen? What are you doing in here?"

"I'm helping you."

"I don't need your help," he protests weakly. "Get out of here. It's too dangerous."

Out of the corner of my eye, I see the tigers' heads snap up at the presence of Donder. They stand at his command and turn back to Hann—to both of us. I reach down to wrap my arm around Hann's waist and help him to his feet. The tigers crouch again, ready to pounce as Donder commands.

I hold out my hand to them. "Down! Down!"

The tigers pause. I can't help the chill that shoots through my spine at their menacing figures so close. Donder yells for them to attack us, but the tigers are confused. They look from Donder to me, not moving.

"Light always overcomes darkness," I shout to Donder, pulling my hood even further down on my head. "You will not win."

The young man's expression registers his surprise. He's not a fighter, I can tell by the lack of confidence written on his face. He looks helplessly up at the King for instruction.

"Kill them," the King shouts to him.

Donder again commands the tigers to attack. Though I struggle to help hold up the weight of Hann, I know better than to move. I stare boldly into the eyes of the tigers, mere feet in front of me. After a tense minute, they lay down in the dirt, bowing their head before me.

Quickly, I turn and shout for Hann to move with me. We make our way to the ring's gate. Arms reach out to help Hann over the gate. Just as I'm about to climb over behind him, I feel hands grasp me from within the ring, trying to drag me off the iron bars.

And then I see Rudolpho appearing in front of my face. He grabs me through the bars to keep me there while other unrecognizable settlers, identity concealed by their brown robes, stand on top of each other and reach over the gate to help yank me to the safety of the masses.

I turn to see several Juuls back away. Courageously, or perhaps obediently, they had entered the ring with the tigers to try to detain me. The tigers rise to their feet as I disappear into the crowd gathered thickly at the ringside.

I hear Donder again command the animals to leave the elves alone. Without my presence to tell them differently, the tigers obey him. They turn and trot back to the other side of the ring and disappear into the structure.

Hann and I are enveloped into the crowd. I crouch down on the ground beside Hann who is valiantly trying to stay alert. Rudolpho and Grandmullie lower themselves beside me.

"Help him, Grandmullie."

She pulls at the bottom of his shirt to rip the bottom half off and presses it against the wound.

"Put pressure on this," she commands Rudolpho.

The Cavaliers painstakingly move through the masses in search of Hann. He's an easy target in his blood stained white linen clothes. And there are no extra brown robes to conceal him and enable him to leave the stadium.

Over the heads of the masses, I can make out a Cavalier pushing through the bodies in our direction. I shed my robe and hand it to Grandmullie.

"What do you think you're doing?" she asks frantically.

"I need you to trust me. I'll be fine."

"I will not allow you to do this," she says, her eyes misting with tears and bottom lip quivering.

"Please, Grandmullie. Put the robe on him."

"You would sacrifice yourself for this boy?"

"I love him," I say simply.

The words slip out of my mouth. My grandmother is speechless, unsure of what to think about my declaration. *I'm* not sure what I think about my words right now, but I know they're heartfelt. I'm grateful that Grandmullie hands the robe to a man who swiftly helps clothe Hann.

"You don't have to be brave, Vixen," she says, placing her hand on my cheek.

"Someone has to, Grandmullie. How else are we going to change things?"

"Oh, child," she says and wraps her arms around me in a tight squeeze.

I look over her shoulder at Rudolpho who can't contain his tears. "See that Hann gets out of here."

He nods to me. I extricate myself from Grandmullie's hug and back away from them so they don't discover Hann. I try to push through the crowd in the opposite direction to draw the Cavalier away from Hann. My ploy works. He spies me and starts yelling at the settlers to move out of his way. I don't stop moving until his heavy hand on my shoulder brings me to a stop.

The large knight grabs me and tosses me over his shoulder as though I'm a rag doll. Amidst the cries from the masses, he plows through the crowd to take me back to the ring. Other Cavaliers join him to keep the masses at bay. They unlock the gate and I'm thrown onto the dirt floor of the ring.

"Who are you and how is it that you defy your King?" King Lawrence yells at me from his throne.

I stand to my feet, trying to quell the shaking in my legs. Defiance to the King can cause my immediate execution. I pause, trying to choose my words carefully.

"Gracious King," I begin, sinking into a low curtsy, "may you live forever more. I don't strive to defy my King. I'm unsure why I'm dragged into the ring for all that I desire is peace on earth and good will to all men."

I hold my breath as the King stares stonily at me. I'm in trouble and I know it. But then an unexpected ally comes to my rescue.

Nicklaus steps from behind the King's throne and crosses to the edge of the platform, squinting at me. "I recognize the young maiden, your Majesty. I can personally vouch for her integrity as she's visited me in my sanctuary for my—," he coughs into his hand, "for my wise counsel, if you will."

I hold back my tears and try to smile. I never thought I would welcome the sight of such a scoundrel.

Twelve

I FEEL HIS GAZE UPON ME BEFORE I EVEN open my eyes. The fighting has commenced inside the ring, but I will not be witness to the death of my people—the masses. I have been detained in a small cell inside the structure. I can hear the yells of the masses as each match is fought, but I don't know who emerges as the victors—the young boys or the King's mighty knights.

"You don't seem to be surprised at my presence," Donder says in the darkness of the cell.

I sit up on the small cot where I've lain for the past hour or longer, biding my time till the King decides what will become of me. The King's nephew stands about a foot away from the cell bars as his eyes drill into mine.

"I felt we would meet face to face at some point," I finally say.

"Were you surprised to find out that I'm the Favored One?" he asks with a raised brow.

"Were you surprised to find that there are more than you? That you aren't so special after all?" I counter.

Donder gives a short laugh. "I admit that I was surprised."

We stare at each other for a long minute before I break his gaze. "Is there a lot of blood being shed in the ring?"

"Yes," he replies simply, "but I want to talk about the identity of the other Favored One—the girl that entered the ring and was able to command the animals right in front of me."

"How should I know that?"

"Because she's one of you—one of the masses. She may very well be you."

I force a laugh even though it's the last thing I feel like doing at such a time as this. "If I were one of the Favored Ones, don't you think I could call upon the animals to come rescue me? Isn't the Favored One supposed to have the ability to do that?"

Donder studies my face, trying to see if I can be believed. He's like an open book. For one being of royal lineage, I'm rather surprised to see a lack of manipulation in the young man.

"Do you know who the girl is?"

I sigh. "How can one possibly know that? There are so many people crammed into the stadium that it will be much like finding a needle in a haystack."

"My uncle thinks you know. He sent me to question you."

"I'm not surprised," I say.

"What's your name?"

"Vixen St. Ridlington."

He smiles. "*Saint* Ridlington, you say. Like *Saint* Nicklaus?"

"Never," I whisper. "It's merely my last name, unlike the position of bishop that Nicklaus tries to assume."

"You don't find Nicklaus a noble man?"

"Does anyone see him as noble?" I wonder.

Donder laughs. It's a pleasant laugh that makes the corners of his eyes crinkle slightly. "I suppose not. Why my uncle keeps company with him is a riddle that I can't solve. Did you catch my humor? Riddle—Ridlington?"

"I'm sorry, sire, but I don't find anything amusing about trying to link me to Nicklaus."

"I suppose I wouldn't wish that upon myself either."

I stand and cross to him, grasping the iron bars in my hands to stare at him. "Will you kindly release me?"

Donder's eyes grow wide. "Release you? I can't possibly do that. My uncle would have my head on a platter for such an act."

"But I don't understand why I'm being detained."

"My uncle thinks you know the identity of the other Favored One. After talking with you, I feel the same way."

"Because I deny knowing who it is?"

"It's not what you say but how you protest," Donder says quietly. "All my life, I've had an innate ability to read people—not their words but their actions. I think you do know who the Favored One is, yes?"

Donder is not one to be taken lightly. I see that now—that I underestimated him. There is a very quiet danger about the young man standing before me.

"What will become of the other Favored One?" I ask. "Death?"

Donder starts pacing in front of me, his fingertips lighting trailing along the cell's bars. "I don't think death is what the King wishes, but it could well lead to that if the person was unwilling to join him."

"What then?"

He pauses right in front of me and moves in very close. "The Favored One would have the opportunity to join with the King, live a life of privilege inside Oldenwald."

"What exactly do you mean by joining with the King?"

"Joining the King's army," he says with a cock of his head. "I should be quiet now. I've already shared more than my uncle would have wished."

I step back from the bars and drop my eyes so that Donder can't read my inner thoughts. "The masses face such grave starvation that I wonder if your words may entice the Favored One to come forward."

I peek up to see him pondering me, a noticeable expression of uncertainty written on his face. *That's good. Perhaps he's questioning his ability to read me after all.*

"Perhaps that's the message to send to the masses?" he asks.

I nod my head. "Starvation could very well drive even the most saintly person to do desperate things."

"I'll take your counsel into consideration before I raise it to the King."

"Can you at least let me see the fighting inside the ring?"

His brow creases as he looks at me. "Why would you want to see the fighting?"

"So I can pray for the young men."

"I'll have to ask permission," he says quietly. And then he walks away.

I cross back to the cot and sink back onto the straw. There's such a feeling of helplessness being confined like this. I desperately want to find out how Hann is faring. Was Rudolpho able to get him out of the stadium?

I close my eyes to imagine my last look at him. His face pale, eyes sunken as he tried to stay alert and watch me. And I think about my words to Grandmullie, blushing as I relive my declaration of love for Hann. But seeing him again and the way he valiantly opposed the monarchy brought forth feelings I have tried to keep hidden. Feelings of a quiet love pressed into my inner being—not a love based on someone's physical appearance, but a love based on seeing a person's inner self— their soul. Hann's soul, as passionate and fiery as my own.

"What dreams are you reliving that bring a whisper of a smile to your virgin lips?"

Nicklaus. The sound of his voice brings turmoil to the depths of my being. I don't turn to look at him, even when he takes a switch and runs it along the iron bars.

"Did you like that I played the role of your savior today?" he asks in his raspy voice, low and husky.

"I didn't need you to be my savior," I tell him. "I've done nothing wrong."

"Why do you keep coming to my attention at the most unexpected moments?" Nicklaus asks with a throaty laugh. "Fate. Simple fate."

"Not fate," I say as I stare at the ceiling. "Desperation."

"Desperation—fate. Call it what you will, but the stars are aligned for you to be near me."

"Much like a mouse is near a snake before it reaches out and swallows the poor creature in one bite?"

I turn my head to look at Nicklaus and see him smacking his lips with a satisfied gleam in his eyes. "You don't understand my intentions, young Vixen."

Oh, I think I understand the vile man's intentions very well, thank you very much. I stand up and return his stare with my own. Up close, I can see his forehead still wears visible signs of the whack it took against the stone floor during our last time together. The bruise has faded to an ugly greenish-yellow color now.

Deliberately, I start sashaying toward him, humming the same tune I had when he had gotten spun out of control. His eyes narrow as he watches me draw near.

"Did you enjoy frolicking with me?" he asks quietly.

"I've never experienced anything like it before," I say with a small smile and a wink.

Nicklaus' brows crease. The crazy old man can't even remember the events of that evening, but he's trying not to let me see that. Two can play the game of snake and mouse.

"We shall have to repeat that evening."

"Indeed we shall," I say in a coy voice. "But you drank all of the wine and didn't refill my glass."

Nicklaus' eyes are becoming glazed as he stares at me. "I'll make sure I have an abundance of wine."

"And your cape, sire."

He presses his face through the bars, and I have to take a step back from the force of his breath hitting my nostrils. *What does the man eat to make his breath so foul?*

"Would you like to stroke my cape?"

"Perhaps when we frolic again," I reply.

"Liar!"

A Juul stands haughtily behind Nicklaus with his hands on his hips. He stares at me with hatred.

"This is a private conversation," Nicklaus sternly warns the elf. "What is this nonsense about lies?"

"She's the liar," the Juul says, pointing his stubby finger in my direction.

"Her? Oh, yes, of course you're talking about her. She's the liar. Wait—*she's* a liar? What is she lying about?"

"She didn't frolic with you. She left you on the cold floor when you drank too much."

"But we frolicked before that," I try to protest but Nicklaus holds up his hand.

"Shh," he whispers to me with a finger to his lips. "Shh."

I stop trying to offer an explanation and the Juul stands to attention, his body stiff with displeasure as he looks at me.

"What do you know?" Nicklaus asks the Juul.

"I came to see if you needed more wine—"

"He came to spy on us," I blurt out, trying to use Nicklaus' words against the elf.

Nicklaus glares at the Juul. "After I told you to leave us alone?"

"Not only that," I continue, "but he tried to frolic with me himself."

"Is this true?" Nicklaus asks the Juul with a more fierce expression.

"Of course not," the elf sputters.

"He did so," I say loudly. "He even licked my cheek."

The Juul cowers as Nicklaus looms threateningly over him. "Not the switch," he yells.

He takes off running when Nicklaus waves it at him. I watch the elf until he's out of sight, just grateful that he didn't argue with me about the events of that cold, dark night.

"So you left me on the cold stone floor? After I fell into an unconscious state?"

"I tried to help you, sire, but the Juul jumped on me and I had to flee for my life."

Nicklaus paces back and forth in front of the cell, this time tapping the switch in his hand. "Something was stolen from me that night. Something of value. Would you know what happened?"

"Perhaps you should check with the Juuls," I say, trying to speak calmly.

"They told me a tale about a young maiden and a very large man running out of the sanctuary with my goods."

He whirls suddenly to stare at me. I meet his gaze unwaveringly. He knows.

"Were they really your goods or did they truly belong to the more unfortunate?"

"How dare you?" he rages suddenly, his voice thundering in the dark.

"How dare you, sire?" I say coldly. "You stole money and coal from the orphans. Have you no shame?"

His chest heaves as he stares at me. "Have you ever wondered about the name of the land in which we live, young Vixen?"

I don't answer. I'm sure he will enlighten me.

"Think about it for a minute," he encourages in a dangerously quiet tone. "Klaus. Klaus. This is my land."

"This land belongs to the masses," I spit out contemptuously.

"Never," he shouts. "Klaus is my land. Think about it. Nicklaus. Say it with me. Nicklaus. I will always be a part of this land—I can't be separated from it. My legend will be spoken of for a millennium to come. Years from now, children will cry from their want of sitting on my lap during Winter Solstice. Parents will threaten them with a switch if they're naughty and give them a sweet if they're nice."

"Your story may become twisted over time, but right now, I see you for who you are. You're nothing but a creepy old man who makes the children cry and the widows cringe to come near you."

A bright red color creeps up Nicklaus' neck and fills his face. Spit flies from his mouth as he yells at me.

"You insolent young maiden," he snarls. "And I could have made your life one of silver and gold. I make the decisions for Klaus. Do you hear me? Not the King, but me! Did you hear the bells ringing this morning? Ding dong, ding dong. Announcing glad tidings for all our guests that soon some boys will be laid to rest."

"You're mad," I whisper.

"Go tell it on the mountain," Nicklaus shouts with a harsh laugh.

"And you, sire, have yourself a merry little Winter Solstice," I say coldly.

Nicklaus whirls, and with a sweep of his cape, he leaves me. My eyes travel to the floor, and I see the switch that he had brought with him now discarded within arm's reach. Before anyone can see me, I rush to the cell opening and stick my arm through the bars as far as I can reach. My fingers can barely touch the switch. I press against the bars with all my might and able to roll the thin twig between my fingers until I can grasp it in my hand and pull it into the cell.

I place the switch out of sight under the straw mattress and lay down, awaiting my next visitor. Someone will come. The

King wants answers from me, and he will stop at nothing until he has them.

Of course, I'm somewhat disappointed by the next guest sent to me to extract information.

"Stratton," I say sadly when he appears at my cell.

"You don't seem surprised to see me," he says, puzzled.

"I'm disappointed to see you."

Stratton nods his understanding. "Aren't you the least bit surprised that the King would send me of all people?"

"No," I reply. "You told him you knew me."

"Only so I could get to see you," he says softly.

"No, Stratton. You want favor from the King."

"But not at your expense, Vixen. Otherwise, I would have told him about you—your ability with the animals."

I chew on my bottom lip as I consider his words. "What do you hope to gain from seeing me?"

"I just want to know the whereabouts of the boy who won in the ring. The one was rescued from the ring."

I feel a sudden jolt at his unexpected request and sit up on the cot. "Why would you want to know that?"

"The King will reward me greatly if I bring him in."

I try not to show emotion, but I'm not sure if I'm successful as Stratton's eyes harden the longer I take to respond to him. I stand and move toward him.

"I'm stuck in this cell, Stratton. How could I possibly know where he is?"

"Ah, but I can get you released," Stratton says. "You're one of them—the masses will trust you. If you tell me where to find him, then we both get what we want. You get your freedom, and I get a fat reward from the King."

Stratton must surely read the displeasure I feel at his words—nay, the anger his words cause. Would he really think I would agree to that? That my freedom would be worth more than another's life?

"You already know my response, Stratton."

He shrugs with a smile. "What if I told you that I would inform the King about your special abilities with the animals— the very same ability his nephew has."

"Are you threatening me?"

Stratton gives a strained laugh. "Of course I would never tell your secret, Vixen. But I need to find that boy. It's not just the matter of a reward. Unfortunately, we lost the boy while me and two other Cavaliers were on guard at the gate. Our heads are on the chopping block unless we can bring him to the King. You must help me, Vixen. I could marry you and bring you to live in Oldenwald with me."

In wonderment, I take in the beads of perspiration that line his upper lip. Stratton is only concerned with himself. I don't doubt that he imagines himself in love with me to an extent—

or else why would he have saved my life from the stampeding animals not so long ago? But at the core of Stratton is selfishness. He will willingly sacrifice others to get what he desires.

"Vixen," he asks in my silence, "do you personally know the boy I'm searching for?"

"He's not from my settlement."

"That's good. It's easier if you don't know him."

Easier to betray an unknown person than one of your own? I must escape this cell so that I can warn Hann, make sure he's safe.

"If you can get me released then I'll see what I can find out."

Stratton grins and pounds his hand on the cell bars. "That's my girl. I will have you released in no time. You'll see."

He reaches his arm through the bars, extending his hand to me. I hesitate for a split second before placing my hand in his.

"Don't delay, Stratton. With each passing minute, the boy is probably hiding himself more securely."

Stratton releases me and hurries out of the cell. I can only hope that he is able to convince the King to free me. Of course, I'll then have to plan how I will evade Stratton once I'm released.

I'm imprisoned for what seems like hours. I've stopped trying to count the number of times the masses suddenly shout—at well over a hundred. I don't know if that's the number of victims or if the young boys are prevailing.

Finally, a Juul appears at my cell. The same one who showed up when Nicklaus had made his appearance. The elf peers through the bars at me, his small face screwing up as though in pain.

"I have a hankering for you to frolic with me," he says suddenly.

"Pardon me?"

I sit up on my cot and look at the vile elf before me. His tongue snakes out and he hisses at me. Some kind of love call, perhaps? But one that only a fellow Juul could appreciate.

"Frolic with me," he insists.

"How can I possibly frolic with you when I'm locked up in this cell?"

The elf raises up a ring of large, rusty keys. "One of these is for your cell."

I try not to smile and show my excitement. It may only drive the Juul away. This may be the only chance I get to escape.

"Aren't you a clever elf?" I say with a smile.

"Clever? Yes."

The Juul starts pushing keys into the lock but he's unsuccessful. I refrain from rushing to help him. If I'm caught doing that, I will be tried for treason. Better for the Juul to struggle with the keys—a seemingly endless task with him inserting the same key over and over in the lock. Unexpectedly, a key clicks in the lock. The Juul clicks his tongue excitedly as he removes the lock and swings open the cell door.

"I have just one question," I ask him. "How do you exactly frolic?"

The question stumps him for a second. "I don't rightly know, but it will be fun to find out!"

He closes the cell door behind him and picks up the lock to secure himself in with me.

"Stop!" I shout. "What are you doing?"

"I'm locking us in so you can't escape me," the Juul says with a devious smile.

I pull out the switch from under the cot and raise it above my head with the most menacing frown I can muster. The Juul screeches and drops the lock and keys on the cell's floor.

"Where did you get that?" he cries.

"It was a gift from Nicklaus," I say quietly. "Now step away from the door and move very slowly over to the cot."

The elf tiptoes in my direction with his hands raised. Simultaneously, I slowly move toward the cell's door with the switch positioned in front of me. *It's a good thing he's petrified of the switch.*

"You're missing out on the time of your life," the Juul tells me, planting himself stubbornly in the middle of the room as though refusing to budge another inch. "I came to frolic with bells on my shoes."

I look down at his small shoes, and sure enough, he has a tiny bell attached to their pointy tips. Any other time I may find the sight amusing. Right now, my hands have started shaking at the prospect of escaping—so much so that I can barely open the cell's door.

"Giddy up," I tell him, "pick up your feet and jingle on over to the cot."

He crosses his arms and glares at me. "I'm going to pounce on you when you turn your back to me."

"You're such a strange little elf," I say.

For good measure, I take a step toward him and wildly wave the switch. The Juul screeches again and runs to the cot.

I use the momentary distraction to grab the lock and ring of keys and fling open the cell door. The elf suddenly realizes that my intention is to lock him inside the cell. He runs full force toward me just as I slam the door shut. I frantically wave the switch between the bars at him so that I can re-lock the door.

I leave the furious Juul, the sound of the bells on his shoes tinkling against the iron bars. It should have been a festive sound. Right now, it sounds as ominous as the sanctuary bells still droning in the distance.

Thirteen

THERE IS NOT A SOUL TO BE SEEN AS I MAKE
my way down the dark hall of the structure. My cell was at the
back of the structure and the closer I creep toward the entrance
of the ring, the louder the crowd's deafening shouts become.

I still clutch the heavy ring of keys in my hand and am about
to lay them on the floor when I have a sudden thought. A
dangerous thought. What if—what if I search the structure to
find the young boys and Kringles still awaiting their match,
hope already departed from their minds, and release them?
What if I carry their hope to live another day in my very
hands—in the rusty ring of keys?

A sudden spasm of yells to my right draws my attention
away from the ring. I retrace my steps back to the cell in which

I was locked. The startled Juul jumps up from the cot to face me.

"How do I get to the other side of the structure?" I ask him.

He crosses to the bars and clutches them in his small hands. "You've got to get me out of here. If Nicklaus finds me in here because of your trickery, he'll give me twenty lashes with the switch."

"My trickery? You're as dishonorable as Nicklaus."

"Thank you," the Juul replies.

"That wasn't a compliment—how could you possibly take that as a compliment. Never mind, I don't have time for the likes of you."

I turn away, but his imploring stops me from leaving. "Please, wretched soul. Please take me with you. Please don't leave me here to receive twenty lashes."

"I'll let you out if you take me to the Kringles and the boys who are held captive."

"Yes, yes!" he screeches, jumping up and down.

I pick the switch back up from the ground and hold it out as I search through the key ring to unlock the door. It swings open within a couple of minutes. The Juul emerges with a hiss at me.

"Take me to them," I order him, holding the switch as though I may give him twenty lashes myself.

The Juul leads me to the very end of the structure and opens a door concealed by the darkness. "This way to the captives."

With a slight shudder, I follow him. The entire area contains cells of young men, most silently bowing their head in prayer. Only a handful of Kringles remain, tucked into the corner of one cell, quietly meditating with closed eyes.

They eye me curiously when I enter. I hand the keys to the Juul. "Start unlocking the cells."

He gasps and drops the key ring to the floor. "I will not be part of your trickery—again! It's far better for me to receive twenty lashes from Nicklaus."

"Oh, really?"

I swipe at his small legs, coming within a mere inch or two of bringing a sting with the switch. He quickly retrieves the key ring and starts trying to match a key to the locks.

"Vixen?"

I turn at my name, and sudden tears fill up my eyes at the sight of a familiar face. "Wilfre!"

Wilfre and Weldon, the twins from my settlement, clutch the bars. They're painfully skinny beneath the white linen clothes that hang on them as though cloaking skeletons. Most of the boys look like this with their eager eyes staring at me with hope.

I snatch the key ring away from the Juul who isn't really trying to find the proper key anyway. Grabbing him by the scruff of his neck, I lead him to Wilfre.

"Hold him here so he doesn't run off and tell on me."

The Juul starts kicking his feet through the bars to try to make contact with Wilfre's legs. The boy grasps him in a tighter hold and raises him off the ground.

"Trickery!" the elf shouts.

Wilfre clamps his other hand over the Juul's mouth and struggles to hold onto the squirming figure. Their lives depend on the Juul not getting loose though. Weldon reaches out and bops the elf on the head. It's enough to silence him.

"What are you doing here?" Weldon asks.

I'm not having good fortune in finding the proper key. "Let me concentrate," I bark at him.

The lock finally releases, and the boys slowly emerge from the cell, unsure of what to do.

"Stay here until I get all of the cells unlocked," I order.

"Stay here? You're out of your mind," a boy tells me. "We'll be caught and executed on the spot if we stay here.

"Silence," I say sharply, trying not to raise my voice. "Leave at your own peril if you must, but there's strength in numbers. If you'll be patient for a little longer, I may have a plan to get us all out of here alive."

The boys gather in a cluster, nervously watching as I move from them to unlock each cell. A Cavalier seems to show up out of nowhere. He stops in surprise at the sight before him. Before he can move, a group of boys jumps on him, bringing him to the ground and silencing him before he can alert others.

"We have a sword," a boy declares, holding up the knight's abandoned weapon.

"Careful. Do you know how to use that?" I ask him.

He slowly shakes his head no. He probably hasn't even held a sword before. An older boy reaches down to pick it up. "It can't be too different from a spear."

He doesn't understand the increased risk of wielding a weapon. And I don't have the time to try to explain it to him as my shaking hands continue searching for the right key to match each lock.

Another Cavalier enters the area and is overpowered by the boys before he realizes what is happening. More will come. Tension rises further.

I finally release Wilfre and Weldon and they push with the others through the cell's door, already tasting freedom. Hope can make a person drunk with anticipation. They gather together, whispering excitedly, trying to figure out the best course of action.

"We go to the platform," I tell them, "and take the nephew."

"We can't do that," a boy says. "We'll all be slaughtered within ten feet of the King."

"Not if you go in the back way."

I turn at the voice. It's the Juul. In all of the commotion, I forgot about him. I don't understand why he didn't just leave and I'm not sure I trust him.

"What about the back way?" I ask him.

"It's down the hall and up the stairs. There are only two knights guarding the entrance. They would never expect anyone to go up there."

"I don't trust you," I say. "Not one bit. Why would you try to help us?"

"Because it will take Nicklaus' attention off me," he says gleefully.

An older Kringle hobbles out of their cell while the others remain. He crosses to stand in front of me, his piercing blue eyes staring at me with fondness. It takes a minute for me to recognize him. My childhood friend, Sir Throck.

"Vixen," he whispers in a hoarse voice.

I bend down and throw my arms around his neck with relief. He hasn't expired in the ring like the others.

"Sir Throck, you must come with us," I plead. "I can't bear to think of you getting killed."

"My child, these old eyes just wanted to see you one last time. I'm not afraid of death. It will visit us all at some point, and I've made peace with it."

"No——," I start to say, but he holds up a hand to silence me.

"Your time is not yet, Vixen. I feel it. You must lead the young men the way the Juul has said. I've seen their patterns, and the knights will come to gather another victim. Go quickly."

I grab his hand and plant a kiss on his withered fingers. But I have no time to mourn. That will come later.

"Follow me," I tell the boys.

Just as we're about to depart, two more Cavaliers arrive. They're immediately attacked and knocked unconscious by the boys. We now have four swords.

I'm joined on either side by the boys who are brandishing the swords. I can only hope they know how to use them. We stride in the direction the Juul instructed, boys linking arms to form chains that can't be broken.

Up the stairs we fly. I'm passed by a group of boys, courage filling their bellies as they push past me to take out the Cavaliers protecting the King and his guests.

The Cavaliers don't stand a chance. They aren't prepared for the onslaught of bodies that overpower them in a few seconds.

Onto the platform we assemble, loud and bold and shouting at the King. Amazingly, he keeps his composure as the others scream and huddle together for safety. I'm surprised the King holds up so well—it's not like he ever enters into battles. It will be only a matter of time before his knights, the mighty men of war, arrive to make an end of us all.

"Grab the nephew," I yell to Wilfre.

He and Weldon, always close beside him, grab the young man who is scared out of his wits. He throws his hands over his head in an attempt to shield himself against blows that don't come. Instead, the twins drag him back down the stairs and I follow.

"You won't get out of here alive," Donder yells.

"Then you won't either," I tell him.

Donder starts shaking so badly that his teeth begin chattering. "Please don't kill me."

"Help us get out of here," I demand.

He looks around helplessly for a second then snaps his fingers. "The animals. Release the animals."

I shake my head no. "They aren't the answer."

"But if you bring them to the platform and they attack the foreign guests, the knights will be distracted and attention taken off the masses."

"We'll try that," I say impulsively. "Where are the boys' robes? We need to hide them among the masses."

"Follow me," Donder shouts, moving hurriedly back the way we had just come. I motion for Wilfre and Weldon to lead the others to follow us.

Donder's pace is quick, and I have to run to keep up. He flings open a door to reveal the stacked brown robes of the boys. I hear the boys trailing just seconds behind us stopping to grab their robes. We move swiftly from there to another door. The door that leads to the animals.

"Have you ever been up close to wild animals before?" Donder asks before he opens the door.

"I was close to a bear once and a deer."

"Prepare to be scared out of your wits."

He opens the door to mayhem. The animals are locked in individual cages—several bears and a multitude of tigers. They jump against the cages in their attempts to escape, their cries both frightening and sad.

Donder is right. Their massive presence up close is a formidable sight to behold. I step back in alarm. Just because I can communicate with them doesn't mean the large beasts don't frighten me.

"Do you trust me to release the animals?" Donder asks me with a smile—the kind of eerie smile that speaks of mischief and distrust.

"Should I doubt your intentions?" I ask.

The boys can be heard right outside the room, stopping short of entering when they hear the animals roar. Donder cocks his head as though waiting for all of them to join him and seems disappointed when they don't.

"What if I release the animals and command them to attack you and the boys?" he taunts.

"I'm believing you to be a man of honor and keep your word."

"You trust too much," Donder says and moves to open the cages.

"Wait," I shout at him. "What are you doing?"

"I can't betray my uncle, Vixen. You really didn't think I would, did you?"

He stares into the eyes of the large animals as he unlocks the first cage. Quietly, he speaks to the first two tigers to emerge from their cages. They snarl in response and look my way.

"Attack her," Donder yells.

The tigers lunge at me, and I instinctively hold up my hand and shout for them to stop. They pause, their bodies taut with tension. Donder intently watches the exchange, his eyes gleaming as the tigers slowly crouch to a sitting position as they await my next command.

"I knew it was you," Donder says quietly.

"You were trying to kill me," I accuse, my heart beating so fast in my chest that I feel as though I may pass out.

"Not so," he says. "I just wanted to prove to myself that I had found you—another Favored One."

"We don't have time for this."

"I know," Donder says. He looks around him, his mind swirling. "We can run the animals through this other door to get to the platform faster. Cavaliers will be swarming the platform by now, so keep down among the animals. I can't let my uncle see me helping."

"Why are you helping now?"

"I never knew there was another person who shared the unlikely gift I never asked for. I will find you again, outside Oldenwald. Go quickly."

I don't tell him there are other Favored Ones besides myself. I simply nod and take a deep breath. Being so close to the large animals is frightening, but I try to stay focused on the task at hand.

Wilfre sticks his head through the door and lets out a yelp. "What's this?"

"Tell the boys to go the other direction and get ready to escape through the ring," I yell to him. "I'll provide a distraction with the animals from the platform. Wait for the commotion to begin and then get out of here."

Donder moves to the other door and opens it, calling out commands to the animals. I run in the midst of them, crouching. Down the hall and up the stairs we sprint. I shout praise to the animals for their courage, for their beauty, for freeing the captives.

One of the bears raises on his hind legs and roars before knocking down the door separating us from the platform. A gunshot rings out, striking the bear in the shoulder. He roars louder and leads the pack of animals onto the platform.

Donder was right. The platform is filled with the presence of the knights. The foreign guests are being hurriedly lowered to the ring by a couple of Cavaliers. The King and his queen are nowhere to be seen—they were probably the first ones to be lowered to safety.

The assault from the Cavaliers upon the animals is savage, brutal, as they swing their swords to slash the animals. The knights cloister together to plunge their swords into the thick fur of the bears.

I move low in the middle of the animals, ordering them to stop the knights. Despite their wounds, the animals ferociously defend themselves and me, ruthlessly ripping their teeth into any part of the knights' bodies that get too close.

I shout for a tiger to bite the remaining two foreign guests trying to get off the platform. Historically, battles between lands have been caused by a visiting foreign dignitary getting wounded or killed. We'll have to bring war to Klaus and the only way to accomplish that is to send foreign leaders home with wounds. The Cavaliers will be sent to the battle, so the last thing on their minds will be hunting the young men when they escape today.

The rampage lasts only minutes, but time seems to stand still as the butchering of the animals takes place. When I see the boys running with the monarchy and guests through the ring, I know the end is near. Their brown robes don't slow them down as they scurry to freedom over the iron bars of the ring.

The entire stadium is filled with chaos. The masses have started rebelling—exactly what the King was trying to avoid. They clamor out of the stadium, trampling over each other in their state of shock and fear.

I see the smoke rising inside the stadium, and I know it's time to make my own departure. I look for a means to escape, but the platform rope has been cut. It's probably too far from the ground for me to jump off the platform as I would surely break a leg.

"Over here! Over here!"

A head peers over the edge of the platform. It's the gypsy boy, Gallius. He's clinging to the side of the platform on the other side. I move in his direction, and two tigers instinctively turn with me despite their bleeding wounds.

"Climb over my back," he shouts.

I dutifully climb onto his back and look down. The gypsies have formed a human chain to the ground—one person clinging to the ankles of the person above them until they reached the height of the platform.

The tigers fight the Cavaliers that rush toward us. My last look at the creatures is them pouncing on the knights with such intense ferocity that the men turn to flee. I am grateful beyond measure for the animals' sacrifice out of obedience to me.

I slide down the bodies to the ground. The gypsy girl is waiting for me. She grabs my arms and pulls me with her and her clan as they run up the bleachers to escape the wrath of the King's knights.

The gypsies are nimble on their feet, leaping over obstacles and maneuvering through the bodies of the masses. I'm determined to stay up with them though. I need to get out of Oldenwald to find Hann.

The smoke fills our lungs as we move through the stadium doors. The large yule logs are roaring with a vicious fire, being fed debris by the masses. It's the only way we can show our rebellion for the King's activities.

"Don't stop," the gypsy girl shouts at me when I stumble in the midst of the masses.

I can't keep up with the gypsy clan and soon lose sight of them in the upheaval of bodies and smoke. My eyes tear up and I start coughing. I try to cover my mouth and nose against the thick smoke. The masses need to move, or we'll all be killed by inhaling the smoke.

A young girl sits on the ground in front of me, wailing as people push past her. I grab her in my arms, looking around to see if her parents are close by. There is so much noise and frantic cries that it's impossible to try to identify anyone. She clings to me as I push toward the gates of Oldenwald with the masses.

Cavaliers are stationed along the way, defending themselves with their swords and arrows. Occasionally, a gunman fires a shot in the crowd to disperse the people and keep them on the defensive. I stay toward the center of the crowd to avoid being cut by one of the knights' swords. Many unfortunate souls suffer slashes to the limbs as they pass by the Cavaliers.

Through the gates we flee until we reach freedom outside the forbidden premises. Nothing good came this Winter Solstice. I look at the masses, screaming and running for their lives. *You better watch out—for Nicklaus knows where we sleep.*

Fourteen

THE ICY FOREST HAS BECOME THE HOME FOR many of the masses too scared to go back to their settlements. I hide with them, all the while searching for a sign of hope that Rudolpho, Grandmullie, and Hann escaped. It's been three days of searching throughout the vast forest and no sign is forthcoming.

Fortunately, I found relatives of the young girl I had rescued in the madness of the sporting event. Now I sit alone under a large oak tree, my nerves on edge like the other settlers. We're awaiting word of the King's decision to pursue us.

Hann is the single victor to emerge alive from the sporting event. The total number of boys and Kringles who died ranges from seventy-eight to one hundred twenty, depending on who is telling their side of the story. It doesn't matter what the number—too many innocent lives were lost in the ring.

"Are you hungry?" a woman asks softly.

I look up into her worn features, eyes laced with sadness. I don't have to ask if she's lost a boy in the sporting event. As with the others, their expressions tell of their loss.

"Yes," I reply.

She holds out a piece of dried meat, but I shake my head. "I don't eat the flesh of animals."

"Is that right?" she replies, taking a bite of the meat. "You're likely to go hungry then. There's nothing else to eat out here."

"Then I'll go hungry," I say softly.

"What rational person won't eat meat if she's starving?"

"My family doesn't eat the flesh of animals that have a soul."

She looks perplexed as she considers my words. "Animals don't have a soul."

I smile politely at her. It's not a conversation I want to have right now. The thought of eating meat is rather distasteful. Perhaps it's because I can communicate with the animals—I don't know.

The woman moves away from me. Most people feel uncomfortable with others who don't believe as they do. That's why I usually keep my mouth closed about matters of food.

I have a sudden memory of the chocolat hidden in my brown robe. I do hope that Hann found it and the three of them were able to enjoy the treat—that is, if they're safely tucked into a safe place.

My ears prick up at a hushed conversation to the left of me. Three men sit huddled in the thick winter brush, their brown robes blending in with the drab surroundings that await a burst of color that spring will bring.

"The Cavaliers are assembling for a battle along the territory boundaries," one man whispers.

"Which land is attacking?" another one asks.

"The land of Chaak. They have threatened to call on the spirits of their ancestors to seize the land of Klaus."

I turn to look at the men. One catches my eyes and motions for the others to silence. I frown at him and turn to crawl on my knees to reach them in the brush, fielding thistles as I make my way closer.

"Excuse me," I say, evidently far too loudly for I'm instantly hushed by all three men.

"Don't you know that any loud sound could be the death of us all?" one of the men ask me with a scowl.

I crawl over and position myself right beside them, determined not to let myself be intimidated. They are forced to shift their positions, which give way to several expletives uttered under their breath.

"My grave apologies, gentlemen. I couldn't help overhearing your conversation."

"Keep your meddling to yourself," one the men grumbles.

"I shall not," I tell him sternly. "Your conversation involves all of us. If you know something, you should share it with everyone."

The oldest man hesitates with a grim expression. Finally, he speaks. "There's word in the land of Klaus that the priest attending from Chaak was badly wounded by one of the tigers. Their King has called for a battle to avenge the priest."

"So the Cavaliers are preparing for war?"

"That's not the worst of it," he says in a low voice. "There's talk of forcing the young men to join the King's army—those who didn't die in the sporting event."

"He can't do that," I whisper, feeling the blood drain from my face.

"He's the King. He can do whatever he wants. If the talk is right, the Cavaliers will stop at nothing to round up the boys—again."

I had thought I was protecting the boys—that war would safeguard them from the King's dictatorship. My heart races as I crawl out from the brush. I have no time to lose. I must find Hann. He will be killed on the spot if the Cavaliers find him. They won't take his victory in the ring lightly. Two knights perished because of him.

I start moving through the forest. The snow has started falling again, so thickly that I have to move slower to keep my bearings. It's easy to get lost in the forest's great size— stretching out for miles in every direction. I have stayed in the area where my settlement is, thinking perhaps Grandmullie would come back there to find me. After three days, it's time to move on.

And then a thought springs to my mind. Only one other place in the forest makes sense where they may have gone— where the forest meets the desolation lands.

I feel foolish for not having thought of that before. Of course Hann would potentially hide there. The masses are superstitious about the area and the Cavaliers are frightened, though they would never admit it.

It's a long trek to the desolation lands, and I don't have two days to walk to it, especially in the snow. I need help. I need transportation. The large deer are my only hope, but I'm not sure they will come to my rescue with so many hunters around. And the masses are starving, so their senses are more alert to the presence of the deer.

Knowing the King is preparing for battle brings some relief to the masses. The adults and small children can go back to their settlements. The young boys, however, will stay in hiding.

I start spreading the news to the masses in the forest so they will depart for their homes. As word spreads, droves start making their way back to their settlements, a bittersweet welcome after being detained in the frozen forest without proper clothing and food.

As night falls and fewer settlers can be seen in the forest, I feel safe to call upon the aid of a deer. I position myself on an open log, shivering. A woman had given me a shawl since I didn't have a brown robe. It doesn't offer much protection against the cold.

A cold has settled in my chest. I understand the dangers of getting sick in the frozen temperatures. If I don't find warmth soon, I could very well be facing the end of my life.

I stifle a cough and wait, the snow now turning into ice and pelting me like miniature daggers. Would any animal come out in this weather?

"Help," I whisper.

My eyelids droop as I feel my body slowly starting to shut down. I'm about to succumb to the elements when I hear a snort right behind me. I turn my head and look directly into the face of a black bear—perhaps the only animal who will venture out in the snow and ice to come to my aid.

"Can you take me to the desolation lands," I ask.

My voice is barely above a whisper, but the bear seems to understand what I desire. He comes closer and nudges me with his snout. I use what little energy I have left to roll over onto his large back. Under the collection of ice gathered on his outer fur is warmth. I press my body down into his coat as he carefully raises and begins moving. My hands grasp his fur tightly as I hold on for dear life. He advances swiftly through the forest, far faster than I could ever have hoped.

I become oblivious to time as I fall in and out of sleep. At one point, I open my eyes, drenched in sweat, and it's daylight. Snow is still falling, and somehow, I'm still on the bear's back.

Then we stop. I open my eyes and raise my head to look around the gray landscape. The tall grass of the desolation lands is covered with ice. It's ghostly quiet with nothing moving. Nothing.

"I need to find my grandmother and friends," I say softly.

The bear snorts in response and lowers himself to the ground. I crawl from his back, feeling weak from hunger and sickness. My body shivers from the onslaught of sudden cold that whips at me.

"Hann?" I call out. "Grandmullie?"

The bear stares up at me. There is no warmth for me in his eyes, only obedience. And intelligence. I reach out and lightly touch his nose. He gives a quiet snort in response.

"Can you help me find them?" I ask the bear.

He looks out over the desolation lands. I wish I could read his mind. Up close, the bear is quite scraggly with several scars stretching across the top of his head. He's leaner than the bears I'm accustomed to seeing. He should be hibernating right now, but the upheaval in Klaus is affecting all of the animals' normal routines.

It's several minutes before he lowers his body back down to the ground as an invitation for me to climb back up on his strong back.

I have no idea where the bear takes me. I don't know where to direct his path, so I blindly trust he will get me to safety somehow.

The forest gives way to a rocky incline as the bear bounds through the snow. I fall in and out of consciousness on that long journey. *Did it possibly last days or was it only hours before I'm aware of my surroundings again?*

It's dusk now when the bear comes to a stop. The high peaks of the mountain we've just ascended extend beyond my sight. I look down the path from which we came and feel dizzy for a second. It's very steep and quite dangerous. I don't know how the bear managed to keep me on his back through such a treacherous climb.

I look at my companion. The bear's hard breathing causes steam to rise from his nostrils. He's stopped at the edge of what appears to be a mountain village about a mile from us. Smoke rises in the distance promising warmth—and hopefully nourishment.

I'll have to walk by myself into the town. It's too dangerous for the bear to venture any further. I lean into him and whisper words of thankfulness and blessings for coming to my aid. I have little doubt that I would be a frozen corpse if it hadn't been for him.

The bear turns and quickly runs back down the path and is soon out of sight. I set out on a slow trip to the mountain town. The wood bark I had wrapped around my shoes just days earlier, quickly gathers ice from the sleet that falls from the heavens. My toes quickly become so cold that I cease to have feeling in them.

Tears slip out of my eyes, drying to ice on my cheeks when I finally find myself close enough to the small village to breathe in the smoke coming from chimneys.

A dozen or more small huts have been erected into the mountainside. Candles softly glow from small windows, instantly bringing a feeling of warmth to my soul.

I knock on the door of the first hut I come to. Lacking strength, I cling to the side of the hut for a minute before the door creaks open a few inches.

"Yes?" comes the voice of a woman, as cold as the temperature outside.

"Please, I need help," I say weakly.

She opens the door a little wider, and I can see her face now. She's surprisingly young, maybe in her thirties with her drab brown hair caught in a bun at the nape of her neck.

"Where did you come from?"

I'm sure I look a fright with ice clinging to every exposed area of my body. Shivers have overtaken me so that I cannot speak. I point down the mountain.

She opens the door wider and looks behind me as though searching for a companion. Satisfied I'm alone, the woman moves aside and waves me into her small hut.

Inside, a fire roars in a modest fireplace along one wall. I immediately make my way to it, seeking its warmth to take the chill out of my bones.

The hut is very tidy with only a table with two chairs and a large straw cot tucked in one corner, covered with a red, white and green homemade patchwork quilt. It's the large copper sink in the small kitchen that arouses my curiosity—gleaming in the light of the fire and small candles placed throughout the hut.

"Some hot tea?" the woman asks, using a hand towel to remove a small cast iron kettle from the side of the fireplace.

I nod my head and watch her move. She walks with a slight limp and a stooped posture. I can only imagine the toil upon the bodies of those living in this mountain town.

I've never even heard of people living up on this mountain. I expect the Council of Elders must live in a village much like this one—neatly tucked away from prying eyes.

I take the tea mug from the woman and hug it in my hands for a minute before slowly sipping at the hot liquid. My throat welcomes the heat when I finally do take a gulp.

"Thank you," I say gratefully.

"Are you one of the settlers?" she asks, taking a seat at the small table and picking up knitting needle with a ball of blue yarn.

"Yes."

"Where's your robe? It would have kept you warmer out here."

I nod my head in agreement. "It's a very long story."

Silence falls between us as she resumes knitting and I sip on the hot tea. My shawl falls to the floor, leaving a puddle of water on the wood planks.

"Who do you seek up here?"

"My grandmother and friends," I reply quietly. "But I don't believe they would come all the way up here."

"Then why did you make the journey?"

The woman stares at me with a hint of suspicion. I can't tell her the truth—that a bear carried me up the mountain to save my life. Perhaps I just leave out the bear part.

"I'm sure you heard of the King's sporting event?"

She nods her head, her jaw visibly tightening. "Yes."

"The masses rebelled and the young men escaped. We are feared for our lives and have hidden ourselves from the Cavaliers."

She stares at me for a very long minute. "I wasn't aware of that."

"Did you have any boys forced to participate in the sporting event?"

She avoids my gaze and looks down at her knitting project, though I notice she doesn't resume knitting. "No."

"Do you have any boys up here?"

"A few," she replies shortly.

I get the sense she wants to change the subject, but something doesn't feel right. As a matter of fact, I sense something is very wrong.

"Why did the Cavaliers not come for your boys?"

"Why do you ask so many questions?" she snaps. "We aren't part of the masses. Our sons weren't expected to participate."

"If you live outside Oldenwald then you're part of the masses," I argue, but she shakes her head no.

"Not true."

"Then who are you?"

A long pause trails my question before she speaks. "Blacksmiths."

Blacksmiths. Men skilled in the art of metal. That explains such a fine copper sink in the modest hut. But it doesn't explain why they don't consider themselves part of the masses—why the King doesn't consider them part of the masses. How were their boys kept from being taken captive this Winter Solstice?

"No more questions," she says when I open my mouth.

I close my mouth with a sigh. "Forgive me for my curiosity. I just don't understand."

"You're young," she replies, as though that explains the situation with the blacksmiths. "Are you warm now?"

I nod my head and take the empty tea cup to the sink. "I'm most grateful for your hospitality. If I may ask, can I sleep the night here and depart first thing tomorrow morning?"

"You'll have to sleep on the floor if you're granted permission," she says briskly. "My husband will be home soon and I'll ask him."

"I don't want to intrude. If there's another place I can stay—"

I stop talking as soon as she shakes her head vehemently. It's obvious she wants to tell me something, but she's carefully trying to choose her words.

"You seem like a decent girl—respectful. I will tell you only the information you need to know so that you do not die."

I swallow the sudden lump of nervousness that rises in my throat. Those words could strike fear into even the most courageous of people.

"I can leave right now. It's really not a problem."

"Nonsense. The weather will kill you before you would get back down the mountain. How you survived in the thin clothes you wore here is a miracle. Take a seat. There are things you must know."

I sit down opposite her at the small table, folding my hands in my lap. I had felt warm before her words set my nerves on edge. Now I can't tell if my trembling limbs are due to stepping away from the fire or the news she is about to impart.

"It is well that you came to my door instead of another in our village. I'm assuming you've never heard the tales of the blacksmiths?"

I shake my head no. Should I have? My eyes grow large from sudden fright, and I feel like I can't even blink right now.

"The older masses have. The blacksmiths were an angry group of men that used to serve in the King's army—not as knights, but as an elite group of assassins. Of course, they weren't called the blacksmiths then. They were called Anonymia—the nameless ones. They would sneak undetected into other lands near and far to take out certain powerful leaders."

I had never heard Grandmullie talk about such men before. If they were so feared, surely she would have warned me.

"What do you mean by 'take out?' Do you mean they would kill them?"

"Precisely," she says in an even tone. "Of course, they were never identified with Oldenwald, or with Klaus for that matter. They were a bunch of renegades with a passion for killing. They were strong men, large, muscular. I've heard stories of how they would rip the limbs from anyone who stood in the way of their missions."

"I don't understand how that puts my life in danger."

"Let me finish my story. Then you will understand. They left their role as assassins, and the King allotted them this side of the mountain to live their lives out in peace. But the King still needed their services and would call upon them for special favors. The men took up the skill of metal-working to aid them. You see, they needed weapons. And the only way to make weapons was from the iron ore from the mountains. So a life was forged in this mountain where the blacksmiths cultivated the metals and made swords and machetes and other strong weapons of war."

"Do they make the Cavaliers' swords?" I ask quietly.

She nods her head solemnly. "Yes, they keep the monarchy armed. But that's not the dangerous part. What you need to know is that they started stealing young women and dragging them to the mountain. They were lonely men and no willing woman would move up here."

"Were you—" I almost hesitate to ask. "Were you stolen?"

She inclines her head. "But not by my husband. Many of the women were stolen and given to the blacksmiths. Of course, there are now young women born in the families, and the young folks marry each other now, but still, they go and search for wives among the masses."

"Why don't you run away?"

"Where do I go? I have no idea where my settlement is as I was only eighteen years old when I was taken from the forest. I'm fortunate, however. My husband is a caring man."

I slowly rise from the table. "A caring man would never steal you from your family."

"He didn't steal me. He stepped in to save me. I have a life I'm satisfied with now. My belly is full every night I lay my head down to sleep."

"But you were stolen," I whisper.

I'm appalled that she seems to accept her fate. And yet, she's trying to warn me from the very fate that she has accepted.

"My husband can be trusted," she tries to assure me. "He's a good man. He'll let you stay the night with us."

"And then what? I'm forced to marry one of the boys from your village?"

"I don't believe that would happen. Not in my house anyway."

"I thank you for the hot tea but I must be on my way," I say, as I scoop my shawl from the floor and head for the door.

"It's too late, you know."

Her words send a frightened chill down my spine. I stop and slowly turn to face her.

"What do you mean?"

"They already know you are here. They have eyes everywhere. My husband is the only hope you have now."

"I'll take my chances out in the snow."

"Nicklaus will find you."

I freeze. "Nicklaus?"

"Have you ever met him?"

I nod. "He's a most vile man."

"He's on his way to pick up fresh weapons. Rumors circulate that Klaus is on the verge of war."

"It's already been declared," I say softly.

"I wasn't aware of that. I'll have to warn my husband lest Nicklaus tries to trick the men into fighting again for the King."

"I thought they did special favors for the King."

"That was years ago when the men were young. Time has caught up with them and they can't fight the battles they once did. No, Nicklaus will seek for young blood that can be splattered in battle for the King. But the young boys don't know the ways of war like the original group of men did—the Anonymia."

"They only know stealing women now, hmm?"

She glares at me. "You wouldn't understand."

I can't risk Nicklaus finding me here so I must not make the woman upset. So I take a deep breath and try to look pleasant.

"I'm sure I don't understand. I only hope your boys aren't forced into the King's army like the masses were forced to compete against the Cavaliers with no weapons."

"No one said the King was fair."

"We were hopeful the new one would be," I tell her.

The woman calmly crosses to the kitchen and opens up a cabinet. She extracts a loaf of bread and places it on the counter to slice.

"My husband will try to help you when he comes home. I'm sure of it. Stay for supper at least."

I cross back to the table and sit back down. I feel trapped on all sides, and I fight the nagging thought that something is bound to go wrong. Very wrong.

Fifteen

DARKNESS HAS SWEPT OVER THE MOUNTAIN by the time the woman's husband comes home. She throws a blanket around her shoulders and greets him outside when we hear his heavy footsteps crunch in the snow.

The woman has not bothered to introduce herself to me, and after spending the afternoon with her, I no longer find it odd. She's a very private person—a lonely person in the mountain village. Interaction with one another is only encouraged in times of dire need. Even then, it sounds like she only has one or two other women she can call on for help if needed.

I'm surprised by the man who enters the hut behind the woman. His skin is very dark, the shade of the black walnuts the Kringles provide to Grandmullie and me every fall. His frame is large and muscular as would be expected for a blacksmith. Black curly hair interspersed with silver strands is confined in long braids. It frames dark features—brooding eyes set in a wide face with a large nose and thick lips. But it's his expression that takes me aback—warm and kind as he stops inside the doorway to peer at me.

"So you are the guest that Pallia has invited to stay the night?" he asks in a deep voice.

In his opening remarks, I finally learn the name of the woman with whom I've spent the past six or more hours. I give an awkward curtsy, banging my knee against the side of the chair.

"If it pleases you, sire. I can be gone first thing in the morning."

The man opens his mouth and laughs—heartfelt and guttural, his white teeth glowing in the candle light. "In this weather? A snow storm is expected to come upon us in the wee hours of the morning. No one will be leaving tomorrow."

"Does that mean Nicklaus won't come?" Pallia asks quietly, taking his thick cape from him and hanging it near the fire.

The man's face turns cold. "Nicklaus will come. Nothing will stop him from making it up the mountain."

Pallia sighs and helps him remove his boots. She takes his cold wet socks and hangs them from the mantle to dry before moving to the kitchen to serve the stew she's prepared. It smells delightful, but I'm sure there is meat in it. Perhaps I could enjoy a slice of the bread she unwraps from a towel on the counter.

"Thank you, Pallia," the man says gratefully as he takes the stew and moves to stand in front of the fire.

He motions for me to take a seat, but as there are only two chairs, I politely smile and murmur, "No, thank you."

"I can't have our guest standing while she eats. What did you say your name was?"

"Vixen."

"Vixen—a gypsy's name. You don't look like a gypsy though."

"No, I'm not a gypsy."

"I'm Blitzen. This is my wife, Pallia."

I smile politely and take the bowl of stew from the woman and sit back down. Surprisingly, it's a vegetable stew that contains no flesh of animals. I'm not aware I've shown my surprise until I feel Pallia's eyes upon me.

"Something wrong?" Pallia asks.

"Oh, not all," I say. "I don't eat meat and I'm surprised—happy to see there's none in the stew."

Blitzen's eyes narrow into slits as he looks at me. "Why don't you eat meat?"

"I've been raised not to eat meat."

"Not too many other people like you."

"I know,' I say quietly and dip my spoon into the vegetables.

"We don't eat meat," Pallia says suddenly.

I cast a quick glance at Blitzen. "You don't eat meat either?"

He shakes his head no. "I've never been able to eat meat. My father used to beat me, try to break me down, force me to eat meat. But I was stubborn. He eventually gave up, but not before my hide received several lashings from Nicklaus, let me tell you."

"Nicklaus hit you with a switch?"

He laughs. "Not with one, but more like five switches at a time. He tried to break me, but instead, he broke his switches. So Nicklaus turned me over to the King to join his army."

"And now you make weapons of war for the King."

"It's an honest living," he says with a slight scowl.

"How honest is stealing people?"

Blitzen looks at Pallia who quickly ducks her head, scooping a large bite of stew into her mouth. Instead of looking angry, his face lightens.

"I keep company with some pretty bad men," he acknowledges. "But I'm not like them. I've never stolen anyone."

"My grandmother used to tell me that someone could tell a lot about you by the company you keep."

He smiles even broader. "Wise grandmother. But that's not always the case—at least with me. These men I've known since my youth. Most come from even harsher upbringings than me. We've fought together, killed together, saved each other's lives more times than I care to remember. When you find someone willing to give their life for you, you've found a brother for eternity."

"But that doesn't excuse their behavior," I insist quietly.

"Quite right," he replies. "There is no excuse for cruelty."

And that is the end of the conversation for him. We sit in silence with only the sound of the spoons scraping the sides of the wooden bowls filling the room. When we're finished, Pallia silently takes our bowls to the copper sink and washes them, shooing me away when I try to help.

"Can you sleep on blankets on the floor?" Blitzen asks. "We can put you right in front of the fire."

"Yes, sire. Thank you."

"I'm no sire," Blitzen laughs. "Just Blitzen."

He grabs a thick quilt from a wood chest and lays it down on the floor. A soft wool blanket is tossed on top of it.

"Thank you," I say. "Thank you both."

Blitzen kindly pats my shoulder. "Don't be too quick to thank me. You're the closest to the fire, so you'll need to keep throwing logs on it all night so we stay warm."

"I will do that."

Pallia has finished cleaning up after supper and makes her way to the straw bed, snuffing out candles along the way. I quickly lay down on the quilt and turn my back on the two of them as they settle down for this cold winter's night.

"Do you believe in fate?" Blitzen asks in the stillness of the room.

"I think so," I reply.

There is a long stretch of silence while I stare into the flames, flicking and sizzling as they cast off their heat. My eyelids slowly close and I'm just about asleep when Blitzen's next words send a shockwave reverberating down my spine.

"I saw you today. Riding the bear."

I feel vulnerable on the floor, blocked by the fire in front of me and the storm starting to rage outside. I lay motionless; even my breath seems to be suspended.

"Do I need to fear for my life?" I finally ask, my voice sounding shaky and insecure to my own ears.

"Not from me," Blitzen says, "but if others find out, you will not find peace."

I don't know how to respond. I can't deny riding the bear. I can try to pass it off as a horse, make Blitzen think he had not seen the animal properly. I open my mouth, but he starts talking again.

"When I was sixteen, I climbed up the cliffs to seek answers from the Council of the Elders."

I sit up and turn to face him. He's also sitting up in his bed, a dark silhouette against the wall. I know that what he's about to share with me is of great magnitude.

"You know why I can't eat meat? It's the same reason you can't. We are able to interact with animals in a way that no one else can."

"You're a Favored One."

"Yes. But I didn't know that in my youth. I thought there was something wrong—seriously wrong—with me. So did my father. He said if I ate the animals' meat, then I would get over this fantasy that I could communicate with them. Even at such a young age, I knew that wouldn't be true. If I ate their meat, I would bring sorrow to my soul."

"And so the Council of Elders told you there were more like you."

Blitzen sighs in the darkness. "That was a relief—to hear there were others out there like me. I wanted to find the others. I even looked at a map and made an effort to seek other Favored Ones. But the Elders told me that I would seek and not find until the fateful day one would be brought to me. And here I am living on this remote mountain for years, knowing that it would have to be fate for any other Favored Ones to show up here. And it's fate that you came directly to my house."

"And here I am," I say quietly.

"Here you are," he echoes. "I have never felt such adrenaline running through my body as when I saw you riding up the mountain on the bear."

"I didn't choose to come here. I trusted the bear to take me to safety. Do you think anyone else saw me?'

"I don't think so or I would have been told. I can offer protection while you're under the shelter of my house, so don't allow yourself to be seen trying to make the journey back down the mountain alone. Nicklaus will get you if the other blacksmiths don't."

Nicklaus. Just the sound of his name produces a bitter taste of contempt upon my tongue. He would not extend kindness to me were our paths ever to cross again.

"You know about the sporting event then?"

"I know that Klaus is going to war and will require weapons. That's all I need to know."

"Do you know that a lot of young men died in the great stadium—from the swords you make?"

"I'm not responsible for how the sword is wielded," he counters quietly. "I've lived many years longer than you. Careful how you cast judgment lest you become judged as well—but on a much greater scale."

His words silence my tongue. Perhaps the reason I've been connected to Blitzen is to learn wisdom. He's well into his sixties. He surely must have some wisdom to share.

"I need your help, Blitzen."

"Ask, and it shall be granted."

"I believe my grandmother got out of the stadium alive with my two friends, but I can't be sure. I need to find them."

"They wouldn't go back home?"

"Until news of the war arose, the King was searching for all the boys that escaped the sporting event," I explain softly. "Everyone was too scared to go back to their settlements. The only place I think to look is the desolation lands. There was no sign of them though."

"One of the boys—he's more than a friend?"

I gasp. "How did you know?"

"Only love will drive a person to the desolation lands," Blitzen chuckles. "I'll make some inquiries."

"But you may arouse suspicion."

I can hear the smile in his voice. "You have to know who—or what to ask. Didn't the Council of the Elders tell you about the birds?"

"I think so—I don't remember."

"If a snow bird is out, I'll send it for answers."

"Time for sleep," Pallia interrupts quietly. "I feel in my bones that tomorrow will bring challenges all its own."

We stop talking and can hear the wind howling outside the hut. Would the snow storm be enough to hinder Nicklaus' efforts to get up the mountain? I can only hope so as I wanted to be far gone from the mountain when he shows up.

A heavy pounding on the hut's door jerks Blitzen out of bed. Who would come in the middle of the night? He strides by me, briefly placing a warning hand upon my shoulder as he crosses to the door.

"Who's there?" he barks sharply.

A muffled voice responds, but I can't make out what is said. Blitzen can though. He opens the door, and the severe wind pushes another large man through the door. He stops abruptly at the sight of me sitting on the floor, hugging the blanket to my chest.

"Don't ask questions," Blitzen orders as he pushes the door closed.

The man is just as old as Blitzen, but his hair is completely silver and woven into a long braid down his back. His heavy black cape is covered with snow and ice.

"We can't deliver. You know that," the man says.

Blitzen yawns and stretches his arms above his head. "We have enough."

"I just did the count, and we're shy of about a hundred or more swords."

"What does that mean?" Pallia asks, a tremor running through her voice.

"The men have grown soft," Blitzen says. "No one expected war, especially not in the dead of winter. Nicklaus will collect on the King's agreement with us—one way or another."

Pallia starts crying softly, burying her head in the pillow to mask the sound. I'm curious what Nicklaus will try to collect that makes Pallia so upset. But I'll wait until the large man leaves before I ask questions. Besides, I don't like the glances the man throws in my direction—sidelong glances that remind me of Nicklaus' interest in me.

"First thing in the morning, round up everyone's personal weapons and we'll see what we have."

"You mean, what we don't have."

"Hide the boys with the dogs. Nicklaus won't go in there. Neither will the Juuls."

The man gestures in my direction. "What about her?"

"What about *her*?" Blitzen asks coldly. "She'll hide with the dogs."

"Protection for an outsider?" the man challenges. "She may very well fulfill the agreement with Nicklaus."

Blitzen's response is to open the door. The man throws an angry look in my direction before heading back into the winter storm.

Pallia jumps from the bed and rushes to him, throwing her arms desperately around his neck. "You can't leave me, Blitzen."

He holds her in his large arms, softly caressing her hair. "I'm in no danger of going—I'm too old. It's the young ones we have to worry about now."

"How many will they take?" she asks quietly.

He whispers to her, and I turn to stare into the fire. I think I understand. Nicklaus has an agreement with the blacksmiths. If their weapon production is too low, the blacksmiths will have to send their youth to fight in the King's army.

Of course, I may very well find myself fulfilling the agreement as the man suggested. And that makes me want to vomit.

"You won't be taken," Blitzen tells me. His gaze is unwavering as he makes the promise. He will fight to keep his word to me.

I close my eyes and focus on the angry wind whipping through the mountain village as though wreaking vengeance— vengeance on creating weapons of war that shed innocent blood. Now judgment has come to the blacksmiths.

Sixteen

THE GRAY WINTER SKY BRINGS NO SUN TO
welcome our day. It's a grim reminder of what we are about to
face this day. I'm sure my eyes must have closed at some point
last night, but the weariness and sickness that my body feels
makes me wonder.

Blitzen throws me trousers and a thickly knitted sweater.
"Put these on."

I slip them over my clothes for added warmth. I've started
hearing a wheezing every time I take a breath. Pallia doesn't
acknowledge it, but she shoves a mug of hot tea in my hand
and whispers for me to drink it quickly.

Something in it soothes my chest. Too bad I can't take it
with me to the dog pen. Pallia tells me it's cold and dirty in

there. The animals are like mad dogs because the blacksmiths never allow them to be petted. They use the dogs to hunt people. I try to calm my fears by reminding myself that the wild animals have never felt a human touch either. Perhaps my fear also comes from being forced to hide with the boys. They may give me up to save themselves.

"Thank you for everything," I tell Pallia and give her a quick hug.

Her eyes are swollen from crying all night, and she chokes back a fresh set of tears. "Be careful, Vixen. Trust only Blitzen."

"Trust only *yourself*," Blitzen says in a low voice. "I won't be in the dog pen to protect you. Keep your wits about you—it's all you have right now."

I nod my understanding and follow him outside. We're instantly hit by below-freezing temperatures. But at least the wind has subsided. Large banks of snow are left in its wake— evidence of the wind's visitation.

Blitzen grabs my elbow and walks at a quick pace through the village. It's already brimming with activity. Women with hollow eyes move in and out of the huts, depositing personal weapons into a large pile collected in the center of the village.

A large, crude wooden building is erected on the outside of the village. The dog pen. I can hear the howling and barking well before we draw closer to the building.

Blitzen isn't the first to arrive. Two other men, younger than Blitzen by about twenty years, are already in the building, throwing chunks from dead animals' carcasses into several rows of cages. The dogs are more like ravenous wolves, fighting each other for the raw meat.

As soon as Blitzen enters the building, the dogs calm down. His mere presence is enough to bring peace to the tense animals. I stand by the door, shivering, while he walks down each row of cages.

"Thanks, Blitzen," one of the men say. "I don't want the boys scared to come in here."

"She will stay in here with the boys," Blitzen says, gesturing in my direction.

The men look at me, somewhat surprised.

"Where did she come from," one asks, as though I can't hear them talking about me.

"She is my visitor," Blitzen says firmly, "and under my protection."

End of conversation. The men turn their attention away from me and resume feeding the dogs. Blitzen motions for me to join him by a cage.

"See the large black and gray dog in the corner?" Blitzen asks when I join him. "He's the leader of all the dogs. Notice how the others stand back and let him eat until he's filled? They follow him."

I stare at the dog, laying on the floor while he gets his fill of the carcass thrown into the cage. His mane is matted, much like all of the other dogs who have longer fur. His size is massive and muscular. By just the look in his eyes, he warns the other dogs sharing his cage to stay back.

"Why are you telling me this?"

"Because I'm going to take him out to guard you."

"From Nicklaus?"

"From the boys right now. You are an outsider. They will not trust you and will throw you out of the pen for Nicklaus."

"But there are other girls here. Why would they think Nicklaus would be interested in me?"

Blitzen reaches out and grasps my long braid. "Because Nicklaus adores maidens with red hair."

Ah, now everything makes sense. That explains Nicklaus' strange fascination with me. I've not seen many girls with red hair in Klaus. It's too late to try to change the color now. Besides, Nicklaus already knows who I am.

Blitzen softly whistles and the large dog immediately rises and crosses to the cage door. The other dogs cower as he passes them.

"I don't know how you do it, Blitzen," one of the men calls out. "They don't listen to anyone like they do you."

Blitzen doesn't respond. Instead, he waits patiently for the men to finish feeding the meat to the last row of dogs. As soon as they leave the building, Blitzen opens the cage door, and the large dog walks through the opening. The other dogs respect the hand Blitzen extends to them to keep them contained in the cage.

"He is called Gund. It means war."

A fitting name for the large dog in front of me. He bears scars all over his face and has an intense look in his eyes. I imagine he's had to prove himself in fights many times to stay the alpha.

"Take him to the corner and wait. The boys should arrive soon."

I look into the dog's eyes. He stares back at me, challenging me, but I don't back down. Within three seconds, he averts his gaze and submits by lowering himself to the ground.

Blitzen's eyes widen. "That's a first. Why did he do that?"

"Do what?" I ask.

"Lay down on the ground like that. He's always obeyed me but never like that."

I shrug. "I don't know."

Blitzen mumbles under his breath and snaps at the dog. "You stay close to her, understand?"

Gund stares at him. Oddly, I feel he understands exactly what is happening. I take a deep breath and give Blitzen a small smile.

"I'll be fine. I've been in some dangerous situations before and somehow escaped death. Go do what you have to."

Blitzen places his heavy hand on my shoulder and whispers a prayer over me. And then he leaves me alone with the dogs. But it isn't the dogs I'm concerned about. It's the blacksmiths' offspring—boys bred to carry on their lineage.

The boys look like they've been raised by warriors, I decide when they eventually start filing into the dog pen. Instead of the corner of the building as Blitzen instructed, I have positioned myself in between the two rows of cages. Better to open the cages if I need reinforcement.

I mentally count twelve boys when they enter the building, ranging from about ten years of age to eighteen. They all wear their hair back in a ponytail and the same black capes the men wear drape their thin shoulders.

The dogs start barking and snarling ferociously. It's clear the boys don't spend much time in the dog pen. As soon as they see me, the boys stop in their tracks. I extend my hands toward the dogs and they cease all noise.

"Who are you?" the oldest boy asks.

"A guest of Blitzen and Pallia."

The boy eyes me suspiciously. He's very tall and lanky with brown hair and eyes. Not someone whose appearance would turn heads, but by his age, I can tell he leads the other boys.

"Why do you have Gund out of his cage?" a younger boy asks.

"He's guarding me," I reply.

My remark receives a few snickers from the boys, but the oldest one shows no emotion. Instead, he moves away from the group and advances toward me. Gund growls as a warning, causing the boy to stop.

"Why isn't he attacking you?" the boy asks. He holds out a hand protectively in front of his body as though to ward off an attack by Gund.

"He's my protector. Why should he attack me?"

The boy slowly turns in the dog pen, looking back at the younger boys with a vicious little grin on his face. "Looks like we have a situation on our hands. A challenge if you will. What say you?"

"We fight her, Marcus," the boys shout in unison and start to advance.

Gund lets out a ferocious snarl and moves toward the oldest boy. I place my hand on the dog's back and he freezes, his body still taut with tension. The older boy reaches into his cape and withdraws a long dagger. He waves it in my direction.

"I wish you no harm," I say as calmly as I can. "It's not me you should think about fighting. Nicklaus is bound to arrive at any moment."

Marcus smiles cruelly. "You don't understand the situation. You are placed in the dog pen simply to test our abilities as warriors."

"What are you talking about? You aren't warriors—you're blacksmiths."

"We come from great warriors—the best the King has ever had. Our fathers train us every day to be prepared for any situation. You are just a situation put in front of us to overcome. Isn't that why Blitzen brought you here?"

"No. I'm his guest, and he's hiding me in here with all of you so we aren't taken by Nicklaus."

"Nicklaus doesn't scare us," one of the younger boys shouts out.

"He should," I say. "He has a black heart."

"Nicklaus won't come here," Marcus says confidently. "At least, not today. He won't be able to make it up the mountain."

"Your mothers and fathers are preparing for him to come."

The boy shrugs. "What do they know? They're letting fear make them do foolish things in their old age. But enough of them. Let's discuss why you're here."

"I've already told you."

He laughs, but his eyes are void of humor. "Gund doesn't frighten us. We all have weapons and can bring a fatal wound to him if we need to. But you have no weapon. You're like a coyote, defenseless. Our fathers train the dogs to hunt by capturing coyotes and releasing them on the mountain for the dogs to find and devour. It keeps their hunting instincts sharp."

The other boys laugh tauntingly at his words. I straighten my shoulders and stare into his eyes, refusing to show intimidation. *I am no coyote. I'm more like a fox, quick on my feet with my wits about me at all times.* Today is no different than any other challenge I've encountered in my life.

Marcus is waiting for me to make the first move. To run. All the boys are poised to chase after me. But this fox doesn't run. Instead, I carefully open one of the cages near me and four other dogs lunge out, growling menacingly as they gather protectively around me.

Alarmed, Marcus steps back to join the other boys who have drawn their own daggers. They're scared. I can tell by their wide eyes and the younger ones' trembling.

"Do I need to open more cages?" I ask quietly.

"You must be a witch," Marcus says, never taking his eyes off me. "What do we do with witches, boys?"

"We burn them," they shout in response.

"Aelos, go fetch our fathers. A bonfire on such a winter's day will be much appreciated, I should think."

One of the older boys takes a step to the door, but I tell him to stop. He pauses and looks back at their leader.

"You will not fetch your fathers," I say firmly and open another cage. "Get back with the others."

The boy steps back into the crowd as more dogs surround me. We're at a standoff. Marcus has no other options, but he's prideful and refuses to show any sign of weakness to the younger ones.

"I am no witch," I say loudly. "Drop your weapons to the floor and push them with your feet in my direction. If you don't, I'll have these dogs attack you. You may be able to cut some of the dogs, but rest assured, you will probably lose an eye or a limb in the attack."

The boys hurriedly drop their daggers to the ground. Even Marcus is quick to comply at my words. But he's seething. He crosses his arms and stares defiantly at me. His father has taught him the look of intimidation very well.

"What now?" he asks.

"We sit and wait for Nicklaus."

The waiting is mentally and physically exhausting. The dogs circle the boys who are gathered in a cluster on the floor. I sit away from them with Gund on guard beside me. They whisper amongst themselves, no doubt devising a plan to distract the dogs and me so at least one of them can escape and bring their fathers to rescue them. All I need to do at this point is stay safe in here until Nicklaus leaves—if he comes. Then I need to find Grandmullie and my friends.

The dogs in the other cages cluster at the doors, waiting for their chance to join us. *And I think that's exactly what I'll do.*

Conscious of their eyes upon me, I slowly rise with Gund and move from cage to cage to release the rest of the dogs, whispering commands to them as they dart out.

"Why are you doing that?" a boy yells out.

"I'm protecting myself," I tell them. "Let me ask you a question. How are the dogs trained to hunt people?"

The boys stare at me, unsure if they should answer my question. So I repeat it.

"Why do you want to know?" Marcus asks. "Are you planning to have the dogs hunt us?"

I smile at him. "I'm not cruel. I'm just curious."

"I think you're cruel," he says with a scowl. "You're holding us prisoner. What would you do if one of our fathers came to check on us?"

"I would ask him to join you on the floor."

"You have the dogs sniff a piece of clothing of the person you want to hunt," a boy tells me. He immediately receives a punch in the arm by Marcus.

I look thoughtfully at the dogs, probably fifty or more in number. They may be my answer to finding Hann and the others.

"It's Nicklaus," one of the boys exclaims.

Sure enough. The distinct sound of bells jingling in the distance alert us to his arrival. My stomach tightens and I cross to the door to peek out.

Through the heavy snow, a team of mules pulls a massive log to flatten the snow and pave the way for Nicklaus' gold carriage following them, being pulled by six pristine white horses. About a dozen Cavaliers accompany the carriage, riding their own horses on either side. Six Juuls, bundled in thick, green knitted clothes, cling to the side of the carriage. Their cheeks are red from the cold, and they drop rigidly to the ground as though frozen stiff.

The carriage remains closed for several long minutes. Finally, the villagers start filing out of their huts to gather round about. Now that he has an audience, Nicklaus is ready to make his appearance, and the carriage doors are thrown open.

"It's the happiest time of the year," Nicklaus shouts gleefully as he's helped down from the gold carriage by the Juuls who stagger to hold up his weight until he finds his footing in the deep snow.

Nicklaus is wearing the same red satin suit with the cape I had seen him in last. This time, he's donned knee-high black leather boots to keep his feet warm.

"Nicklaus," one of the older men say with a bow.

"You were expecting me, I hope?" Nicklaus asks loudly.

"Yes," the man says. "Your message came through. I must say, we're surprised you made it through the mountain pass."

"Why?" Nicklaus asks, looking out over the crowd.

"The storm—" the man begins, but Nicklaus waves his arms to shut him up.

"Learn this lesson from me," he shouts. "When you say you're going to do something, do it. Neither rain, nor sleet, nor—nor a little snow storm will keep me from fulfilling my word."

The crowd gathered before him claps their hands. That's what Nicklaus wants. That's what Nicklaus expects. Adoration.

He rubs his hands together expectantly. "Do you have my goodies?"

The older men look at each other hesitantly. Finally, Blitzen steps forward.

"Nicklaus," he says with a stately bow. "We have your swords."

"Two hundred of them?" Nicklaus asks, his eyes narrowing with suspicion.

"Most of them. We're about sixty short. But we've added our personal weapons to your collection. I think you'll be most pleased."

"Personal weapons?" Nicklaus asks. "What personal weapons?"

"Daggers and spears and axes—"

"Axes?" Nicklaus screeches. "Axes? Do you really think Klaus' knights will enter into battle with axes?"

"Axes make fine weapons," Blitzen counters. "We've used them effectively in many battles. Our young sons even hunt for food with them. They kill just as well as a sword."

With a devious grin, Nicklaus turns to the knights still perched on their horses. "Would you want to wield an axe in battle?"

The men shake their heads no. Two of them climb from their steeds to start loading up the pile of swords into the back of the carriage.

"And what about daggers or spears?"

Again, the men shake their heads. Nicklaus turns back to Blitzen and places his finger on the side of his nose as though considering the situation.

"Hmm. What to do? What to do? Our agreement states that you will have one hundred of the finest swords always ready for our gallant knights when the King requests."

"But you took fifty swords last month for the sporting event."

Nicklaus clicks his tongue. "Ah, but the agreement states specifically that one hundred swords will *always* be ready at the King's request. That's why you get to live on this god-forsaken mountain in peace."

"Give us two weeks, Nicklaus—"

"*Saint* Nicklaus," he corrects. "We don't have two weeks, unfortunately, but I'll tell you what I'll do. I'll take your sons into battle with me since they're such experts at using the axes to kill already."

The older men take a threatening step toward Nicklaus. Swiftly, four of the knights move in front of them to shield the old man from their heightened emotions.

"You won't take our sons," one of the men declares with a sinister expression.

"What's going on?" Marcus whispers.

"Nicklaus wants to take you all to fight with him in the battle," I say quietly, keeping my eyes on the scene outside.

"Our fathers won't let them."

"Shh," I say. "I can't hear what they're saying right now."

The wind has picked up so that I can't hear the group's words now. I don't need to. I see Blitzen and three other older men step forward and say something to Nicklaus. Pallia then runs from the villagers and throws herself in the snow at Nicklaus' feet, pleading.

Blitzen and the men have volunteered to fight in the King's army. So much for being too old.

I turn to look into the frightened eyes of the boys. I feel like I'm looking at the boys who were forced to participate in the sporting event.

Gund stares at me as though reading my thoughts—what I plan to do next to save Blitzen and the boys—and my grandmother and friends.

I move quickly through half of the dogs, pressing my shawl to their noses, whispering for them to find Hann who must still be wearing my brown robe in the freezing temperatures. The dogs, accustomed to hunting humans, are my only hope to find them.

The boys look at me as though I have lost my mind. Perhaps I have. Perhaps what I'm about to do next will backfire. *But what if it doesn't?*

I snap my fingers and the dogs leave the boys to gather around me. I instruct them on their next move—half to find my loved ones and the other half to help me get Nicklaus off the mountain.

I take a deep breath and fling open the door. The dogs begin barking ferociously as they lunge into the open, cold air. Half take off in the opposite direction to search for Hann wearing my brown robe. They should be able to pick up the scent of me still on it.

The other dogs make a mad dash in Nicklaus' direction. He turns at the commotion, his face registering both surprise and alarm.

I follow the dogs, running full force toward the vile man. The knights seem frozen in place for a second, unsure how to react. That gives the dogs just enough time to reach them before they're attacked.

"You!" Nicklaus screams at me—right before two of the Cavaliers tackle him in the snow in an effort to shield him from the onslaught of ravenous dogs.

Gund keeps pace with me as I race up to the team of mules still attached to the log. The sudden appearance of the dogs makes them shift from fear. I duck in between them, narrowly escaping the sharp blade of a sword one of the Cavaliers swings at my head.

I scramble through the mules' legs until I reach the other side, all the while yelling for the powerful beasts to take off down the mountain. As soon as I'm cleared from their path, the mules spring into action and begin running, the log still attached behind them bouncing precariously over the snow as they bound down the mountain.

The knights kick off the dogs and drag Nicklaus back to the carriage. A dog has managed to bite the old man's hand, and he grasps it with an anguished expression. As soon as the Juuls and horseless knights board the carriage, they take off after the team of mules.

The villagers don't know how to react with all of the commotion. The boys charge out of the dog pen, throwing accusations at me. I have to get out.

Blitzen grabs my arm and starts forcing me to run with him and Pallia. I don't ask questions, and neither does Pallia. We let the dogs keep the villagers from pursuing us as we run. Only Gund follows. His loyalty runs deep.

"Run like your life depends on it," Blitzen yells at Pallia and me.

So we run with all our might. Because our lives truly do depend on it. And we don't stop until our lungs are bursting and we feel we're a safe distance from the village. We bend over for several minutes as we try to catch our breath. Finally, Blitzen whirls on me, frustration written all over his face.

"What were you thinking? You can't attack Nicklaus like that! Do you know what danger you've put yourself in?"

"That's right," I say calmly. "I put *myself* in danger. Actually, I was already in danger with Nicklaus before today."

"He will not stop until your blood stains his cape too. You realize that, right?"

"He's old," I reply. "I'll outrun him until he expires."

Blitzen shakes his head. "That's not how it works. Don't you realize that what happens to Nicklaus affects the whole land?"

"I don't understand," I tell him. "Nicklaus was rambling something about that at the sporting event, but he's mad and his words made no sense to me at the time. They make less sense now."

"It makes no sense to me either, but then again, neither does me communicating with animals. All I know is that all of our destinies are intertwined with Nicklaus somehow."

Instinctively, I know Blitzen's right. We're in Klaus. Nothing is as it seems.

Seventeen

FEAR DROVE US TO CLIMB TO THE TOP OF THE
mountain. From there we could see the rolling hills of the
settlements below, covered in a thick blanket of snow. I decide
that life is often like that. Overcoming the greatest challenges,
the most fierce obstacles, requires confronting the mountain
head on. Nicklaus is a mountain, and this is the second time I
have conquered my fear of him. He will kill me if we meet
again.

"We have to rest," Pallia's voice calls out weakly. "I need
to eat something."

Blitzen has led us the entire two days it has taken to reach
the top of the mountain. I have stayed back with Pallia the
entire trip but left her with Gund when we were nearing the

mountaintop. She had started running a fever the day prior. My sickness left me to settle upon poor Pallia. And we left so suddenly that we are without teas and oils that may help her recover.

Blitzen ignores Pallia, his attention arrested by a movement to the right. "Soldiers," he says in a low voice.

"How can you tell?" I ask.

"The sun is glinting off their shields. I don't think the King is aware of their presence this close to Klaus."

I feel my heart starting to thump harder in my chest. "Will they invade our lands?"

"Not right now. They've called for a battle outside Klaus. They'll camp outside our territorial boundaries until the Cavaliers show up. If they win the battle, they'll invade Klaus. That's when we have to worry."

Blitzen turns to wade back through the snow to reach Pallia. "You need help so we have to keep moving."

She looks at him and all of a sudden, her eyes roll back in her head. She swoons and would have fallen had Blitzen not scooped her up in his large arms.

I push back through the snow to join them. "I'm so sorry. I brought this sickness to her."

"'Tis that time of year," he says quietly. "Sickness is permeating Klaus. Why don't you move on ahead of us to get help? I'll stay back with Pallia."

"You'll both die on this mountain if you linger. No, we stay together. It'll be easier going down."

I help Blitzen put Pallia on his back. He clutches her arms over his shoulders to carry her unconscious body. Gund circles us nervously but allows me to rub his head to calm him. Secretly, I think he's beginning to enjoy feeling my hand petting him.

Blitzen struggles under the weight of Pallia and pushing through the heavy snow that he's carved a path through with his body this entire time. I grab a thick branch that has fallen from a tree and move in front of him to clear the snow so he can move easier. We don't speak for well over an hour. It's enough of a struggle for us to even breathe in the cold air and keep moving.

Our descent off the mountain does hasten our pace. I throw occasional glances over my shoulder at Blitzen but he's in some kind of personal place—eyes closed, mouth murmuring silent prayers, one foot moving methodically in front of another. Occasionally, he'll trip over something protruding through the snow, but he persists in keeping his eyes closed and moving forward.

"We're about a couple of hours to the first settlement," I yell back to him. "I see some smoke rising from some houses."

I would have thought Blitzen would have expressed joy, but he doesn't react to my words. He just keeps moving toward me. Something doesn't feel right.

"Blitzen, how is Pallia?"

Again, no response. I take a deep breath and wait for him to join me. It's several minutes before he catches up. He passes without acknowledging me. And then I see why. Pallia's body is hanging lifelessly on his back. Her eyes are closed, and her skin is a dull gray color.

"Pallia," I exclaim, following him.

"She's dead," Blitzen says dully.

"When?"

"Over an hour ago. I felt her spirit leave her body."

"Stop, Blitzen. We should bury her."

"Not here. Not on this mountain. She always talked about the rolling hills she came from. I want to lay her to rest off the mountain. It's the least I can do."

So we continue our trek through the snow without words. Hunger gnaws at my stomach and guilt devours at my soul. I brought the sickness to Pallia. It was because of my actions that we had to flee the mountain village without supplies. I choke back tears. I can't afford them right now. There will be time later to mourn for many people who have lost their lives this winter in Klaus.

At the edge of the first settlement, Blitzen finally lays Pallia's body on the snow. I stand back with Gund to give him privacy to say goodbye to his love. He closes his eyes and spreads his hands over the snow. When the trembling overtakes his body, I know exactly what he's doing. He's preparing the soil to greet the body of Pallia.

The snow melts before my eyes and springs of dead grass slowly reawaken to stand in the cold air. I work silently alongside Blitzen to use rocks and sticks to dig a hole. By the time we've dug deep enough, we're both sweating profusely—not healthy in the frigid temperatures.

"She would have liked this," Blitzen finally says. "It's good you were here too."

So we lay Pallia's body to rest under a large oak tree. Blitzen says a prayer and sings a small hymn. His voice is filled with loneliness, yet hopeful, and it breaks my heart for his loss.

After long minutes of sitting silently before Pallia's grave, Blitzen rises.

"You can find shelter in the settlements. I'm heading back to my village."

"You're going back?"

He gives a half smile. "They may appear to be savages, but I know their hearts, and they're my family. They will receive me with open arms. Besides, I need to warn them of the Chaak army."

"They are already aware, Blitzen. They just supplied Nicklaus with swords."

He looks at me with a tightened jaw. "But they don't understand the magnitude of the army. You don't understand. It isn't just the Chaaks coming to battle. They've enlisted the forces of other lands."

"What? How can you possibly know that?"

"You can see at a great distance from the top of the mountain. I saw forces from all corners making their way to battle us. Klaus has never had foreign enemies on its land. There are a number of them who would like to overthrow our monarchy."

"I want to overthrow our monarchy," I tell him.

"That will come at a later time. Right now, we have to make sure we win that battle so our borders aren't opened. I will fight with my comrades in the battle."

I glare at him. "You will fight for the King?"

"No. I will fight for Klaus."

I stare at the man before me. He has become an ally—a friend. I wonder if we will ever lay eyes on each other again.

"Find your loved ones," Blitzen says gently. "Give them one last hug before the end comes."

"One last hug? No, there will be many hugs to give our loved ones, Blitzen. I'll find reinforcements and meet you on the battlefield."

He nods. "We'll meet on the battlefield, young Vixen. Take Gund with you for protection and listen for the ram's horn to be blown the day before the battle is scheduled. When you hear it, you'll know it's time to attack."

I watch Blitzen walk away from me until he becomes a dark spot in the winter wonderland. Then I turn my attention to the settlement before me. Hann's settlement. I'll make my way to his homestead on the outskirts. Perhaps Grandmullie has taken him home.

Gund gives a low, warning growl. I lay my hand on his back. It's just the presence of settlers in the distance that's alarming him.

"Let's move, Gund."

We cross through the village, through the curious eyes of a couple of women gathering dead tree limbs to keep their fires burning.

"Where do you hail from?" one of the women asks.

I point to the mountain. "I just came from there."

"You live up there?"

I shake my head no and point in the opposite direction. "I live yonder."

The woman smiles. "So you're a settler. Where's your robe?"

"I lost it at the sporting event."

She looks at me with sadness clouding her eyes. "That was a dark day."

"It was," I agree somberly. "I am seeking my grandmother and friends. We were separated."

"You'll find them," she says softly. "My husband just made his way home yesterday."

"Klaus is going to battle, you know."

"We heard that."

"Have you heard that it isn't just with Chaak? There are other lands joining them so they can have the victory. Our lands will be overtaken if they're successful."

The women look frightened. The quiet one whispers to the one who has done all of the talking.

"Best you be on your way," the woman says sharply. "Stop trying to create fear so our boys will join the Cavaliers. Haven't we lost enough lives as it is?"

"But more blood will be shed—women and children too— if the Cavaliers aren't successful. We all need to fight for Klaus."

"Did the King send you? Or Nicklaus?"

I spit on the ground at their feet. "Nobody sent me. I have no dealings with evil."

"Then don't bring evil to our lands. Keep your news to yourself so our lads are safe. Let the King fight his own battle."

They quickly gather their wood in their arms and stride away from me. I call out to them to explain further, but they have already closed their ears to my cries.

I waste no time in moving through the settlement to get to Hann's home. Gund strides beside me, his eyes darting back and forth nervously. *I feel it too, Gund. I feel the tension of war in the air.*

Hann's home looks deserted. No smoke rises from the modest house like the others I've just passed. The snow surrounding his property is untouched by human footprints.

He isn't here. I feel it in my soul before I even approach the house. As a matter of fact, no one is here. I imagine fear drove his parents away. If the King ever found out who Hann is, his parents would be in grave danger.

I yell "hello" outside the small house, but after several minutes of silence, I feel comfortable to enter the dwelling. It stinks inside. Like rotting food. No one has been here in days.

I search the cupboards for some kind of edible food and am delighted to find a small jar of grains tucked into the back of a cupboard.

The cold has settled into my bones, so my hands tremble as I light a fire in the fireplace. Sir Throck taught me how to build a fire in the worst conditions when I was seven years of age. He said it could save my life one day. I say a silent thank you to my friend as a small flame leaps up from the small twigs.

As the grains cook over the fire, I think of the Kringles slaughtered in the sporting event. I don't know if Sir Throck escaped the stadium that day. But I feel a stirring inside me that I need to go to Kringle, to enlist the help of the elves of light.

But right now, I need rest. And nourishment. I eat the cooked grains slowly, saving a small portion for Gund. He eats quickly and paces about the small room. He's always on edge, never feeling peace. I'm counting on that right now as I close my eyes to rest.

I don't really sleep, but my body responds to just lying motionless on the straw cot in a separate room. I wonder if this is Hann's cot. That thought brings a smile to my lips and a warmth to my heart as I snuggle deeper under the quilt.

I'm on the verge of succumbing to sleep when Gund suddenly growls. He lays on the floor at the end of the cot, but his head is cocked as though sensing something amiss.

I climb off the cot, and he walks with me to the outer room. I don't hear anything, but I trust Gund's instincts. His ears are pushed back in alarm and a quiet, steady snarl in his throat is waiting to be unleashed.

"Quiet, Gund," I whisper, pushing the dirty curtains away from the house's single, small window to peek outside.

Dusk is falling, but I don't see anyone. Carefully, I move to the other side of the window and catch my breath. Two fresh sets of footprints are embedded in the snow. The footprints are made by boots—Cavaliers. Only the knights are afforded the luxury of boots in the winter.

They know someone is in here. The smoke from the fire I built gives my presence away. I fully expect they will burst through the door.

I look at my options for a weapon. The iron pot I used to cook the grains is all I can find. Gund is also a weapon they won't expect. With an old towel, I wrap the handle of the hot pot and move to the door, pressing my back against the wall beside it. Gund plants himself right in front of the door. He'll attack the first knight and I'll take on the second one.

I swallow the lump of fear that has settled in my throat as the door slowly opens. As soon as a figure enters the house, Gund attacks with a savage growl. A Cavalier is knocked to the floor by the dog and a second one enters right after him, sword raised to slice Gund open.

I swing the pot at the Cavalier's legs with all my might. He howls and sinks to his knees, still clutching the sword. Swiftly, I bring the heavy pot down hard on his head. He slumps to the floor, not knowing what hit him.

I whistle to Gund to stop his attack. That Cavalier is curled in a ball in an effort to protect himself. Blood gushes from the wounds Gund has inflicted upon him.

"There will be more," I tell Gund. "We have to get out of here."

I wrap the blanket around my shoulders to depart. There is no more food for me to take with me. I know Gund is hungry. I see him eyeing squirrels darting through the trees. He'll have to wait till we get to Kringle. Hopefully, Lady Sysselye is still there. She'll provide nourishment for both of us.

So we venture back out into the frigid air. Night will be upon us soon. Snow has started falling again, soft flakes gently caressing my face as we move. I know if I pass through a section of the forest from where I stand, I'll reach Kringle quicker. And animals may be in the forest to help me. But so are Cavaliers.

It isn't long before I start feeling the cold penetrate my body again. Wading through the snow forces me to move much slower than I need to and doesn't allow my body to heat.

"Gund," I say softly, "I want you to leave me. I need to find an animal to ride and you'll only get hurt. Go find Hann."

I press the blanket to his nose. He should be able to track Hann's scent from the blanket or my brown robe. He sniffs eagerly at the blanket and then looks up at me with a sadness in his eyes as if we're saying goodbye. I sigh.

"Stop. I must do this. Please. I'm going to Kringle. Bring me word of where I can find him."

I can't watch Gund leave me—I've quickly grown attached to him. The silence reminds me how alone I really am.

My face is numb, as are my feet and hands. I call out softly for any animal to come to me, but not even a bird is venturing into the snow. It's dark by the time I reach the forest. I don't know this section of the forest but I have a general sense of which direction to walk to reach Kringle.

I see a small light, barely visible in the falling snow, ahead of me. Friend or foe, I have no idea. My teeth are chattering so loudly that I press my fist against my mouth to still the noise.

The light draws closer, and I move behind a tree for cover. The soft sound of a horse's whinny reaches my ears. The rider can only be a Cavalier.

I can take one of two courses of action. I can remain hidden from the knight until he passes on his way or I can risk making my presence known. I need that horse. It's the only animal forced out in this freezing cold night.

The knight is almost upon me when I step from behind the tree. My sudden appearance startles the horse, and he rears up in alarm, knocking the young Cavalier to land with a groan into a snow bank.

Before the Cavalier can stand, I whistle to the horse. He pauses, snorting in my direction before crossing to me. I've noticed that the animals seem to be more responsive to me now—perhaps it's my awakened state to who I really am.

"Help me," I whisper.

The horse leans down for me to climb on his back. As I swing my leg over, the knight grabs my ankle and yanks me down off.

I kick at him as he tries to wrestle me down into the snow, pushing my head into the hard-packed white powder to suffocate me. I'm cold and tired and hungry. But something rises up inside me—that feeling I used to get when I would beat up the twins or George in my youth. That feeling of desperation that I will not be overpowered by another.

I relax my body and lay very still, holding my breath so the Cavalier will think I'm either dead or unconscious. He releases his pressure on my head and rises. I can hear his boots crunching in the snow as he crosses back to the horse. I give him just enough time to mount the horse before I rise from the ground with a vengeance.

I scream at the horse to help me. The great steed's eyes widen and he rears up again—this time out of obedience to me. The Cavalier tries to cling to the reins, but cannot hold on when the horse starts bucking. He is thrown off the horse and lands hard against the tree I was hiding behind.

I waste no time in clamoring on top of the horse, clumsily grasping the reins in my hands as he takes off. As with the bear, I lean against the horse's torso and drop the reins to cling to his mane. It takes time to get accustomed to the horse's movements, but he provides warmth to my frozen body and the hope of getting me to the safe haven that Kringle offers.

Eighteen

"WILL THE TWINKLE LIGHTS EVER COME BACK
to Klaus?" I ask quietly.

Lady Sysselye looks up from the potatoes she and I are peeling in her small kitchen. My questions make her lips tighten and her eyes harden.

"I don't know," she says.

It's an honest reply but it makes me sad. Will Klaus ever return to normal? If normal is the way the King has ruled with such a heavy hand and Nicklaus is allowed his creepy behavior, then I hope for a return to the balance Grandmullie experienced in her youth. She didn't grow up hungry or scared for her life. The Kings during her youth had respected the masses in Klaus and peace was his reward for the duration of his rulership.

The sun has started peeking through the dark clouds, a reminder that not everything is controlled by humankind. I slept on Lady Sysselye's floor for the night, grateful she was still safe in Kringle. She had listened to me in the darkness of her small house and then sent word to the elves of my warning of the Chaaks early this morning. The Kringles won't participate in slaying those rising against our land, but they are adept at traps. Perhaps that skill can be useful at a time such as this.

The sliced potatoes sizzle in the small pan and the smell makes my stomach growl. Lady Sysselye smiles and hands me a biscuit. I sink my teeth into it and decide I've never tasted anything so good. She pats my head affectionately.

"Your grandmother is fine, Vixen. I feel it."

I nod my head. "As do I."

"You've changed," she whispers softly, her aged eyes studying my face intently. "You look like you've experienced a great deal of life since you last visited me."

"Most of it pain, Lady Sysselye."

"Yes, there is much pain inflicted on Klaus right now. But just like the twinkle lights, I'm hopeful that tomorrow will bring a new beginning."

We fall into silence, each of us lost in our own thoughts. Lady Sysselye gently turns the potatoes in the pan until they are soft. Without a word, she dishes them onto a plate for me.

"Aren't you going to eat some?"

"No, dear child. I'll eat later. You need your strength right now."

So I delve into the potatoes, blowing on them quickly before shelving large bites into my mouth. Every morsel is devoured in less than two minutes.

"I'm hopeful Grandmullie will come to Kringle," I say, leaning back against the small chair with a satisfied sigh.

"You should stay with me until she arrives."

I shake my head no. "I can't, Lady Sysselye. I must keep moving, warn others about the battle."

"What others will you warn?"

"The gypsies."

Lady Sysselye sniffs disapprovingly. "That wild bunch only serves themselves. They won't join in battle, you'll see."

"They were most helpful to me at Winter Solstice."

Her eyes widen. "Really? So there may be hope for them after all."

"There's always hope for the human spirit, Lady Sysselye. You taught me that. But I don't know where to find them now."

They gypsies are renowned for being a nomadic people, never staying in one place for any stretch of time. With the upheaval in Klaus, I wonder if they have hidden themselves from the trouble.

"If anyone can find them, it will be Sir Throck."

I have to let her words sink in before I can speak. "You mean—"

She nods. "He's alive and kicking."

I feel tears well up and blink rapidly to prevent them from slipping onto my cheeks. "I prayed he would survive. I couldn't bear to think of anything bad happening to him."

"I had a dream once—of Throck standing beside me while I held your child. I've never told anyone that before, but that dream gave me hope that he would survive the sporting event."

I feel the heat rise in my cheeks. "That must mean you both live for a very, very long time for that to happen."

"Is the dream so very far away?" Lady Sysselye asks quietly.

I think of Hann and my cheeks burn even brighter. I'm sure she can't help but notice my embarrassment. Thankfully, she doesn't press me. She turns to washing my dishes and changes the subject.

"When you're ready, you'll find Throck in the home on the hill," she says quietly. "Mind yourself so you don't get hurt."

I cross to her and grasp her wet hand to hold next to my cheek. "I'll be fine, Lady Sysselye."

She smiles and flicks water at my face. "Go now. While the morning is yet young."

I wrap the blanket around me and let myself back out into the bitter cold. The sun has hidden itself again. I had hoped to see it sparkle on the fresh snowbanks covering Kringle.

The house on the hill is easy to find because there is only one gentle slope in Kringle. The house belongs to a Kringle scribe who spends his days compiling the history of Klaus from a multitude of writings into a single book. He's worked on the compilation for years with seemingly no end in sight.

Sir Throck stands outside with a fur coat snugly belted about his torso. He's expecting me. Word of me seeking him must travel faster than I can walk.

"You should wear a fur," Sir Throck chides me when I draw near.

"You know I can't do that," I respond cheerily and lean down to kiss his weathered cheek.

He grumbles under his breath but doesn't say anything else about it. I have to grin. Despite his age, he's still as spritely as I recall from my childhood days. His hair may be thinner and more white and his face lined with far more wrinkles, but the youth and vitality are still evident in the spring to his step.

"Gypsies, huh?"

"Can you help me find them?"

"I'm probably the only one foolish enough to help you. They can hide themselves better than any other group I'm aware of," he says with a sigh.

"Where do we start?"

"At the coal mines."

"Why do you say that?"

"Because that's where they were hiding two days ago."

His words catch me off guard for a few seconds. Then I smile. "You already knew where they were."

Sir Throck chuckles. "Follow me."

I follow him silently down the hill and through Kringle. The coal mines are close to the tip of the forest, at the base of a smaller mountain range outside the elfin village. They are dangerously close to the forbidden premises.

"We won't see any living souls today," Sir Throck tells me. "All of the knights have been summoned into Oldenwald."

To prepare for the battle, no doubt. I'm hopeful the gypsies will join with the masses to enter the battle, as well. Throughout the history of Klaus, they have avoided any hint of wartime activities. Not out of peace, but rather out of self-preservation.

We hear music from lyres and harps before we reach the coal mines. For a group that is trying to hide, they're remarkably loud.

Sir Throck leads me around several wagons with large pieces of canvas thrown over their contents to prevent curious eyes from viewing their goods. We come up on the gypsies, about twenty of them, suddenly. Startled, the group stops their music and stares at us.

"It's only me," Sir Throck calls out. "I brought a guest, but she means no harm."

"Is Gallius or Cupid here?" I ask them.

Immediately, they relax. One of them steps forward and I recognize him from the crowd at the sporting event that fateful day.

"They're inside the coal mines," he says, pointing toward the mountain.

"Follow me," Sir Throck says and moves through the gypsies toward an opening in the mountain. The cave looks dark, and I shudder as we approach it. Undaunted, Sir Throck marches through the snow into the dark opening. I follow at a slower pace, listening to him greet those inside.

Suddenly, a large body bolts from the cave and rushes full force toward me, unable to stop and knocking me to the ground.

"Vixen! Vixen!"

I'm in shock—possibly hallucinating—as I look into the round, bearded face of Rudolpho. It seems like a life time ago that I last laid eyes on him.

"Grandmullie?" I manage to whisper. "Hann?"

"Both are safe. We're all safe," he yells exuberantly, his loud voice bouncing off the mountain wall in a deep echo. "And we ate the chocolat you hid in your robe. I hope that was all right?"

Rudolpho doesn't wait for a response. He clamors to his feet and reaches down to grasp my hand and yank me to my feet. As if in a dream, I let him lead me into the cave. Into the safe arms of Grandmullie and Hann—except Hann is stretched out on a pile of straw in the corner of the cave, blankets piled over him to shield him from the cold. Gund lays at his feet and sits up, whining, when I enter.

A fire burns in the center of the cave, but it doesn't really provide much warmth. It seems only to keep the severity of the winter cold at bay.

Grandmullie leaves the warmth of the fire to greet me, wrapping her arms around me tightly, sobs causing her frail shoulders to shake as she buries her head in my shoulder.

"Grandmullie, I thought I had lost you."

"I didn't know how to find you—didn't know if you were alive, my precious child."

After several minutes of enjoying hugging my grandmother, I gently ease from her arms to make my way to Hann. His eyes watch me closely. He's weak. So weak he can't even sit up.

"You don't look so good," I say in a low voice as I crouch down beside him.

Hann manages a small smile, his eyes drinking in my features. "You look as beautiful as I remember."

"Are you trying to flatter me?" I tease with a smile. It's a sad smile and Hann knows it.

"I will walk out of here, Vixen," he says with a determined gleam in his eyes.

"I know you will, Hann. But you must rest now—your body must heal."

"What about you?" he asks softly. "Will you stay with me?"

I lick my dry lips and take a deep breath. "So much has happened. Klaus is in real danger of being invaded. I must go to the battle."

Despite his pain, Hann gives me a weak smile. "You're never one to run away from the battle, Vixen."

"I came to enlist the help of the gypsies," I tell him.

"They saved our lives."

"I know," I say. I carefully raise the blankets higher around his neck. "We need all the reinforcements we can find right now."

"We have them," comes a voice behind me.

I whirl at the sound of Cupid's voice. Gallius stands beside her, along with none other than Donder van Rycke Sinter, the King's nephew.

"What are you doing here?" I challenge Donder, ignoring Cupid and Gallius.

He holds his hands up defensively. "I'm here to help."

"Are you sure your loyalty to the King isn't bringing you here to spy on us?"

Cupid steps in between us. "We need him. We need each other. You know that. He's done good, Vixen. We have to learn to trust at a time like this."

I stare into her deep brown eyes. "You trust him?"

She nods. "Yes."

"Then I'll follow your lead," I say quietly. "He did offer assistance at the sporting event."

"Thank you," Donder says gratefully. "The battle has been formally called to commence in two days, and I'm here to help."

I nod my head. "I know. I met a man, another Favored One, on a mountain—his name is Blitzen. He has a plan to attack the foreign armies with animals the morning before the battle—scatter them, perhaps scare them so that Klaus has a fighting chance."

"Of course we will win," Donder replies with a smug smile. "Our knights are the finest of any of the neighboring lands, especially the one we're entering into battle within two days."

"You don't understand, Donder." My voice is sharp as I explain the situation. "Blitzen and I saw other lands coming to join the battle against Klaus. It isn't one land we're fighting—

it's more like four or five. If they're successful in that battle, Blitzen says they will invade our land."

The cave is quiet as my words sink in. They're now fully understanding what is at stake.

"Right now," I continue, "there are five of us—five Favored Ones—Cupid, Donder, Blitzen, Rudolpho, and myself."

Donder gives me a surprised look. "I don't understand. There are more than two Favored Ones?" He looks at Cupid and Rudolpho and swallows the lump in his throat. "You two are Favored Ones?"

Rudolpho grins. "You're not so special after all."

I clap my hands. "You'll have to meet up for a conversation later. Right now, it's crucial we're at the battleground by dawn tomorrow. The plan is for us to break up and surround the armies on all sides. Each of us will be responsible for bringing animals at dawn. The armies won't expect to be attacked by animals—especially in winter when they should be hibernating."

Donder scratches his chin with a perplexed look. "I still don't understand how there are five Favored Ones."

"There are actually nine Favored Ones," I tell him. "When this battle is finished, I will seek out the others. For now, we use our favor with the animals to unleash fury upon the foreigners with every wild beast that bows to our command."

The others nod in agreement. Donder nervously takes a step to the center of the group and clears his throat. It's obvious he's scared. His lack of bravery is as pitiful as Rudolpho's cowardice.

"We need to try this," Cupid says quickly. "I don't want to ask my clan to join the King in the battle if it can be avoided."

"If we can scatter the foreigners, no battle will even come close to Klaus," I assure her. "But we must be successful in our efforts."

I bend down to the dirt and quickly sketch out a map, detailing from which direction Blitzen will attack, which is due west. I tell Rudolpho to meet up with Blitzen there, bringing animals as reinforcements. The rest of us will have to await the ram's horn Blitzen will blow—our signal that the time is at hand to wage war against the foreigners.

Cupid will hang back and move in with animals from the south. She has Gallius assisting her efforts to usher in the animals.

Donder has at his side a young knight, his best friend, who has not knelt his knee in submission to the King. The two of them will move quickly through the evening to penetrate from the east.

Sir Throck will accompany me far north. We'll have to move swiftly to be there by dawn. We can't afford to leave any direction open for the foreigners to escape the animals' attack.

Rudolpho hangs back by me as the others file out. I already know he's suffering anxiety from my decision to send him without a companion.

"I can't do this alone," Rudolpho whispers. "I get scared being out by myself at night."

I frown at him. "How is that possible? You told me you lived in the forest with the animals."

"Not in the middle of winter," he protests. "They're all asleep, and it scares me to wake them up from hibernation."

"You accompany Sir Throck to attack from the west with Blitzen," I urge. "I'll travel alone to the north."

"Absolutely not," Grandmullie breaks in. "You should be ashamed of yourself, Rudolpho—making this young maiden traipse by herself out into the dangers—"

My laughter stops her words. "Grandmullie, I have been traipsing by myself since the sporting event. I'm not scared."

"Can't the three of you go together?" she asks.

I can't be angry with Rudolpho. He's soft on the inside, but his way with animals will be greatly needed in the task before us.

"To appease you, Grandmullie, we'll travel together to get Rudolpho and Sir Throck to their destination, and then I'll branch off from there to chart my path. You keep Gund here to protect you and Hann. He'll give his life for you if needed."

She nods her head, relieved that I'm not traveling by myself the entire time but still unsettled for the danger that lurks before us. I give her a quick hug and leave the cave quickly. I don't even look at Hann. It's killing him that he can't accompany me.

The gypsies lend us some older horses that are accustomed to moving on the mountain trails. Rudolpho offers up loud lamentations when he sees the path that will take us to our destination. Very narrow, harrowing trails, barely a foot wide and covered with snow, lead down the mountain. The sheer drop off on one side of the trail causes even my stomach to tighten.

I give Rudolpho a warning glare, and he promptly closes his mouth, steadfastly holding his tongue from further complaining as his horse steps onto the dangerous path at the cliff's edge. One slip of the horses' hooves in the snow could very well have us falling to our death below.

My heart beats with fear as I grip the horse's reins. I close my eyes on the narrow paths and breathe a sigh of relief when we finally make it safely to the bottom.

Rudolpho's eyes are red from crying silent tears on the terrifying parts of the path down. I pretend I don't notice as he swipes his runny nose on the sleeve of his brown robe.

Sir Throck points in the direction of the ground the battle will wage. "We *will* get all the animals there by morning."

"I'll ride north and be there by dawn," I tell him. "Stay close by Rudolpho and guide him."

I click my tongue at the horse and he carries me onward, away from my friends. I gently whisper in his ear. He's tired from the treacherous climb down the mountain but valiantly keeps pushing through the snow. After expending his energy for several hours, I draw him to a stop at the outskirts of the forest. I'm not familiar with this section of the forest. The horse neighs softly and prances in a circle as a show of his nervousness. I stroke his mane reassuringly and climb down from his back. When I peer into the thick brush before me, I spy a large deer peeking through the bushes at me. *So that's why the horse is nervous.*

"It's fine," I whisper, both to the horse and the deer.

If anyone would see me talking to the deer, directing the massive creature to rally his help in our plan, I would be labeled as having an unsound mind. But the deer understands and abruptly leaves me to gather other animals.

I dislike calling on the bears. Their size makes me feel they are unpredictable. But it's that size and their aggression that is needed at this crucial time. And my bravery is needed. I'll have to lead the animals into the fight.

I continue riding the horse through the night, hearing the wild animals assembling all around me—the screeching of the panthers, the low, unmistakable growling produced by the grizzlies, the jaguars' anxious grunts, the howling wolves gathering in a pack.

It's still dark when I slide off the horse's back and mount a smaller bear to carry me to the battle. I shoo the horse back in the direction from which we came. He will only get hurt in the battle.

And we move—together, and yet, alone. The animals run with their own species, keeping careful distance from each other as they heed my commands. We're within a couple of miles from the designated battleground when we hear the drums. They're already beating a triumphant sound. The foreign armies feel they have already won before the battle has even taken place. They will be surprised by the animals who are coming together to protect Klaus. But I must wait for Blitzen's signal. I only hope the others have been successful in rallying animals too.

I shiver in the darkness—as much from fear as from the cold. The bear snorts at me as though offering a warning for me not to lose my courage at this time.

I close my heavy eyelids to relieve them of their weariness. Just a small rest. Almost instantly, I'm jolted awake by the blare of the ram's horn. Blitzen is somewhere near as the horn sounds loud to my ears.

I clutch a handful of the bear's fur and shout with all my might for the animals to attack. Blitzen's voice can be heard shouting as well. The bear lunges forward with a mass of animals toward the battleground. It's anarchy—utter destruction as the animals move onto the unsuspecting soldiers, awakened out of their sleep and unprepared for the onslaught of the animals.

"Vixen! Vixen!"

I hear Blitzen's voice yelling to me. I look to my left, and he's riding a bear as well. He waves for me to stop before we reach the soldiers.

I command the bear and wait for him to draw near me. "Why are you stopping?"

"Because we aren't going into the battle. The animals will wage this war."

"But I told the others to meet me there."

Blitzen laughs and reaches out to pat my back. "You're one of a kind, Vixen. I doubt anyone is going into battle with the animals. Only you would have the courage to accompany them. Only you."

I hope he's right. I don't want to let the others down. I climb off the bear and Blitzen joins me.

"You would have joined the animals too, Blitzen."

"Once upon a time long ago," he answers. "But I'm too old for this now and you have too much to look forward to in life."

We can't see the attack of the animals, but we can hear the scream and cries of the soldiers. A great number of them are able to escape the animals. They rush past us with terror-stricken eyes, breathing heavily. We let them pass without incident. They will carry the story of Klaus' victory back to the other lands. Besides, there will be a great many victims left behind, their blood covering the battleground where they sought to overthrow Klaus.

I cover my ears to mute the screams of the men being attacked. Blitzen wraps his thick arms around me, his low voice telling me to stay calm, that it would all be over soon.

And he's right. Within twenty minutes, the animals depart, leaving behind an ominous silence. I don't dare go to the battleground now. The blood and carnage would only cause terror in my mind for my remaining days. I've seen too much blood shed this Winter Solstice.

"It is finished," Blitzen says at last and releases me.

Klaus is safe for now. The foreign armies will be forced to concede victory when the Cavaliers show up to a battle that won't take place tomorrow. Klaus will come to be known as the land protected by animals.

And so we assemble back at the coal mines—five of the Favored Ones, the remaining four yet to be identified. No one will know our names, but our actions will indeed affect history.

My brave Hann will live to see another day. He is my gift; I know this. But I must continue to seek out the remaining four

Favored Ones. We will find each other; I'm confident of that. Now is the appointed time for all of our destinies to intertwine.

Right now, there are chestnuts roasting on an open fire, and my stomach is growling in tune to the popping sound of the wood burning. I look at my friends gathered around the fire, making merry—Blitzen, Cupid, Donder. But the most affection I hold is for Rudolpho, my red-nosed friend.

Epilogue

"SHH," RUDOLPHO WHISPERS. "CAN YOU HEAR snow bells ring?"

"Are you listening?" I ask him with an irritated sigh.

"I'm listening," he says quickly, "but I tell you, I hear snow bells."

I have spent the past hour trying to show Rudolpho how to knit a scarf. His thick fingers have somehow knotted the yarn and twisted it about his hands. If he will but listen to my instructions, he'll be able to salvage the mess he's created.

"He's right," Hann says quietly from across the room. "I hear the bells too."

Only one person travels with bells on. Nicklaus.

"You better watch out," Rudolpho whispers, "Nicklaus is coming to—"

"Stop," I say sharply.

I throw a worried look at Hann. We both know that I can't allow Nicklaus to see me. It's been exactly three weeks since the battle that never was. We heard tales of the fabled knights of Klaus arriving at the battleground with swords drawn and flags raised proudly in the air—only to find dead bodies of slain soldiers greeting them.

There were no accusations against Klaus—that they had attacked early. No, only the outrageous stories of animals arriving from the four corners of the lands to attack the armies. It's a grand story and one that will live on in the legendary land of Klaus—recited at every Winter Solstice.

Right now, I have every reason to be nervous as the galloping of the six white horses carrying the gold carriage trollops through our settlement.

Hann, dear Hann, rises unsteadily to his feet and crosses to me for my protection. He will never be the same physically again, but he's gaining strength and his courage will forever be a testament to the masses. Grandmullie approves of my choice for a husband one day. His bravery won her over. She anxiously awaits our marriage, but we're in no rush. Hann needs to heal and I want to find the other Favored Ones first.

"He knows when we are sleeping," Rudolpho whispers in my ear, pressing close to me to peek through the curtains as well.

"He knows when we're awake," Hann mutters.

I grasp Hann's hand and peer through the small window to see Nicklaus emerge from the carriage—stepping heavily into the snow.

"All ye pious ones," he bellows, holding a burlap bag over his shoulder. "Have yourself a merry krist, masses."

Nicklaus turns his head to look directly at my window as though fully aware that we're watching him. He touches the side of his nose with a sniff and gives a wink. He's up to no good.

Children of my settlement slowly leave their small homes to make their way to Nicklaus, hopeful for a piece of chocolat. He throws the burlap bag on the ground and waits for them to assemble. When they have eagerly gathered around him, rubbing their little hands in anticipation, he reaches into the bag and draws out a switch.

"Little children," Nicklaus cackles, "have you been naughty or have you been nice?"

THE END

ACKNOWLEDGEMENTS

As always, I want to thank anyone who takes their time to invest in reading one of my books. I'm grateful.

Four editors that I must acknowledge are Savannah Wise, Emilee Tucker, Marissa Sivill, and Kendal Wise. Your input was much appreciated and invaluable in producing the final story.

All my siblings who have encouraged me with words and actually purchased my books. I love you all.

Dear friends who always have my back and make me belly-laugh: Amanda and Tess.

My friend, Tivo, whose description of me as an adventurer is, hopefully, prophetic this next stage of my life's journey.

Finally, my Heavenly Father who provides all creativity and spiritual and physical sustenance for my life's journey.

www.julietpiercebooks.com